The Last Ride of Jed Strange

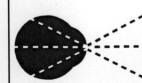

THE LAST RIDE OF JED STRANGE

FRANK LESLIE

WHEELER PUBLISHING
A part of Gale, Cengage Learning

GALE
CENGAGE Learning·

Detroit • New York • San Francisco • New Haven, Conn • Waterville, Maine • London

GALE
CENGAGE Learning

LIBRARY OF CONGRESS CATALOGING-IN-PUBLICATION DATA

Leslie, Frank, 1963–
  The last ride of Jed Strange / by Frank Leslie. — Large Print edition.
    pages cm. — (Wheeler Publishing Large Print Western)
  ISBN-13: 978-1-4104-5578-9 (softcover)
  ISBN-10: 1-4104-5578-5 (softcover)
  1. Large type books. I. Title.
PS3552.R3236L37 2013
813'.54—dc23   2012041986

Published in 2013 by arrangement with NAL Signet, a member of Penguin Group (USA) Inc.

For Sherman and Sharon Langehaug
of Grand Forks, North Dakota —
for their friendship and support
over all these years

CHAPTER 1

The bullet nipped the crown of Colter Farrow's hat and blew it off his head before smashing into a stone scarp with an echoing *wham!* and a shrill whine.

The whine was almost instantly drowned out by the crash of the rifle up the hill on the left side of the old Indian trail that Colter and his horse-breaking partner, Willie Tappin, had followed out from Tucson.

"Down, Willie, down!" Colter cried, throwing himself out of his saddle as his mustang gave an indignant whinny, then buck-kicked and galloped on up the trail, reins bouncing along behind him.

Colter rolled as two more bullets plowed up dirt around his head and shoulders, and threw himself behind a small cedar and a rock. Willie Tappin — older and slower — swung down from the back of his pitching horse and dropped to one knee beside a rock on the other side of the trail. As his piebald gelding ran up the trail after Colter's coyote dun, Willie poked back his Stetson's broad, flat brim and looked over the rock toward the source of the gunfire.

"What in tarnation?" the older man exclaimed.

"Keep your head down, Willie!"

"You don't have to tell me twice!" Tappin looked at Colter. "Hoss thieves, you think?"

Colter jerked his head down behind his covering rock as two more bullets smashed into it and a third whizzed past his right shoulder to hammer a gnarled cedar behind him. The shooting continued for nearly a minute, bullets whistling and hammering and the ricochets whining, until a lull drifted down over the Arizona desert, in the shadow of the Rincon Mountains. Colter glanced at Willie, crouching low behind the boulder, his hat down over his eyes. None of the bullets had appeared to land anywhere near the older horse breaker. Most if not all had churned the dust and rocks around Colter.

"Good God Almighty!" Willie said, lifting his head now, directing his long, horsey face toward Colter. "Whoever they are, there's a few of 'em, and they don't like us a heap!" He had his Schofield revolver in his gloved hand, but he didn't appear overly eager to use the weapon, which he wore mainly to guard against rattlesnakes and for smashing coffee beans. Willie's specialty was horses, not gun work. It had been for nearly all of his thirty-odd years.

"You stay here and keep your ugly head down, Willie."

"I heard that!"

Colter slid his Remington revolver from the soft leather holster on his left hip and flicked open the cylinder's release tab. He pinched a .44 cartridge from one of the loops on his shell belt and slid it through the loading gate, filling the cylinder that he always left empty beneath the Remy's hammer, so he wouldn't inadvertently shoot himself in the leg.

He flicked the loading gate closed and spun the cylinder. The gun was old and tarnished and prone to rust, but he kept all its machined pieces well oiled and free of debris.

Wanted as he was by the law as well as by bounty hunters, the eighteen-year-old redhead kept the pistol ready for work at all times. Now he lifted his battered tan hat, ran a hand through his shoulder-length, sweat-damp hair, and cast a glance around the rock to the high, rocky hill on the other side of the trail.

Smoke puffed around a rifle maw about halfway up the hill, the shooter himself concealed by the rocks. The slug hammered the face of Colter's covering boulder, and he jerked his head back behind it as rock shards flew in all directions.

The rifle's crack flatted out across the valley, chasing its dwindling echoes.

"Colter, you all right?" Tappin yelled.

"I ain't hit, if that's what you mean."

"Them boys seem to have a bone to pick with you."

Colter tried to keep the tone light, not wanting to give away any information about his previous and ongoing trouble, which neither Willie nor anyone else at Camp Grant, where he was currently employed as a horse breaker, knew anything about. "They're probably after my hoss. Must've seen Northwest back at the stage station."

He and Willie had been out scouting a herd of wild horses south of Soldier Gulch, and had stopped for water and coffee at a swing station about five miles back. Several other men had been there — a couple of Mexicans, a half-breed Indian, and two white men including a plug-ugly midget — eating lunch on the station house's front porch. Colter had kept his distance but he'd

10

thought he'd glimpsed a couple of the ragged crew favoring him with lingering gazes. All, including the midget, were a savage-looking lot bristling with guns and ammunition. Either game hunters for the railroad or bounty hunters, Colter had figured.

"What's your hoss got that my hoss ain't got?" Willie wanted to know as more rifles hammered away on the slope.

"That horse of yours is a beat-up old cayuse ready for the glue factory!" Colter shouted. "You stay here. I'm gonna work around behind 'em."

"There's too many of 'em, Red. Let's hightail it!"

"You hightail it," Colter shouted. "I'm gonna work around behind 'em, see if I can discourage 'em."

"Damn it, Colter — *there's too many of 'em!*"

Ignoring the warning, Colter took advantage of the lull in the shooting to bound up from behind his boulder and run crouching across the trail. Two bullets licked up dust behind him as he scrambled into the thick brush and stunt cedars lining the base of the hill and running around the hill's shoulder. After only a few yards, he could no longer see the nest of rocks from which the dry-gulchers were slinging lead, which meant they couldn't see him, either.

A pistol popped behind him. Willie was triggering shots at the bushwhackers, keeping the brigands distracted.

As Colter moved along a rocky wash that angled around the side of the hill, partly concealed by saguaros, spindly cottonwoods, and mesquites, he wished he'd had time to grab his Henry rifle from his saddle boot before he'd left his horse. All he had was the six-shooter. It had done for him before, though. It would have to do for him again.

A rattling sounded. He leaped to his left, grunting with a start, for anyone who'd been raised in rattlesnake country had an instinctive horror of such a warning. He turned to his right, where a diamondback lay coiled atop a rock in the shadow of the ridge, flicking its forked tongue toward Colter while shaking the hard rattle at the end of its tail. Its flat, pelletlike eyes regarding him devilishly.

Colter lowered the Remington and stepped back away from the viper, out of range of a lunging strike. "Easy, feller. You're not one of the snakes I'm after."

He turned and continued walking along the wash, noting that the cracks of the dry-gulchers' rifles had fallen eerily silent. Slowing his pace, he moved more quietly, ratcheting back the Remington's hammer and holding the pistol straight out in front of him. Just ahead, a notch was dug into the side of the hill — a narrow, dry watercourse filled with dead weeds and jumbled rock left by previous monsoon floods.

Colter turned into the cut. It should take him right up behind the shooters. When he'd walked a dozen yards, he heard someone moving down the slope on his right and turned to see the midget he'd seen at the swing station skip-hopping down the rocks, angling toward him from the crest of the rocky hill. Colter swung his pistol toward the midget, who was dressed in a pinstriped shirt and auburn vest trimmed with a gold watch chain and a miniature tan slouch hat. His leathery face with its pinched little nose and a blond patch beard gave him a goatish look. He wore whipcord trousers and the black boots of a ten-year-old child. He'd been reloading the pistol in his doll-like hands when he saw Colter, and now he flicked his pocket pistol's loading gate closed.

"Hold it there, shorty," Colter said, keeping his voice pitched low.

The midget snarled, stopped on a flat

13

boulder, and swung his pocket pistol toward Colter. "Hold this, Red!"

Colter's Remy barked, leaping in his hand, sending the midget tumbling backward off the boulder. The goatish little man dropped the pistol as he clutched his bloody neck and fell down out of sight.

"What a rotten thing to do!" The voice came from Colter's left.

He froze, his powder smoke still wafting in the air around his head. In the corner of his left eye, he saw several figures step up onto the rocks on that side of the cut.

Slowly, he turned just as the fifth man was stepping onto a boulder, all five holding pistols down low in their gloved hands. Three of the four wore long dusters that blew around the tops of their scuffed, dusty boots. An Indian near the middle of the pack wore a deerskin vest under crisscrossed cartridge bandoliers, and a black sombrero. His face was cadaverously narrow and crooked, with a long nose against which were set two incredibly small eyes, the left one angling inward as though perpetually staring at the end of the man's beak.

"You just shot my brother, Red, you son of a bitch!" he told Colter, jutting the gun in his hand in the direction of the unseen midget.

A man at the far left of the line of five wore a dusty white frock coat. His bearded face was broad and fat beneath the brim of his straw sombrero. He held a long-barreled Colt Navy down low by his left thigh clad in white- and red-checked trousers with green-patched knees. He smiled, showing the black nubs of his teeth. "Bill Rondo done sent you a message in care of us, Red."

Colter turned slowly, making no sudden moves but keeping the Remington held tight in his right hand, aimed at the ground near his right boot. "That right? Well, I got one to send back to him."

He hadn't finished the sentence before he swung around, bringing up the Remy. He fired from a crouch, the old pistol roaring and belching smoke and saffron flames. The bushwhackers went down like dominoes. Screaming dominoes spewing blood from the wounds in their chests or heads, but dominoes just the same. One after another, they flew back off the rocks as though they'd been lassoed from behind, hitting the ground with grunts, groans, and crunching thuds.

After they were down, none made another sound except a single, short gurgle. The rowel of one of the dead men's spurs spun.

Colter straightened. His heart beat slowly

but now, in the aftermath of the killing, it began to quicken. That's how it had been lately. When he'd been forced to kill, it had come easily to him. He'd approached it as calmly as a poker player dealing cards. Only later did his nerves start to twang, his mouth go dry, his hands shake. He wasn't sure what to make of it all. On the one hand, the calmness meant he'd grown comfortable with killing. On the other hand, it made killing easy. At least it made the killing of men who would otherwise kill him easy.

And that was how it should be, shouldn't it? Otherwise, after all the men who'd hunted him down over the last, long two years, he might be dead.

Still, something bothered him about it now as, looking around warily, making sure no one else was about to dry-gulch him, he plucked the spent brass from the Remington's cylinder. He slipped .44 shells from the loops on his cartridge belt and punched them through the Remington's loading gate, then flipped the gate shut and rolled the cylinder across his forearm, having the gunman's appreciation of the gun's smooth action and the solid-sounding clicks.

A fluttering, rasping sound rose from the rocks on his left, and he aimed the Remington in that direction, clicking the hammer back. When no one appeared, he climbed the bank and walked around the large boulder the midget had been standing on, and stopped, aiming the pistol straight out from his right shoulder, angled down.

The midget lay back against another rock. His little paunch was rising and falling sharply. His hat was off, and sweat dribbled down his wizened face, his thin lips capped by a scraggly blond mustache. His eyes were a depthless gray brown and they bored into Colter as he said, "You sure are fast with the smoke wagon, Red."

Colter didn't say anything.

"Good thing you are, 'cause there's gonna be a whole lot more . . . from where we come from." Then the midget died, his head rolling to one side and his belly behind the gaudy vest falling still. He gave a jerk and his little tongue slithered out from between his lips.

Then the rest of him fell still, as well.

CHAPTER 2

Colter frowned as he studied the savage-looking little man. The midget had a scrunched-up piglike nose. A piece of paper fluttered inside his auburn vest, angling out from a pocket of his pin-striped shirt. Colter crouched and plucked the paper from the midget's pocket.

He unfolded the single sheet until his own image stared up at him — an inked sketch of his face looking exaggeratedly menacing beneath his hat brim, his eyes more heavy-lidded and intimidating than they actually were. Or, at least, than he thought they were.

The artist had dabbed in a few freckles across his nose. Colter's mouth was depicted as a thin knife slash. The sketch included the S that had been branded into his right cheek by Sheriff Bill Rondo at a slight angle from left to right and starting an inch down from the inside of his eye. Unconsciously, Colter lifted a gloved hand to his cheek, touched his index and middle fingers to the knotted scar, feeling his ears warm as he wondered if the brand was really that stark and hideous.

The rendering made it larger and darker than it really was. He knew from appraising it in a looking glass that it wasn't quite that large, and it was more pink with knotted scar tissue than black. But to him it often seemed just as big and bold and threatening as on the paper before him. Especially lately, when he'd been fooling with Miss Lenore, the pretty daughter of the commander at Fort Grant who often came out to the stables to watch him and Willie breaking horses.

Across the top of the page in large, blocky letters, the circular read REWARD: $1,000 DEAD OR ALIVE. Beneath the picture was his name, COLTER FARROW. Then: NOTORIOUS YOUNG PISTOLEER WHO MAIMED AND SCARRED SHERIFF BILL RONDO OF SAPINERO, COL. TERR. In slightly smaller letters the reward proclaimed that Farrow wore "the mark of Satan" on his cheek and had "murdered countless numbers in an ongoing bloodbath across the West!"

Colter tore up the paper and tossed the bits into the hot, dry breeze. He ran a thumb under one of his suspender straps and stared off in anger. "Mark of Satan, huh? The mark of Sapinero, more like."

Indeed, it was the "mark of Sapinero" that Sheriff Bill Rondo had burned into his cheek after Colter had discovered that Rondo and several others from Sapinero had killed his foster father, Trace Cassidy. He till couldn't quite work his mind around all that had happened up in Sapinero, all that he'd discovered after Trace had been sent home in the back of his own wagon, dead, his clothes nearly whipped off him, his hands and ankles nailed to the wagon bed.

A grisly, horrific crucifixion — an act of unspeakable brutality even for a man like Rondo and the ranching king of Sapinero County, Paul Spurlock.

Colter had been taken in by Trace and Ruth Cassidy at six years old, when his parents had died in a milk plague that had swept the Lunatic Mountains of south-central Colorado, where they'd ranched. Trace and Ruth had owned a ranch not far from where Colter was born. They'd raised the orphaned boy like their own, and he'd grown up as an older brother to David and Little May, though after he'd turned twelve he'd moved out to the bunk-shack and worked as a puncher right along with the other men Trace had hired to keep up his fences, cut hay, and tend his growing cattle and horse herds.

It had been a good life, and Colter had intended to marry his sweetheart from a neighboring horse ranch — Marianna Claymore — until that fateful day on which Trace had been carried home dead in the wagon he'd driven to Sapinero to buy supplies.

So Ruth had sent Colter and his Remington pistol to Sapinero to seek out the responsible parties behind Trace's murder. That's how things were done in the Lunatic Mountains populated mostly by the tough, intransigent men and women from the Tennessee and Georgia hills. A tooth for a tooth, an eye for an eye. Colter had been old enough to shoot and ride, so in Ruth's way of thinking he'd been old enough to avenge his foster father's brutal murder.

Ruth had sent him to Sapinero to find out who had killed Trace and to exact vengeance where vengeance was due. Lead had flown. Colter'd gotten out alive but wearing the Sapinero brand on his cheek — the brand that Rondo had used to mark those he barred from his town. Yes, Colter survived but not before killing Deputy Bannon, crippling Rondo with a bullet to his back, and branding the sheriff with his own iron . . . and earning a hefty price on Colter's head.

Of course, he hadn't been able to go back home to Ruth and David and Little May. Not with the price on his head.

So Colter had run. First to Wyoming. When his trail had grown hot up there, he'd ridden down here to Arizona, where he was now trying to live quietly, unassumingly earning an honest living by breaking horses with Willie Tappin at Camp Grant, a dusty little military outpost on the hot, desolate banks of the San Pedro River.

Certainly no bounty hunters would find him there. . . .

Colter walked away from the dead midget. He surveyed the five other men he'd left dead atop the blood-splattered bank of the wash, then stomped around until he found their horses. He unsaddled the mounts and spanked them free, to be picked up by one of the area ranchers.

Hot and dusty and thirsty, he found Willie riding toward him, leading Colter's coyote dun by its bridle reins.

"Heard the shootin'," Willie said, his eyes looking wild. "You all right, boy?"

"I'm all right, Willie." He took his hat, a bullet hole in its crown, from Willie.

"What the hell happened?"

Colter shrugged as he grabbed his canteen off his saddle horn and pried the cork from the lip. "Managed to scare them dry-gulchers off with a few shots from my Remy."

Willie's angular, deeply lined face looked skeptical. "You did?"

"They was just after our horses, I reckon." Colter feigned a rueful chuckle. "I reckon their hearts weren't really in a lead swap."

"Coulda fooled me." Willie leaned forward and patted his piebald's neck. "Well, I reckon we'd best get on back to the camp. We got us a hoedown tonight, remember."

"Ah, hell," Colter said, scowling as he stepped into the leather. "I can't dance a lick. *Can't* dance and I don't *wanna* dance!"

Willie chuckled as he followed Colter back toward the main trail they'd been following when they'd been bushwhacked. "I bet Miss Lenore'll have the last word on *that!*"

His chuckles broke into coughs from too many cigarettes rolled with spicy Mexican tobacco.

As he rode, Colter fingered the "mark of Satan" on his cheek and thought about the midget's warning.

CHAPTER 3

"Colter Farrow, you're gonna dance with me whether you like it or not," the girl whispered in a breathy, intoxicating, Deep South accent. Her mouth was so near to Colter's ear that the young cowboy could feel the moistness of her warm breath pouring through his head and rushing clear down to his boots, making his toes tingle.

Even though Colter had never been east of the Mississippi — had never, in fact, been anywhere but West — Miss Lenore Fairchild's raspy voice conjured images of sprawling, white-pillared plantation houses, rolling green hills studded with mossy oaks, and mist-enshrouded creek banks lush with blooming laurel.

Before the redheaded cowboy could protest, Major Fairchild's daughter ground her fingers into his right biceps and pulled him out onto the dance floor. Several groups of dancers — the young women of the fort dosi-do-ing with well-groomed, young officers — made way for the major's ravishing, bubbly, and roundly adored young daughter, while raising incredulous eyebrows at her choice of a dancing partner. The lanky, long-haired, blue-jean-clad Colter Farrow occupied the lowly though indispensable position of bronc breaker at Camp Grant. While an indispensable position, it was not an esteemed one.

A bony shoulder clad in blue wool and capped with a lieutenant's polished brass bar appeared out of nowhere, ramming into Colter's chest and stopping the young cowboy and Miss Lenore dead in their tracks. "Now, Miss Lenore," said Lieutenant Pres Belden, "you know this boy can't dance. Why, I don't think he even scraped his boots off before he entered the hall."

The lieutenant — tall and square-shouldered, with a coal black dragoon-style mustache, belligerently jutting jaws, dimpled chin, and cobalt blue eyes that always owned an angry, condescending cast — worked his nose, sniffing, then made a dismissive face. "Why, I know he didn't!" He glanced at Colter before giving his back to the young horse breaker and hooking his right arm for Miss Lenore. "Allow me."

"I do apologize, Lieutenant," said Miss

Lenore, not influenced a bit and just as relief that he wouldn't have to dance was beginning to ease the tension in Colter's shoulders. "But I've promised this and possibly the next dance to Mr. Farrow."

Smiling and radiant, the pearls around her creamy neck setting off the chocolate brown of the sausage curls dancing around her pink cheeks and the amber brown of her sparkling eyes, Miss Lenore Fairchild stepped around the slack-jawed lieutenant. With Colter in tow, she continued out onto the dance floor where, Colter noticed with a horrific shudder, the music had suddenly changed and the dancers were now dancing face-to-face and hand in hand, only two or three inches apart!

"Miss Lenore," Colter said, hearing the nervous quaver in his voice, "I'm afraid Lieutenant Belden is right — I can't dance. Oh, I've barn-danced a few times back home, but mostly I whacked an empty kettle with a kitchen spoon, keeping time for the banjo picker." He gulped as she grabbed both his sweating hands in hers and held them up between them, smiling warmly at him, showing all those perfect white teeth sheathed in rich, ruby red lips.

"Nonsense, dear Colter," Miss Lenore said, her head just a little lower than his.

"The waltz is the very picture of grace and simplicity. Follow me. Watch my feet. Hold on tight, and I'll step you through it." Her laugh sounded like snowmelt water chiming along a cedar-lined creek bed high in the Colorado mountains, which was where the young cowboy wished he were right now.

She put her moist lips up close to his ear once more, and he could feel her breath again, soft as a butterfly wing. "And we'll no doubt win the jam-and-apple basket at the end of the evening!"

"Oh, Lordy," Colter muttered as the girl began sidestepping and swinging her hips, tugging his reluctant, six-foot-tall body along like an extra, oversized appendage. "I just don't think I can do this, Miss —"

"No, you're doing well, Mr. Farrow," the girl encouraged.

"I'm liable to hurt you and face a firing squad in the morning."

She laughed heartily. "Just watch my feet and do what I do, and I've no doubt you'll be leading in a minute. See — it's not so awfully hard, now, is it?"

Colter concentrated on the girl's metallic green, elastic, side-zipper shoes showing below the swirling pleats of her cream ball gown, and, ignoring the other dancers he felt himself running into frequently, forced himself to learn the steps lest he should stomp all over this poor girl and likely send her sailing into the punch bowl yonder. It was pure fear rushing through his veins like miniature arrows that kept him on his own feet and off hers as well as off the hem of her obviously expensive dress as they shuffled this way and that about the dance floor.

After one song Miss Lenore insisted they stay for another — he was catching on so quickly it would be a shame to stop now! — he found himself growing more aware of the others around him, and how out of place he must look in this crowd of handsome soldiers with their waxed mustaches, red sashes, and gilt-braid tunics, and the be-ribboned, curly-haired, cream-skinned girls in their colorful ball gowns hand sewn from the finest cloth shipped from St. Louis to Tucson.

There were a few enlisted men and non-commissioned officers who lumbered around the floor nearly as awkwardly as Colter Farrow was, but it was the handsome officers and equally attractive dance part-ners he was most aware of — them in all their charm and grace and formal cavalry attire, and he in his crude, faded albeit freshly washed Levi's jeans with deerskin inseams, pale blue chambray shirt with its collar frayed from many scrubbings, and ancient green neckerchief. His copper-red hair hung straight down to his shoulders; he kept it long to hide the grisly scar on his freckled right cheek as much as possible.

His three-year-old brown leather boots with their undershot heels had not been polished, just rubbed down with a damp rag. They looked as worn as Indian moccasins, but, contrary to the lieutenant's comments, he had taken a stick and scraped the shit from the heels and from the stitching between the uppers and the soles, by God. Colter himself had had a bath only the day before, so if the lieutenant had indeed smelled any horse shit, it had come from his own heels, though Colter doubted the arrogant officer had ever visited a corral or stable, much less mucked either out with a bucket and a pitchfork.

Colter had been breaking horses here at Camp Grant — on the banks of the San Pedro River in the sun-blistered valley of the Gila — for only a month, but he'd known after two days that Belden hailed from a moneyed family from a West Virginia tobacco plantation, and that his father, a Unionist during the Civil War, had been a close friend and associate of General Grant.

Colter had also learned quickly that Belden had firmly set his hat for the delectable Miss Lenore.

That bit of information could not be ignored. Several times as they danced, with Colter even beginning to enjoy himself a little, he glimpsed the lieutenant glaring at him amongst the crowd milling at the edges of the dance floor or sitting in cane-bottom chairs back against the adobe walls or around the cloth-covered mess hall tables appointed with small ham salad sandwiches, coffeepots, and cakes. The lieutenant stood alone, like an angry bull, turning a cut-glass punch cup around in his beringed right hand.

His anger must have been as plain to everyone else in the wooden-floored dance hall as it was to Colter, for no one came near him much less tried to engage him in conversation. His anger was plain to everyone, that is, except to Miss Lenore herself, who appeared completely oblivious, engaged as she was in counting the steps aloud for Colter and helping him twirl her with more and more adeptness under his arm.

Colter himself was as confused as everyone else in the dance hall. Why was she paying so much attention to him — a lowly horse breaker from the Lunatic Mountains in south-central Colorado Territory? True, it was no secret to anyone at Camp Grant that Miss Lenore both knew and loved horses, for she could be found milling about the holding and breaking corrals whenever she managed to slip away from her family's impressive home quarters and the watchful, ever-protective eye of her mother. Was she so enamored of horses that she'd become enamored of Colter, who broke and trained them?

Colter had no illusions it was a serious attraction, as he himself, with the nasty S-brand forever burned into his right cheek at a slight slant starting about two inches below his eye, could never be an attractive prospect for such a girl as Miss Lenore Fairchild. Miss Lenore was a beautiful, cultured girl — "a great room girl," as folks of Colter's humble station knew young ladies like her — who could never be seriously attracted to anyone outside her own moneyed class. She was lured to Colter for the same reason she was lured to a breaking corral — because she was a hemmed-in, romantic girl in need of frivolous diversions.

And that, Colter realized now with admittedly a sinking feeling in the pit of his belly, was what he was. A frivolous diversion. Possibly even an instrument with which she could make Lieutenant Belden even more attracted to her.

"Ouch!"

"Oh, shit — I'm sorry, Miss Lenore!"

"No, it's all right," she said, laughing, continuing to dance despite the slowing of his own boots. "You just lost your concentration. Count, now — one, two, three . . . four!"

She let him twirl her once more, and he stared in heartsick amazement at her brown hair and cream skin and cream skirts and glistening pearls swirling above her corseted breasts in a beguiling whirlwind of radiant femininity so rich that Colter felt his blood rise like a spring stallion's — hot and churning. The rushing, warm air around the girl was filled with the delicate cherry perfume he was sure he'd recall, grinding his jaws, on his deathbed.

"Perfect!" she cried.

Just then another uniformed shoulder nudged Colter, and her father, Fort Commander Major Angus Fairchild, attired in his company grade dress uniform complete with horsehair-plumed helmet and steep rear visor, stepped between the dancers. The metallic gold thread embroidering the chest of the major's brass-buttoned, double-breasted coat became visible as the grizzled but stately old officer glanced with faint admonishment at Colter before returning his fatherly blue gaze to his flushed and breathless daughter.

Lenore's bosom heaved as she stared up at the leonine gent in surprise. "Father, we —"

"Are quite finished. High time you danced with your father, my dear. You know the old knees are a mite creaky, but the boys told me they'd take it easy on the next waltz."

Lenore gave Colter a reluctant, parting glance before placing her hands on her father's shoulders and letting the bandy-legged old graybeard step her stiffly off into the dancing crowd, safely out of the scar-faced shit-kicker's reach. Relieved but also embarrassed for the summary dismissal, Colter turned to see many faces regarding him reprovingly.

The lieutenant, however, was nowhere to be seen.

Colter fought his way to the front of the dance hall, then, grabbing his tan, flat-brimmed Stetson off a wooden wall peg, set it snugly on his head and walked out the open double doors. As he crossed the roofed veranda, a cloud of rich tobacco smoke wafted around his head, and a familiar voice said, "Where you goin', boy? Wear out them boots, didja — on the scout for another pair?"

His fellow horse breaker, Willie Tappin, wheezed a laugh and elbowed the young lady beside him — one of the younger girls from "sud's row," the steamy, baracklike buildings in which the fort's clothes were washed by eight or nine hired women, including the pear-shaped, plain-faced one now standing with Willie, looking as out of place here as Colter felt.

Willie winked, squinting through the fetid smoke cloud billowing around his long, craggy face. "Now, if you could find you a pair of boots with wings, that'd really strike the fancy of Miss Lenore."

"I reckon it would at that. But I'd be too worn out to wear 'em," Colter said, heading down off the gallery steps to the hard-packed yard where the silhouettes of men stood around, the coals of the cigarettes or cigars glowing in the darkness. "This night's about done me in, Willie. I'm headin' to bed."

He threw up an arm in parting and headed in the direction of the stables.

"Hey," Willie called.

Colter heard the horse breaker's boots on the steps, and then the man, a few inches taller than Colter but stooped from too many separated shoulders, was beside him, matching his long-legged stride. "What's got your tail in a droop, Red? I seen you in there dancin' with the princess of southern Arizona. Hell, if you didn't want her, you could have passed her to me!"

"I reckon I feel like a dancin' bear, Willie."

"How do you mean?"

"Ah, hell — I don't know what I mean." Colter slowed his pace, glancing at Willie and jerking his chin toward the long, adobe brick dance hall lit behind them and from which the banjo and violin music emanated clearly on the cool, dry night air of Arizona Territory. "Go on back and enjoy the dance, Willie."

Loud, measured clapping and foot stomping sounded and Colter saw through the dance hall's open doors the silhouettes of the dancers lined up facing their partners for the Virginia reel — the one dance Colter was familiar with and at which he wouldn't have been as likely to make such a fool of himself.

Willie scowled at him, then canted his long, horsey face to one side and brushed a thumbnail across his bristled chin. "Red, you did realize she was spoken for, right? You weren't thinkin' you were doin' anything more than just dancin' with that purty little gal, were you?"

"Of course I did. I ain't a cork-headed moron. Now, leave me the hell alone, Willie!"

"All right, all right. Have it your way, Red!" Willie backed away, raising his hands, palms out, then turned and strode off in the direction of the dance hall.

"At least," Colter muttered to himself, feeling like a lovelorn schoolboy, "I *thought* I did." There'd just been something so damned intoxicating about the girl that he'd found himself, even while counting his dance steps, wishfully believing there might be something more between them.

It was a sparkling Arizona night, the cool air like cactus wine in nostrils and lungs. The greasewood and cholla stood like witches' fingers against the sky lit by a rising powder-horn moon as Colter followed the meandering footpath through the desert, flanking the main part of the fort, out behind the quartermaster's and commissary storehouses, toward the cavalry stables and hay barn and the sprawl of cottonwood pole corrals.

The night's beauty was lost on the young cowboy, who went on into the log barracks abutting one of the stables and that was reserved for the horse breakers. It was more of an Apache-like "jacal" than a genuine building — constructed as it was of upright mesquite logs chinked with mud and straw and roofed with leafed cottonwood branches to keep out the sun and occasional rain.

He didn't bother with a lamp but quickly undressed in the dark and slacked onto his lower, ironwood-frame bunk, forcing himself to sleep.

He was vaguely surprised to find out how easy it was to throw himself into oblivion even after the complicated night with Lenore and after the shootings earlier in the afternoon, his leaving another six men dead behind him. He heard Willie a few moments later when his partner came in and undressed and crawled, rasping and snorting, into his bunk above Colter, making Colter's own bunk quiver. But he was fast asleep soon after Willie had punched his pillow and settled in — until his eyes opened suddenly, his senses alive.

He didn't know how much time had passed, or what had awakened him. Whatever it was, it hadn't awakened Willie, who snored deeply, whistling, in the bunk above Colter.

Maybe Willie was able to sleep so deeply because Willie didn't have a price on his head. Remembering the midget's warning,

Colter reached for the Remington revolver he'd holstered to a bedpost, tossed his covers aside, and dropped his feet to the floor.

A shadow passed outside a near, moonlit window, and Colter clicked the Remy's hammer back, his heart thudding slow but hard in his ears.

CHAPTER 4

Colter pulled his jeans on over his thread-bare balbriggans and looped the leather suspenders up over his shoulders. He wrapped his shell belt, gun, and holster around his lean waist, donned his hat, and glanced at Willie still sawing logs on his bunk. Colter stepped into his boots and then stole quietly over to the door and tripped the latch.

He gritted his teeth as the hinges squawked but continued to slowly draw the door open. When he had the door half-open, he stood there, cocked Remington now in his hand, angling a look into the moonlit yard beyond the brush ramada fronting the shack.

The corrals were forty yards from the shack, their rails looking like black velvet in silhouette though their tops were furred with pearl moonlight. The ground was floury pale. The windmill between Colter and the corrals stood still and silent, the wooden blades unmoving. There were three horses in the corral — three broomtail broncs from California that were up next for breaking — and they, too, stood still as black statues. The water in the stone holding tank glistened like quicksilver.

Nothing moved. The eerie silence pricked the hair at the back of Colter's neck. Not even a night bird called, nor did a coyote howl. The coyotes milling around the washes surrounding Camp Grant usually howled nearly all night long.

Colter caressed his Remy's hammer with his thumb and ran his tongue across his bottom lip. He'd come down here to Arizona to escape the bounty hunters in Colorado. Could more have followed him here? Maybe he shouldn't have been so stubborn, and changed his name to an alias. But he'd thought he'd be safe here at Grant amongst soldiers. As remote as the fort was, and as much as he kept to himself, avoiding most towns, surely his name hadn't spread beyond the fort.

Who cared about a scar-faced young horse breaker who kept to himself?

Of course, no matter what he called himself, the scar on his face would give him away. That's undoubtedly how the midget and the others had identified him at the swing station. It was Colter Farrow's mark of Cain, and he'd wear it to his grave. But it had taught him one thing, he mused now, as he glanced down at the cocked Remy held steady in his work-thickened left hand. It had taught him how to use a gun — in fact, he'd become about as fast, one Colorado newspaper had claimed, as John Wesley Hardin.

Of course that same writer had also said he was as mean and crazy as Hardin, that he'd filed his Remington's front sight off and rigged the hammer for fanning, and that his "demon eyes" matched the "mark of the Devil" on his cheek. You couldn't put much stock in the words of writers. They just wanted to sell stories — the more lurid and exaggerated, the better.

But Colter knew he was fast. He had to be or he wouldn't be standing here now, feeling that sudden, almost unsettling calm float over him again, easing the tension in every muscle and bone, and slowing his heart.

Colter drew a breath, then stepped quickly out under the ramada, putting his back to the wall beside the half-open door. He swung the pistol from right to left and back again, looking and listening. Nothing. He was about to step forward when something moved in the corner of his right eye, and someone gave a short, soft whistle.

Colter swung around to face the man-shaped shadow stepping out from behind the shack to stand off the end of the ramada, his gloved hands raised shoulder-high. "Easy, shit-kicker."

Behind Colter rose a ratcheting click. The familiar sound froze him as would the rattle of a diamondback. A man on the opposite end of the shack said, "Set the gun down, boy."

Colter turned his head a little, saw a tall silhouette in a tan kepi aiming a pistol at him, the moonlight gleaming on the bluing. Colter depressed the Remington's hammer and set the gun down on the bench abutting the shack's front wall beside him.

"What's this about?" Colter asked.

The man in front of him, whose pale face he could not make out beneath the square bill of a dark blue forage cap but whose voice Colter recognized as belonging to Lieutenant Damian Hobart, one of Lieutenant Belden's cronies, said, "The pleasure of your company has been requested behind the corral."

Colter curled his upper lip though he had to admit to feeling relieved that it was merely Belden calling and not a passel of greasy bounty hunters ready to take his head back to Sapinero, Colorado, where the mangled Bill Rondo was holed up in a rooming house, his craggy face sporting the same brand as the one he'd given Colter. "Belden wanna dance with me now, too?"

"Somethin' like that," said the man behind him, whose voice he thought he recognized as that of Lieutenant A. J. McKnight. The three could often be seen together drinking and playing cards in the saloon off the fort sutler's store at night, or heading off to Tucson during weekend furloughs.

Colter stepped down off the gallery steps. As the two men moved to flank him, he began walking toward the corrals ahead and on his left. A breeze came up to churn some dust, straw, and horse manure, and Colter blinked against it. The windmill blades gave a little squeal. Then the breeze died, and Colter walked around the far corral to the back, where he could see a dark figure sitting on the open tailgate of a hay wagon.

The three California broncs didn't move other than to switch their tails, annoyed at being disturbed at this late hour.

Colter rounded the corral's rear corner and approached the hay wagon. Belden sat on the tailgate with his legs dangling, ankles crossed. He had a bottle cradled in his lap the way a woman would hold a sleeping child, and a long black cheroot smoldered in his right, black-gloved hand.

He looked at Colter, dark blue eyes looking white in the moonlight. He didn't say anything and neither did Colter. Another slight breeze rose, blowing Colter's long hair out in front of him, brushing it against his cheeks. McKnight and Hobart stood silently behind Colter. He could sense them grinning, and he could smell the alcohol and tobacco smoke on all of them.

"You know," Belden said finally, cocking his head to one side and blowing out two smoke plumes through his nostrils, "a kid like you, as scarred up and dumb and ugly as you are, really oughta just stay back here with the horses."

Colter shrugged. "Your girl just wouldn't have it, I guess."

Behind Colter, Hobart sighed deeply.

Belden stared at Colter from beneath the brim of his dark blue cavalry kepi with the gold braid encircling the crown. "Is that supposed to be funny?"

"I'm just sayin' she invited me to the dance," Colter said, putting some steel into his voice. "I didn't invite her. So I danced with her."

"You know why she danced with you — don't you?"

"I guess she thinks I'm pretty."

"No. She thinks you're ugly. But, see, she's always trying to save stray cats and stray dogs. The uglier the better. Even had her a crippled coyote for a time. That's just what she does. Everybody knows that."

"Then what are we doin' here?"

"Everybody knows that, it seems, except you."

"What if I said I know that?"

"Knowing that isn't gonna keep you from starin' at her all dog-eyed, next time she comes around to watch you bust your broncs. Or keep you from accepting her invitation to the next dance." Belden set the bottle aside and gained his feet, balling his fists at his sides. "Or thinkin' you might have a chance, as ludicrous as that would be."

Colter chuckled at the absurdity of the situation. Also, possibly, to cover his own chagrin of knowing that there was a kernel of truth in what the lieutenant had said. Part of him had indeed fallen for the girl, and that part of him made the rest of him feel like a damn fool.

He glanced at Hobart and McKnight behind him. "Three against one?"

45

"No, no." Belden removed his hat and gloves and set them on the tailgate beside the whiskey bottle. "I fight like this, kid."

Colter didn't see the straight left jab hammering toward him through the darkness before it smacked him in the mouth. It seemed to shove his lower jaw back into his skull though he didn't feel a thing until the ground came up to smack him hard from behind.

Suddenly, he was sitting in the gravel, his hat tumbling off his shoulder, hair in his eyes. Warm blood oozed from his bottom lip. His head began pounding in earnest though only for about three beats before the pounding dulled and the two images of Belden standing in front of him, slamming his right fist into his left palm, merged into one.

Fury burned hot and wild in Colter Farrow.

He glowered up at the lieutenant as, chuckling, the other two men climbed the corral fence behind Colter, hooking their heels over the bottom rail, McKnight removing the cap from a flask and settling in for the show.

Colter brushed his fist across his lip and spat a gob of blood on the ground. "That was a sucker punch, you son of a bitch."

"What'd you call me, shit-kicker?"

"A son of a bitch. A cheap, yellow-livered bitch."

Hobart chuckled but broke it off sharply when Belden flicked his cold gaze at him. Holding his fists out in the bare-knuckle style, Belden shuffled sideways around Colter. "Get up."

Colter got his boots under him and heaved himself to his feet. Quickly, he appraised his opponent. Colter had little chance. Dripping wet, Colter weighed a hundred and fifty pounds. He stood an inch shy of six feet. Belden had two inches and a good thirty pounds on him, and, judging by the deftness of that first punch, he'd obviously boxed a few times in the past, and hadn't let the rules fetter him. Colter had heard rumors about him using the feckless enlisted men as punching bags, and now he believed them.

Just the same, Colter had no intention of turning tail. He'd get in a lick or two before the lieutenant beat him into a miserable night's sleep.

Raising his own fists, mimicking fighters he'd watched in the past, he crouched and shuffled sideways, bobbing and weaving to avoid a sudden strike from his opponent.

Belden grinned savagely, mockingly. He

came at Colter hard and lightning fast.

Colter tried to duck the first slashing right, but the more experienced fighter had anticipated the move, and the man's bulging right fist clipped Colter on the nub of his scarred right cheek. The blow punched Colter's face into the man's other fist, which caught Colter on the left side of his mouth. Suddenly, he was stumbling backward once more. Either McKnight or Hobart stuck out a boot and Colter pushed off it, regaining his balance and spreading his feet.

He didn't wait for Belden but stepped forward quickly and landed a lucky punch on the lieutenant's chin. The blow did not faze the lieutenant but only evoked a sneer before Belden came forward once more, and Colter felt like a punching bag that the slashing rights and hammering lefts pummeled with merciless speed and force until Colter lowered his spinning, ringing head, feeling both eyes swelling shut and blood dribbling down from his split lips and across his lower jaw and chin.

Then Belden punched him hard in the belly — once, twice, three times — before the ground came up with the force of a runaway freight train.

The wind exploded from Colter's lungs.

He rolled, arms crossed on his battered

ribs, groaning.

He tried to stand. His ribs screamed, nearly drowning out the cracked bells clanging in his ears.

He eased himself onto his back and looked up at Belden staring down at him, the man's head silhouetted against the milky wash of moonlight dulling the stars scattered like glitter above him. The man's hair was mussed. That was all the damage Colter had done. Belden's white teeth showed under his thick black mustache. His jaws bulged.

"Think you're done?" He shook his head. "You're not done." He glanced at Hobart and McKnight. "Hold him."

Belden's two cronies climbed down off the corral. They each reached down and hauled Colter up by an arm, each twisting a limb behind Colter's back. He could have fought them off about as well as an injured sparrow could have fought off a hungry wolf pack, for he hadn't sucked a full breath since Belden's second, gut-busting blow to his solar plexus.

Yep, a miserable damn night's sleep this was going to be.

Belden stepped up within six inches of him, jutting his hard, angry face toward Colter's. "I ever see you talking to Miss Lenore again — I don't care who starts it

— you're gonna get twice as good as what you got tonight. Just remember that, shit-kicker. When she comes around, you turn away."

Colter nodded slowly, exaggeratedly, not complying with the lieutenant's wishes but merely acknowledging to himself that even in his addled state he could understand, with extreme effort, what the man was saying.

Colter tensed when McKnight and Hobart drew back on his arms so hard he thought his shoulders would bust out of their sockets. He tensed again when he saw the first of the next batch of blows coming. The lieutenant worked his face over good, not ignoring Colter's midsection, until Colter felt two Apache war lances thrust into his shoulders. As he hit the gravelly ground, bleeding and swollen and gasping like a landed fish, he crossed his arms on his chest to reach for the war lances.

But there were no war lances. The pain was only from McKnight and Hobart so suddenly releasing his arms that the blood was returning screaming life to the twisted limbs.

Colter gritted his teeth, feeling warm blood oozing out of his mouth and through his lips to mingle with the several thick streams already flowing freely down his chin and lower jaw. Vaguely, he wondered how many teeth were gone and how badly shredded his tongue was.

"Christ, Pres," he heard someone say as though from far away. "The major's gonna be mad as hell if he can't work tomorrow." A face appeared close to Colter's — the long, pale, blond-goateed face of Hobart, the lieutenant's mouth gaping in shock. "And shit, it doesn't look to me like he's gonna be ridin' anything but a bunk for the next *six weeks*!"

"No, and he won't be pestering Miss Lenore for a long while, either," said Belden with a self-satisfied air.

Hobart moved away and then Colter stared at the sky as he sucked more air into his heaving chest and spat more and more blood out of his mouth. Suddenly, Belden was standing over him again. The lieutenant was wearing his hat, cocked at its usual rakish angle. He had one glove on and was pulling on the other.

In his slow, softly rising and falling Virginia accent, he said, "Sometimes it takes some harsh teaching for the stable-mucking ilk of Mr. Farrow here to learn their proper station, and the respect due their betters." Belden got his glove on and let his arms fall to his sides, staring coldly, arrogantly down at Colter. "And that the women of their betters are given a very wide berth. But when you're asked how you got those little cuts on your face, you just say you came out here drunk tonight after the dance and climbed aboard the wrong hammerhead. Hear?"

Colter had no idea where the sudden strength came from. It was as though lightning struck him, filling him with blue-white fury and just as much concentrated energy. He raised his left leg, and, gritting his tender teeth, hurled the leg hard to the right and against Belden's left, high-topped black cavalry boot.

Belden must have just started lifting that foot, because Colter's ankle sliced through it like a knife through lard. And then it sliced through the other one, and both Belden's boots flew out from under the man.

"Oh!" The lieutenant's scream was shrill and short.

Colter stared up dully, incomprehendingly, as the tall, willowy man's upper torso slanted down to Colter's right so fast that it looked like the shadow of a night bird winging over quickly. There was a hard thudding, crunching sound and a dull grunt. And then the heavier thump of a body slamming into the ground.

Silence.

A boot crunched gravel.

Hobart's low, tentative inquiry: "Pres?"

No response.

"Holy hell," whispered McKnight.

He crouched to Colter's left, staring down at something on the ground. Colter didn't have the strength to lift his head. All he could see in the periphery of his vision was a thick black oblong shape on the ground to his left, under the two crouching lieutenants.

McKnight didn't say anything for what seemed a long time until he whispered, "He's not movin'. He's not movin' one damn muscle."

Another short silence before Hobart said, "And he's not breathin', neither."

CHAPTER 5

Colter must have passed out.

All he knew was that time seemed to skip ahead until he was looking around and realizing that both McKnight and Hobart were gone, and that Pres Belden lay on the ground nearby, flat on his back near the wagon's open tailgate. Something dark was dripping off the end of the tailgate and pooling on the ground below it, beside Belden's head.

Then Colter realized what had drawn him up out of shallow unconsciousness — the trilling of spurs and the thudding of boots moving toward him fast. He'd know the skip-scuff shamble of Willie Tappin anywhere.

"Colter, what the . . . ?"

Colter groaned and lifted his head, trying to push himself up to a sitting position against the searing pain in his ribs. As Willie approached dressed in buckskin pants, boots, and underwear shirt with an army blanket thrown over his shoulders, Colter gave up and rolled onto his left hip, spitting more blood from his lips and casting his gaze toward where Belden lay unmoving near the wagon's open tailgate.

Willie slowed his pace and stooped to place a hand on Colter's shoulder, but then, seeing the dark hump of Belden, he stepped over Colter and continued on over to the wagon. He dropped to a knee and placed a hand on the lieutenant's throat, then glanced over at Colter. "Dead. By the way he's lyin' I'd say his neck's broke."

Colter blinked, just now beginning to comprehend what had happened. He'd caught the lieutenant off balance and kicked him off his feet. His head had slammed into the tailgate as he'd gone down. The crunching sound had been Belden's neck breaking. The realization slowly gathered steam in Colter's head.

Belden was dead. Colter had killed him.

"I got up to take a piss," Willie said, walking back over to Colter, "and I'd just stepped out of the bunkhouse when I seen two soldiers running off toward the fort, like two donkeys with tin cans tied to their tails."

"McKnight and Hobart."

"Colter, what for the love o' Jehova happened out here?"

"I got the shit kicked out of both ends."

"I see that."

"Somehow, I managed to give that son of a bitch one helluva mule kick, and" — Colter leaned on an elbow and fingered his chin, still trying to remember and work it all through his mind — "and beefed the bastard."

"Well, beef is what he is, all right." Willie stared in awe at the dead lieutenant, then dropped to a knee in front of Colter. "How bad you hurt?"

"I feel like I still have one of his boots up my ass."

"You look like a bobcat done tried to drag you off down the wash for supper."

Willie stared toward the main fort across about a hundred yards of desert bristling with rocks and cat-claw. The adobe buildings sat slouched and ash-colored in the moonlight. The major's house was at the far right end of the parade ground — a big Victorian affair that looked as out of place here on the Arizona desert as would a peacock in a chicken coop. No lights were on there, either.

Willie said, "And you're gonna look a lot worse if you don't get the hell out of here."

Colter shook his head, rose off his hands, straightening his back to a kneeling position, grimacing as he sucked a little more air into his lungs, both of which felt strangled. But he didn't feel any bones moving around, so maybe no ribs were broken. Bruised certainly. Maybe cracked. But not broken.

"It was an accident. I lashed out, caught him off balance. Besides, he beat me like a rented mule while those two tinhorns, McKnight and Hobart, held my arms."

"Colter, it don't matter. Belden's old man is in tight with the territorial governor of Arizona. They're business partners. Hell, I think they might even be cousins."

"What're you sayin', Willie?"

"I'm sayin' you have to hightail it the hell away from here. Now. The governor and Belden's old man are powerful men, and if you know powerful men, you know they're gonna want blood."

Again, Colter shook his head. "Forget it. I'm gonna tell it the way it happened. Besides, the son of a gutless cur had it comin'!"

Willie stared at him, his eyes round and serious above his beard stubble and below a wing of mussed brown hair. "And what about that price on your head? The one them shooters was huntin' this afternoon?"

Colter stared back in shock. He'd never told Willie anything about Bill Rondo or the bounty Rondo had placed on his head. He'd thought Willie had swallowed his story about that afternoon's bushwhacking, too.

"I spent the last coupla summers in Colorado," Willie said. "Workin' a ranch in the San Juans, just close enough to the Lunatics for word about what happened in Sapinero to spread there like one o' them late-summer lightning fires. I heard what Rondo did to your foster pa, Colter. And I heard what Rondo did to you . . . before you give back the same to him. This is gonna draw a helluva lot of attention, kid. If you don't hang for this" — he jerked his square chin toward Belden, keeping his eyes on Colter — "you'll hang for Rondo."

Colter looked once more toward the main part of the fort. Still no lights. Where had McKnight and Hobart gone? What were their intentions? Were they going to let someone else find Belden or would they spill the beans themselves about the ungallant and proscribed ass-kicking they'd taken part in?

Hard to say. Both men were drunk. They might not say anything, or they might wait and report what had happened out here to

Major Fairchild after they'd sobered up in the morning. Whatever happened, the trump card was always going to be that a civilian horse breaker, Colter Farrow, had killed a young lieutenant who not only hailed from a prominent family but who'd also intended to marry the major's daughter.

And then, as Willie had said, there was the not so little matter of the price on Colter's head, not to mention the federal warrant for his arrest. It seemed that shooting and branding even a scum-wallowing lizard like Bill Rondo was against the law. If he didn't hang for that, he'd hang for Belden.

"Holy shit," he said, turning to Willie with warning bells now clearly clanging in his head. "I guess you're right, partner."

"Ain't I usually?" Willie set Colter's hat on his head, threw an arm around his shoulders, and helped the young man to his feet. "Let's get you fixed up, and then I'll saddle your horse."

"What about you, Willie?" Colter said when Willie had gotten him into the shack and eased him down on the edge of his bunk. "They're gonna ask you a lot of questions."

"Ah, hell," Willie said, grabbing a wool army blanket off a shelf. He did not light a lantern. "Everyone knows how much I drink at those things. They'll believe me when I say I didn't see or hear nothin'. When I woke the next mornin', you were gone, and I figured you was just gettin' an early start at the snubbin' post."

The older horse breaker grabbed his bowie knife off a table and used it to carve a notch in the end of the blanket. He gave a grunt as he ripped the blanket in two, discarding one half while folding the other half once.

"I don't want you getting in trouble over me," Colter said as Willie pulled him to his feet and then wrapped the blanket around the young man's waist.

He pulled the blanket taut around Colter's battered ribs. Colter grunted and drew a sharp breath, cursing.

"This'll hold them ribs in place, kid. If any're broken, ridin' a horse'll likely kill ya, but I reckon it's a chance you'll have to take."

"Like I said . . ." Colter's face heated up like a steam iron as Willie tied a knot in the two ends of the blanket at Colter's lower back.

"Don't worry, kid," Willie said. "You know what a good liar I am."

In the moonlight angling through the window, Colter saw his partner give him a wink. Then Willie turned and grabbed a bottle off the tomato crate standing on end in front of the window, handing it to Colter. "Take a few sips of that. Hell, take the bottle. It was brewed by old Salty over at the store, with a dead rattler at the bottom of the vat, but it'll keep those cuts and bruises from squawkin' loud enough to wake every 'Pache in southern Arizon."

Colter hefted the three-quarters-full bottle in his hand, his stomach recoiling at the thought of the stuff burning the cuts in his mouth. Besides, he'd never acquired a taste for tanglefoot of any kind though he'd taken a beer now and then, just to be sociable. "Thanks," he said, making a face.

Willie walked over to the door, opening it a crack and looking out. He cursed sharply.

Colter's heart thudded. "What is it?"

"There's a light on in the old man's house." The "old man" was Major Fairchild.

Colter set the bottle down, hurried to the door, and shoved Willie aside. "Forget it, Willie. You get in bed. I'll saddle my own horse and ride out. They'll think you were asleep the whole time."

Willie grabbed Colter's arm firmly and hardened his jaws. "We haven't known each other long, Colter, but there's been damn few people in this world I've ever called a friend. Even fewer I'd risk my neck for."

He stared hard at Colter, letting his eyes add the rest. Colter stepped back away from the door. "All right. Hurry!"

Willie bounded out the door and under the ramada and ran limping down the front of the stable. Colter glanced out once more. The major's lower-story windows were lit. The house was a couple of hundred yards away, but he thought he could see shadows moving around in front of the windows.

Colter ran a frustrated hand through his hair to which grit and flecks of hay and straw still clung. So McKnight and Hobart had reported the killing to the major. Why hadn't they just taken him into custody themselves rather than look like a couple of tinhorns? Too drunk to think of it, maybe.

Colter closed the bunk-shack door and stumbled around, dizzy and sore from the beating, filling his saddlebags and remembering to include the bottle though he couldn't yet bring himself to take a drink of the sutler's snake venom. He filled the burlap sack that he used for stowing his cooking supplies, rolled his soogan inside his rain slicker, tied it closed, and headed out the door just as Willie came out of the stable, leading Colter's blaze-faced coyote dun whom he called Northwest for the way the horse had always faced back home when he was grazing.

Colter paused to dipper water out of the olla hanging from the ramada, and swished a mouthful around before spitting it out into the yard, trying to get rid of the coppery taste of blood. Probing his mouth with his tongue, he discovered one tooth missing, one chipped, and another one loose. Most of the blood had come from his lips and his tongue, which he must have bit while being used as a human whipping post by Belden.

That was all right. He was still alive, which made him better off than Belden. Besides, he hadn't been too worried about his looks since Rondo had burned that S into his cheek.

"Thanks, Willie."

Willie handed Colter the bridle reins. "You best head on up to that cave above White Tanks. Water there, and no one'll find you. Be damn hard to track you in that rocky country. I'll check in on you after the dust has settled, bring you some grub."

He helped Colter into the saddle. The maneuver made sweat bead on the young redhead's forehead. "Don't take any chances, Willie."

"Don't worry — I'll make sure the dust has settled before I come."

Voices sounded from the direction of the parade ground. Likely, the major had rousted soldiers and would be bringing a contingent out here in a few minutes.

Colter reined the gelding out away from the bunk-shack. "Have a drink and get back in bed, Willie. They'll be here soon."

Willie tried a grin. "Now, those are orders I don't mind followin'!"

Colter booted Northwest around the bunk-shack, past the privy and trash pile, and across a shallow dry wash angling toward the San Pedro. His ribs grieved him something awful, and it was hard to draw a breath, but he'd had broken ribs before, and Willie had been right. If any were broken, just riding this far would likely have killed him or at least have caused him to pass out.

Without the moon, Northwest would have had trouble picking his way across the desert. As it was, Colter was able to give the horse his head and close his eyes and try to rest as much as he could despite the jostling. Northwest headed toward the Galiuro Range that was a vague black bulk rising ahead of him, toward Aravaipa Canyon.

He and Willie had stumbled across a cave in the Galiuros when they'd been driving a string of broncs they'd trapped on the far side of the range of jutting stone cliffs and massive strewn boulders, and they'd holed up there for a night. Colter had returned to the cave once since then, when he'd been out hunting alone on a day off — because of the bounty on his head, he never went to town, as the soldiers and Willie usually did — and he hoped like hell he'd be able to find the cave again tonight near the White Tanks.

Every now and then Colter glanced over his right shoulder. The fort was growing more and more indistinct in the shallow bowl it sprawled across, surrounded by several craggy mountain ranges. He could see the pinprick glow of a couple of lights but nothing more. If soldiers were on his trail, he couldn't tell it from here.

He thought about Willie and hoped the stove-up horse breaker was as good an actor as he seemed to think he was. The worry was short-lived. A wicked scream rose on a low ridge to his right, and Northwest gave a shrill whinny as he pitched wildly off his front feet. Colter must not have had a good grip on the saddle horn, because he suddenly found himself tumbling ass-over-teakettle over the horse's rump and into open air before once again he met his old nemesis — the cold, hard ground.

Chapter 6

Colter must have passed out again, because when he found himself flat on his back and staring at the stars, his horse was nowhere in sight. He heard low snarling and the rattle of stones sliding down the ridge that rose on his left now, about forty yards away — a steep dyke about fifty feet high and resembling a half-buried dinosaur spine.

Fiery pain consumed the young horse breaker. Its intensity doubled as he rose to a sitting position, gritting his teeth, and slid his Remington from the cross-draw holster on his left hip. Out of the frying pan and into the fire was the phrase that repeated itself in the back of his agonized brain. Now a wildcat was stalking him.

And in his condition, he'd make an easy meal.

"Please stay where you are," he muttered, feeling fresh blood ooze from his cut lips, mingling with that which had crusted on his chin. "Just stay there."

He clicked the Remy's hammer back, aiming at the ridge, not wanting to trigger a shot and give away his position. In the silence of this Arizona night, without a breath of breeze and no yammering coyotes, the shot would easily be heard back at Grant. And he'd be just as easy pickings for a contingent of soldiers — especially those riding out to avenge the death of one of their own at the hands of a lowly horse breaker — as he would for a mountain lion.

Not only had Colter been on the lower echelon of the social scale at Grant, but he'd sensed that his keeping to himself had been taken as snobbishness. That would be held against him, too, when it came time to ride him down and throw a loop around his neck.

He aimed the Remington as steadily as he could at the ridge. He could see no moving shadow, and the rocks had stopped rolling. Faintly, then, he began to hear a soft, contented mewling and the snapping of hungry jaws. His gun hand relaxed. The cat must have already found its supper on the other side of the ridge, and had just come over to frighten off any potential competition.

Colter waited.

When he was fairly certain he was in no immediate danger from the cat, he hauled himself wearily, painfully to his feet and stared back in the direction of Camp Grant. He could no longer see the fort but merely a milky purple wash of light over the bowl in which it sat. There were no sounds except for those of the cat feeding on the other side of the dyke.

Finally, he started walking up the slope to find Northwest. He stopped, turned back toward the fort, pricking his ears. Faintly, he could hear the soft thuds of distant horses. The thuds of the shod hooves grew gradually as the soldiers — who else would they be? — headed toward him.

Colter wheeled and strode as fast as he could up the slope, sweeping the terrain around him for Northwest. Sweat beaded on the back of his neck and slithered, cold as snowmelt, down his back, pasting his shirt to his skin.

He holstered the Remington and moved faster, looking around the low outcroppings, breathing hard from pain and anxiety as well as from the hard upward climb. Nearly a quarter hour later, stopping now and then to listen to the muffled hoof clomps behind him, he found Northwest cropping galleta grass around a dry spring trough angling out from the side of a rocky slope.

He did not berate the horse for running out on him. Horses feared wildcats the way little boys feared bogeymen, and no horse, no matter how well trained, could do anything but run when it heard the dreaded feline scream.

When Colter had made sure his rifle was secure in its saddle boot, he heaved himself bitterly into the saddle, the twisting and crouching making him feel as though a hot, wet blanket had been thrown over his shoulders, then turned his head to listen behind him.

Amidst the clomps of oncoming horses, he could now hear men's low, conferring voices. The deep, raspy one he recognized as that of Major Fairchild. A stone dropped hard in Colter's gut. The major's leading the contingent himself in the middle of the night, with his bad knees and pleurisy, meant the old man really meant business. He'd show Colter no mercy at all for killing his prospective son-in-law, let alone listen to Colter's story of how it had all transpired. Colter knew the man's iron-hard, take-no-prisoners reputation when it came to the Apaches, and he'd likely treat Colter with just as little mercy.

Colter put Northwest ahead, holding the

horse to a trot, as he didn't want to be heard by the riders behind him, who probably realized they were nearing their prey and were stopping often to look and listen. When he gained the vertical jut of sandstone at the top of the rise, Colter picked up the wild horse trail at the base of the rock and followed it down a steep slope to the south.

At the bottom of the slope, he swung Northwest into an eastern-angling, gravel-bottomed canyon and, knowing now he was likely far enough from the cavalrymen that they wouldn't hear him, booted the horse into a gallop that broke the sweat out in earnest across Colter's forehead and shoulders.

He was fairly swimming in pain and fever sweat by the time he'd reached the end of the canyon and loped on up and over a rise, then swung hard to the south. This was rocky country, so by the time the soldiers reached the end of the canyon, they'd have no way to track him — especially in the dark. Only a good Apache scout could shadow him to where he intended to go — up high into the rocky, wind-blasted, and sunbaked reaches of the boulder nest called White Tanks that formed a spur off the southern Galiuro Mountain Range.

Only diamondbacks, Chiricahua Apaches,

and Mexican banditos lived there, though Colter had heard that the Apaches had been chased into Mexico by General Crook. That left the snakes and banditos, formidable opponents Colter would worry about when the time came, after he'd lost the soldiers.

Colter had been through this country three times since he'd come to Camp Grant, looking for wild horses to trap and some to buy from a friendly old *mesteno* who lived near here but whom Colter would not burden with his troubles. No, he'd find the cave. He knew a winding route through deep canyons, and the moon should make for relatively easy traveling as long as he wasn't waylaid by banditos or the odd Apache who'd chosen to remain here in the Chiricahuas rather than run wild in Mexico with the others.

Colter had been traveling alone in remote country for nearly three years now, on the run from the law as well as bounty hunters, and he had developed a good eye and a good memory for landmarks, for he never knew when he'd need a fast, inconspicuous escape route to a remote sanctuary. That's why he'd remembered the cave and the path that led him into a canyon below it and then to a circuitous wild horse trace up a steep ridge, until the cave shone like a velvet, black, egg-shaped shadow in the rocks just above him.

It was surrounded by wiry tufts of brush and cactus, slabs of rock poking every which way, and wagon-sized boulders. There was about fifty feet of sheer granite above it, like a giant fireplace mantel, so it was a hard place to see from any direction unless you happened to stumble on it, as he and Willie had done when they'd been avoiding banditos. He doubted anyone had spent much time in it over the last fifty years or so, including Apaches, because, while there'd been a hole dug for a fire ring inside, until he and Willie had spent a night here there'd been only a trace of ashes in it and the flaky remains of ancient, charred bones.

He half fell out of his saddle and dropped to his knees, sucking air into his battered chest, his ribs grinding as his lungs expanded. He was soaked in sweat. Cursing Belden, he gained his feet and stared off across the jagged slope that was cast mostly in shadow by the west-tumbling moon. He could neither see nor hear anything from the devil's mouth of slashing canyons and gorges he'd just traversed, though from far behind him, on the other side of the ridge, coyotes were yammering.

Odd, how he found comfort in their

distant company. Aside from them and Northwest, he was alone out here, miles from anyone including the old *mesteno* who had a small log cabin about five miles away as the crow flies — a long, hard ride in this devil's playground. He'd grown accustomed to spending long stretches of time alone, sometimes going weeks without spying another soul. But it was always harder just after he'd been amongst people he'd become close to, like Willie and Lenore Fairchild, whom he would likely never see again.

As he led Northwest up around the rocks toward the cave, he supposed she'd learned of the death of her beau. He supposed, too, that she wished she'd never laid eyes on Colter Farrow, and was probably right now cursing his name while she cried into her pillow.

He paused outside the gaping cave mouth, smelling the cold stone within. Touching the worn walnut grips of his holstered Remington, he said softly, "Hello the cave."

The cavern's only response was the faint echo of the redhead's own voice. Quickly, agonizingly, he stripped off Northwest's bridle and saddle and the bedroll and saddlebags, piling the gear in front of the cave, then led the horse around the cave to a small alcove nearby. It was an area about as large as two stable stalls, and it had a small rock tank with some water in it from a recent rain. He placed a hackamore over the horse's head, tied the rope to a pillar of rock, and tossed down a few handfuls of oats near the tank. The water and oats would have to do for now. He'd rub the coyote dun down later, when he'd had some sleep. And he'd take him down to the spring in the morning and let him crop the green grass that grew amongst the rocks lining the seep.

In the meantime . . . he stumbled on the toes of his boots as he made his way back to the cave. He scratched a lucifer to life on his shell belt and ducked inside the cavern, holding the match up to inspect the place, making sure it was empty. Then he dropped the match, dragged his gear inside, spread his blanket roll as best he could, and collapsed into it, drawing the top blanket up to his chin. He was cold as well as hot, sweating so that he felt as though he were swimming underwater, and sleep would not come.

He knew he should build a fire, but he did not want to risk the glow being seen from downslope. Besides, he didn't have the energy to gather wood. Remembering Willie's whiskey, he opened the flap on one of his saddlebag pouches and pulled out the bottle. He grimaced when he thought of that snake floating around on the bottom of the sutler's vat and gave a shudder. Before he could chicken out, he popped the cork and took a pull.

The whiskey set his mouth on fire. He swallowed quickly, and then his throat and belly were aflame, as well. His guts heaved, and he bent forward, nearly vomiting. After a few seconds the burning waned and a faint lightness closed over him, dulling the ache in his lips and ribs. He corked the bottle, set it aside, and laid his head back on his saddlebags before closing his eyes.

He gave a deep, rattling sigh.

Sleep about as restful as a voyage in a small boat on typhoon-embroiled seas boiled over him. He ached and burned and felt an Arctic chill deep in his bones. Several times he half woke to find his teeth clattering until he thought all the rest would crack. He dreamed of fire and snow and fork-tailed devils chasing him through dark canyons and up mountains limned in moonlight and into the waiting arms of snarling, red-eyed wolves. All night he was either running from demons or wolves or fire or icy snowmelt seas.

When one of those wolves had grabbed

his ankle, and the demons were swarming on top of him, one of the demons screaming, *"Killer!"* he jerked his head up off the soaked leather saddlebag pouch with a low, raspy yell that got tangled up in his throat.

Golden-copper light angled through the cave mouth. It could be morning, but judging by the warmth in the air, it was likely later on in the day. Colter blinked against the light as he looked around dumbly, only half remembering where he was and what had brought him here, running his tongue around in his dry mouth that still tasted like copper. He fumbled around for the canteen, and just when he'd gotten the cap off and was taking a drink, Northwest whinnied.

The dun's cry was answered by another horse farther away.

Shod hooves clacked on rock.

Colter dropped the canteen and flailed around with both hands for his pistol. Where the hell was it? Finally, he found his shell belt half concealed by his possibles bag and pulled the Remington from its holster, his hand still shaking from the fever as he heard the rider moving up the slope toward the cave.

CHAPTER 7

As the hoof clacks grew louder and copper dust began to waft in front of the cave, Colter saw his rifle in its scabbard still strapped to his saddle. He depressed the Remington's hammer, set the pistol aside, and grabbed the Henry. He racked a shell into the breech and scuttled forward until he was a few feet from the cave mouth, then, on his knees, pressed the stock to his shoulder.

A girl's scream cut the quiet air.

Colter blinked in surprise as a cream gelding was brought up short, the bit in its teeth drawing its head back as it pranced in place, half turning and showing the profile of the chocolate-haired girl in the saddle, clad in a blue blouse with ruffled sleeves and collar and a spruce green riding skirt. She sat back in the silver-trimmed Texas saddle with a dinner-plate-sized horn, her back taut. Beneath the brim of her straw sombrero, her fearful eyes flicked between Colter's scarred face and the cocked rifle he was aiming at her heart. She held the reins in her gloved hands up close to her creamy neck.

"Don't shoot me!"

Colter lowered the rifle, looking around quickly, then, seeing no one else riding up the slope, depressed the hammer and let the barrel sag toward the cave's floor carpeted in gray rock dust. "Lenore . . . ?"

She swung expertly down from her saddle — no sidesaddle for Lenore, which was one of the things Colter had admired about the girl — and continued the last twenty feet to the top of the slope, leading the cream by its reins. Rocks rattled beneath her dusty black riding boots. Her horse snorted and blew. Northwest whinnied from his alcove, and the cream raised its head and returned the greeting in kind.

Lenore place a quieting hand on the cream's snout, her eyes riveted to Colter. "God, you look . . . *terrible!*"

"What're you doin' here?" Again, Colter swept the boulder-strewn slope with his apprehensive gaze. "Who told you . . . ?"

"Mr. Tappin. He couldn't come himself. My father's keeping a close watch on him."

"Willie's all right?"

Lenore nodded. "He hasn't been hurt, but if my father thought that he knew where you're holed up, he'd likely face a firing squad. My father's very . . . angry . . . about this."

"What about you?"

"I know it's not very ladylike to admit, but I was so sick after I heard what had happened that I retched six times yesterday."

Colter frowned. "Yesterday? You mean last night. Today."

She frowned back at him, shaking her head. "It happened a day before yesterday."

Colter looked around as though to find some indication of how long he'd slept by his natural surroundings. The angle of the sun told him it was midafternoon, probably edging toward three. Could it be the afternoon of his second day in the cave?

Lenore turned and unhooked the rope of a burlap sack from her saddle horn and set it on the ground near Colter. "This is food. Some chicken sandwiches and jerky, a couple tins of peaches. Willie added a bag of coffee, some beans and tortillas, and a pouch of deer jerky."

The image of the food in Colter's mind caused his belly to spasm and rumble. He was surprised how hollowed out and hungry he was despite his aches and pains. But then, if he'd slept for nearly two days, it wasn't surprising.

He set his rifle aside, and with quivering hands — due as much to hunger as the fever, he realized now — he pulled at the knot of rope holding the sacks closed, drawing the neck of the bag open. He froze, remembering Northwest.

"Ah, shit," he said, forgetting himself. "Northwest — he needs food and water."

"You eat," Lenore said. "I'll tend to your horse." She pulled another burlap pouch off her saddle horn and, holding it against her chest, patted it and smiled. "Mr. Tappin thought of him, too."

Colter grabbed his canteen and held it up to her by its canvas lanyard. "He'll need water."

"Of course."

He tossed her his hat, and she took it along with the canteen and started walking toward the alcove in the rocks flanking the cave.

Colter had the smaller pouch in his lap, and he was fishing around inside for a sandwich. "Lenore?"

She turned back to him, brows arched.

"I don't understand. I . . ."

"I know what happened, Colter," she said grimly. "Lieutenant McKnight and Lieutenant Hobart told my father that they and Lieutenant Belden had found you smoking around the stables after the dance. That you were stumbling around drunk. They were afraid you'd start a fire, so they told you to knock off and go to bed. You got mad and wanted to fight them and somehow got Pres . . . Lieutenant Belden . . . off balance, and he fell against the hay wagon and broke his neck."

Colter shook his head and narrowed his eyes angrily. "That ain't what happened, Lenore."

She held his gaze with a firm, sincere one of her own. "I know what happened, Colter. Even before I went over to the stables and talked to Mr. Tappin."

Colter stared at her in confusion.

She shook her head. "I had no intention of marrying the lieutenant. That was my parents' wish, because he came from a wealthy family, and my doing so would be politically beneficial for Father."

"Your father know you weren't gonna marry him?"

"He knew only my protests against it, and that Lieutenant Belden turned my stomach like no other man ever has. I'm sure he and my mother thought that, in the end, I would bow to their wishes. And I even believe they thought my marrying Belden really was the best opportunity for me, as well." She looked off, the breeze sliding loose strands of hair around her cheeks. "For some reason, they couldn't see the monster he really was."

She moved toward Colter, leaned down, and kissed his cheek. "This is all my fault. I shouldn't have tried to parade you around the dance hall, caused you so much trouble and pain. You see, Colter, I really do like you, and I wanted so much to spend the bulk of the night with you. Not him. I was being very selfish."

She turned and walked back toward Northwest, leaving the cream ground-reined just outside the cave.

Colter bit into the chicken sandwich that she'd built thick on crusty wheat bread, with onions and mustard and strips of bacon. Ignoring his chipped tooth and torn tongue, he devoured half the sandwich in under a minute, and was about to reach for the second half when he realized his stomach wasn't quite as happy with the food as his mouth had been.

He set the sack aside and looked around for his second canteen. It lay beside his saddle, against the cave wall behind him, about five feet from the opening. He turned gingerly, crawled over to it, popped the cork, and took a long drink of the water no less refreshing for being stale and tepid. When he'd had his fill, he poured some over his head and ran his hands through his wet hair, shivering as several drops slithered under his collar and rolled down his back.

Footsteps sounded behind him. He started to turn toward Lenore, saying, "Sure do appreciate the grub, Miss . . ."

It wasn't Lenore behind him. It was three men in cavalry blues, all three holding Spencer repeaters — two resting their rifles on their shoulders while the third, a young, yellow-haired sergeant with a darkly tanned face with pinched, belligerent eyes, aimed his carbine straight out from his left hip at Colter. He wore a hard smile. The other two looked just as self-satisfied.

Colter rose slowly.

"Easy, now, killer," said the yellow-haired sergeant, whose name Colter believed was Gustafsson. "No sudden moves or we'll gut-shoot you and leave you here."

Colter studied the three men. One more came up behind them from the direction of Northwest's stone stable. The fourth man was a tall, gangly corporal, and he was holding Lenore in front of him, one hand over her mouth. Lenore was red-faced with shock, and tears dribbled out of her brown eyes. The corporal removed his hand, and Lenore said, sobbing, "I'm sorry, Colter. I tried to make sure I wasn't followed!"

Colter wasn't surprised she'd been shadowed. He wouldn't have expected her to cover her tracks. But these four soldiers were not going to take him back to Camp Grant. They'd have to kill him and take back a corpse tied over his horse.

The blond sergeant said, "Take that six-shooter out of your pants. Slow. With two fingers. Then toss it over here."

Still, blond Sergeant Gustafsson was the only one of the four aiming a gun at him. The others obviously didn't think he'd be much trouble, as beat up as he was. They were likely already planning the furloughs that Major Fairchild would award them with for bringing his late prospective son-in-law's killer back to the fort.

"Please, don't!" Lenore beseeched the solders. "It was all an accident. Won't you please let him go?"

"Let him go? We can't let him go, miss. Your father wants his head. I reckon that's all we really need to take back to Grant."

Sergeant Gustafsson grinned sadistically as he flicked his eyes sideways toward Lenore. It was just a split-second lapse of attention, but it was all Colter needed to close his hand over his Remington's walnut grips and whip the gun up with practiced speed, cocking the gun as he leveled it and then blowing a hole through the dead center of Sergeant Gustafsson's dusty blue tunic. The sergeant groaned and triggered his Spencer into the cave ceiling beyond Colter as he stumbled back on his boot heels and fell.

The casual sneers on the faces of the four others disappeared behind a mask of un-bridled fear and exasperation as they began pulling their own shooting irons off their shoulders. Colter turned sideways, auto-matically making as small a target as pos-sible, and extended the Remington straight out from his shoulder, shooting the private in the middle of the group first, then sum-marily dispatching the other two before any had even gotten the hammers of their rifles drawn back.

One by one, spaced about a quarter second apart, they flew backward, dropping their rifles, hitting the ground, and rolling. The three yelled or screamed curses. The yells or screams were quickly replaced by gasping groans as their shredded hearts stopped beating.

The tall corporal threw Lenore aside and,

sidestepping wildly and cursing, raised the Colt Army revolver he'd managed to claw out of his covered holster while Colter was dispatching his brethren. He raised the gun amidst the dust kicked up by the soldiers still rolling in the rocks and sand around him, and Colter drilled a slug through the middle of the corporal's forehead, just below the leather brim of his forage cap.

The corporal triggered his Colt Army into the ground near his right foot, staggered back as though drunk, eyes rolling back into his head as though to view the bullet that had just killed him. He dropped heavily to his butt, sat there for a time, jerking, before he sagged against a boulder and rolled awkwardly onto a shoulder.

Colter lowered the smoking pistol and turned to Lenore. She was standing with her rump pressed against the boulder behind her, leaning forward slightly, her palms pressed flat against the rock. She stared at Colter, eyes wide with shock, lips parted slightly. Her face was as pale as rock dust.

Slowly, her knees started to shake and buckle behind her skirt drawn taut against them. Colter ran to her and caught her just as her knees touched the ground. He wrapped his arms around her and pressed her face against his shoulder, shielding her from the grisly view of the dead or dying men.

She shivered as though in a January snowstorm. Colter said nothing. There was really nothing he could say to assuage the shock of what she'd seen. All he could do was comfort her for a while before getting her back on her horse and sending her home.

"You," she said finally, her voice quavering as she turned her head to stare up at him, deep vertical lines cut into the bridge of her nose and just as deep horizontal lines slashed across her forehead. "You've . . . you've done that before."

"Yeah." Colter took her face in his hands, smoothed her hair back, nodding. "I have. A few times. I ain't proud of it, but I have."

In the periphery of his vision, he spied movement down the canyon below the cave. Quickly, he pulled Lenore into the cave behind him, grabbed his Remington out of his belt once more, and began shoving .44 cartridges into it from his shell belt.

CHAPTER 8

"What is it?" Lenore said, her voice still trembling, fearful.

"Don't know, but I spied movement down-canyon a ways."

Colter flicked the Remington's loading gate closed, then went over and grabbed his rifle and his saddlebags. He set the saddlebags down, leaned his rifle against them, and pulled his ancient, brass-chased spyglass out of a pouch. He glanced at Lenore, who sat on her knees, hunkered low behind him, hands on her thighs.

"You shouldn't have come here."

The girl said nothing as Colter, staying low, raised the spyglass. The canyon below was a devil's maze of stone escarpments forming several winding corridors. He'd studied the terrain for nearly a minute before he saw a blue-clad soldier atop an army bay ride around a bend in the wall of a corridor straight out from the cave and about seventy yards away. The man was moving fast and staring in Colter's direction, showing his teeth inside a shaggy blond goatee. Colter recognized the man a second before the horse and rider disappeared around another bend in the corridor he was following toward Colter's cave.

"Hobart," he muttered.

Behind Colter, Lenore said, "He and Lieutenant McKnight were leading a patrol out before I left the fort this morning. They were heading straight south. I came east, following Mr. Tappin's direction, and . . . I thought I'd made it through without being seen."

Colter continued to stare through the spyglass. "They must have split up. Probably several groups around here now."

Lenore said in a voice pitched low with self-disgust, "I'm sorry, Colter."

Colter turned to her. Her eyes were still bright with the shock of seeing four men die before her, but the color in her cheeks had returned. She'd been raised on military forts throughout the West, and, while she might never have seen men killed up close, death could not have been new to her.

Colter returned the spyglass to his saddle-bag pouch. "I'm obliged for the grub. Without it, I might not have made it a mile from here." He placed his hands on her shoulders, something he'd only dreamed about doing before this day. Odd, how easy it was now, the emotion compelling it being his desire to send her away. "Leave here," he said with passion. "Go now. Before they get here and the bullets start flyin'."

"But what. . . . ?"

"I'm pullin' out."

Quickly, despite the ache in his ribs and other sundry bruises, cuts, and abrasions, he began gathering his gear.

"I'll help you," she said, starting to roll his rumpled blankets.

He grabbed her arm and shoved her brusquely toward her horse, now standing to the right of the cave, rooting for some spindly brown grass growing amongst the rocks. "No, go!"

"All right," she said, stepping over the dead sergeant as she strode to her horse, a purposeful flush in her cheeks. "I'll go and try to waylay Hobart and the others. "That's the least I can do."

She grabbed the cream's reins and swung into the silver-trimmed Texas saddle. Colter whipped his head toward her as he tied his blanket roll. "Lenore, go back the way you came. Steer wide of Hobart!"

She swung the cream around and turned

once more to Colter. "Good-bye, Colter."
She studied him, her thin brown eyebrows
furling slightly above her penetrating gaze,
as though she were seeing a different person
than the one she'd thought he was. She
tapped heels to the cream's flanks, and the
hooves clattered on the rocks as the gelding
began picking its way down the slope, lifting copper dust behind it.

Colter continued to gather his gear, gritting his teeth and muttering against the
dreadful feeling in his gut. Quickly, he
retrieved Northwest from the horse's stone
alcove and threw his tack onto the horse's
back, adjusting buckles and tightening
straps while his heart tattooed a dire rhythm
against his breastbone and he stared down
the rocky slope.

Lenore had reached the bottom and disappeared behind a pinnacle of towering
rock.

Colter shoved his Henry into its scabbard
and swung gingerly onto Northwest's back.
He put the horse down the slope, following
Lenore's path for fifty yards and then, finding a natural corridor angling south across
the side of the slope, swung onto it.

A pistol cracked, the report echoing.
Colter jerked his head to look over his left
shoulder.

Hobart sat his bay in a sandy-floored, horseshoe-shaped bowl in the canyon floor about a hundred yards away. Lenore's cream was there, as well — pitching wildly and whinnying as Lenore flopped down the horse's left side. Colter blinked his shocked eyes as though to clear them, but when he held his gaze on the clearing in the canyon, he saw Lenore fall from the cream to land on the ground. The lieutenant held a pistol in his right hand as he sat staring toward the girl.

Colter thought that the lieutenant had triggered a shot at him, Colter, and that the bay had been startled by the shot and thrown the girl. But a look of keen horror and disbelief slid across his face as he realized that that was not what had happened.

Hobart had shot Lenore.

"You son of a bitch!" Colter screamed, reaching for his Henry and heeling Northwest across the slope in Hobart's direction.

The lieutenant snapped his head up, facing Colter, and then he turned sharply to stare behind him. As he followed Hobart's gaze, Colter pulled back on Northwest's reins, and the coyote dun's rear hooves skidded across a talus sliding, nearly losing his footing and going down. Behind Hobart, rounding a bend in the canyon, several blue-clad riders were galloping toward the lieutenant. Hobart shouted something that Colter couldn't make out from this distance. Then he saw Hobart jerk his arm and his pistol sharply toward Colter.

As Hobart faced Colter, Colter could make out the shouted cry as the lieutenant waved his pistol at him, *". . . killed the major's daughter!"*

Raw fury was a pack of blood-hungry wolves charging through every vein in the redhead's body. He slid his Henry from its sheath, held Northwest steady, and planted his sights on Hobart's chest.

Ka-bam!

Rock dust puffed from the slope just left of Hobart. The lieutenant jerked his head down and threw an arm up with a start, then cast his exasperated gaze toward Colter. At least, Colter figured it was an exasperated gaze. From this distance he could see only a pale oval beneath the brim of the killer's tan hat. He hoped the look he cast back toward Hobart was as easily read despite the distance between them, because it was Colter's sincere promise that he would kill the man no matter what it took.

He wanted Hobart to know that Lenore's killer was going to die bloody. Like a rabid wolf, he was going to die howling.

Now the six or seven other soldiers put their mounts into ground-eating gallops, heading toward Colter and disappearing amongst the steep stone walls of the canyon. Hobart, recovering from the shock of Colter's near miss, shouted something else that Colter couldn't hear and gigged his bay after the others.

Colter stood with his rifle butt pressed against his thigh, his eyes hard, his nostrils contracting and expanding as he stared at Lenore sprawled belly-down on the ground where the soldiers had left her. He felt a knife twist in his chest, tears of fury glaze his eyes.

Lenore . . . *dead.* He sat feeling slack and dead in his saddle, his shoulders weighing down on him like a yoke. How could such a sweet, kindly, and beautiful girl be dead? Killed so savagely?

Colter would have faced all the soldiers now if he thought he'd had a chance. But they'd likely get around him, and others would come, and he'd be dead and Hobart would still be alive, spreading his lies.

So he reined Northwest around and continued following the path across the shoulder of the hill and down toward the canyon floor. He'd stay ahead of the soldiers for now, until the time was right. And then he'd turn to face them, and they'd wish like hell they'd never known him.

He spent that night in a long-abandoned stone shack a good ten miles from the cave. The shack, likely belonging to a Mexican farmer or goatherd at one time, was hidden in a deep crease between two hills. Its covered well still held cool, sweet-tasting water. There was an old garden patch long since grown up with weeds.

It was a cold, bitter night despite the fire he'd built inside the roofless hovel and the whiskey he'd thinned with the cool well water and sipped from a tin cup to dull his sundry aches. The memory of Lenore lying in a lifeless pile at the bottom of that canyon was crisp in his mind, firing him with a fury he hadn't known since he'd crippled and branded Bill Rondo.

It was a killing fury. He sat with his blankets draped about his shoulders, sitting near the fire but facing the dark night beyond the shack, sipping his whiskey and trying to replace the image of the beautiful, dead Lenore with pictures of a dead Hobart.

No. Of Hobart howling as he died . . .

He ate the last sandwich Lenore had made for him, and for which she'd given her life to bring to him, finished the whiskey and water, and swiped a fist across his nose, trying to puzzle it out.

Lenore.

Such a senseless, tragic killing. Why?

But Colter knew why. She'd been a headstrong girl, and in her zeal to stop more killing she must have told Hobart that she knew the real story of Belden's death. To keep her from revealing his and McKnight's lie, Hobart had shot her. How easy it had been to blame Colter for her death, to say that she'd been killed by the man she'd ridden into the desert to see.

How easily one lie led to another.

Now, because he'd danced with a pretty girl, the pretty girl was dead and Colter was on the run for his life.

He slept fitfully only a few hours, his dreams tormented this time not from pain, but from images of Hobart's gun blasting into Lenore. Rising early, when dawn was a pale, shallow streak behind the eastern ridges, he ate some beans and jerky washed down with water and whiskey, saddled Northwest, and headed out.

He saw no sign of the cavalry all that morning and into the afternoon. They wouldn't give up on him, he knew. He was wanted now for killing not only the major's intended son-in-law but the major's daughter, as well. He especially hoped that Hobart didn't give up on him. Likely, a contingent had taken Lenore's body back to Camp Grant, but there would still be a goodly portion of Grant's soldiers combing south-central Arizona for him.

Something told him he'd see Hobart again soon. The lieutenant would want to make sure that Colter died, so that no one could contest his and McKnight's claim about the night of Belden's death and that it was Colter who'd killed Lenore.

Willie's whiskey made the ride easier on Colter's ribs. But when he stopped in the midafternoon to take a swig, the bottle slipped from his hands, and it shattered on a rock, giving Northwest a start. The loss of the painkilling whiskey grieved him, but he smiled with relief when, an hour later, he crested a low butte and stared down into a hollow before him in which a collection of log and mud-brick buildings squatted in the Arizona sun. Likely, he'd find a replacement bottle there. A stagecoach was pulled up to the side of a barn, its tongue drooping, and there were ten to fifteen horses in the corral off the barn's other side.

A wide, rutted trail came down out of the east, to Colter's left, and split the yard of the place before continuing on up into a jog of low hills in the west. He was looking at a stage relay station, most likely. Maybe one that served food and whiskey. He'd go in out of the sun for a time, give Northwest some water, parched corn, and rest, as well, before continuing on his way.

Colter sleeved sweat from his brow and booted the horse on down the hill.

CHAPTER 9

Colter turned onto the trail at the bottom of the hill, scattering a few chickens pecking at the edge of the yard in which several sun-blistered buildings crouched amongst dusty yucca plants and tumbleweeds.

A windmill stood in the middle of the yard, the blades turning lazily with a dry breeze, the sun making a lemon on the surface of the straw-flecked water in the stone tank. A small dust devil lifted between the windmill and the station house and died against the house — a long, low, brush-roofed shack with a sagging front gallery decorated with bleached animal skulls. Wooden shutters were thrown back from the windows, a few of which were covered with animal skins scraped thin enough to resemble waxed paper. The sign above the gallery's roof of ironwood poles announced DELACORTE STAGE LINE RELAY STATION NUMBER 3.

Another sign nailed to a front gallery post offered BEER AND BEANS 10 CENTS. Yet another warned: NO APACHES. NOT EVEN TAME ONES! "Tame" had been underlined twice.

Three saddled horses stood on the far side of the windmill from Colter. As he angled past the windmill and the water tank, he saw a young boy standing with the horses, one hip hiked on the edge of the tank, his sunburned face turned to regard Colter over his right shoulder, squinting one eye.

No, not a boy, Colter saw as Northwest clomped toward the station house, the horse's hooves kicking up little puffs of dust, some of which the breeze tried halfheartedly to lift and spin into devils. The person with the horses was a sunburned girl in a gray wool skirt and plaid, overlarge work shirt, its tails sticking out. She wore a brown felt hat with a bullet crown, and she had a homemade burlap satchel slung over her shoulder, like a purse.

Colter pinched his hat brim to the girl, who — with her tomboy's face and bony body, she looked more like a boy in a dress than a girl — stared at him out of frosty blue eyes set wide below a shelf of straight blond bangs. He led Northwest around to the shaded side of the shack. Here, the horse would be out of sight from the front. He'd water the dun later, once the horse had cooled.

As he grabbed his Henry and swung down from the saddle, he noted the abating of the severe ache in his ribs and guts and even around his eyes and lips, and supposed there was nothing like rotgut whiskey and a ride in the hot, dry sun for healing. He threw the reins over the worn, silver cottonwood pole hitch rack on that side of the shack and set his rifle on his shoulder as he walked back around to the front and mounted the gallery steps.

"Hey, bucko."

He half turned to see the puzzling youngster dropping the reins of the three horses and stepping away from the water tank, moving toward him. Beneath the hem of her long skirt, he saw that she wore brown, lace-up ankle boots like those a boy would wear, which also gave him the vague impression that he was looking at some strange boy in a skirt.

Colter waited as the kid came on, stopping about ten feet beyond Northwest's switching tail, the coyote dun craning its head around to get a look at the kid, the dun's expression as skeptical as Colter's.

"Do me a favor?" Even the voice belonged

to a boy.

"If I can."

"Inside, you'll find two scoundrels. One fat and old. The other young and skinny." The girl-boy raised her dimpled chin toward the station house behind Colter. "I'd be obliged if you'd inform them that their employer has directed them to hustle their lazy, worthless carcasses out here to their horses, so we can lift some dust before sundown." She narrowed her blue eyes, and an angry flush rose in her tanned, lightly freckled cheeks. "Please add that if they continue to imbibe in spirituous liquids and cavort with fallen women, which I strictly forbade at the start of our trek, I will dock their pay if not terminate their employ altogether and continue on to Mexico myself."

Colter studied the sunburned little urchin, incredulous lines digging into his forehead. He turned, continued up the steps, crossed the gallery, and stepped through the door that was propped half-open with a rock.

Inside, a stocky Mexican sat behind a split cottonwood log bar on the right. He was perched on a stool, softly strumming a mandolin, and humming. A bottle sat on the bar with a grimy glass half-filled with the clear liquid. He had jade green eyes set below heavy black brows, and he let the rheumy orbs drift slowly to Colter as he continued to strum and hum.

His flashy handlebar mustache with waxed ends curling upward toward his nostrils was in sharp contrast to the stained apron he wore over a grimy wool tunic. A fat tabby cat lounged on the bar to his right, eyes closed, head dipping toward its paws, as though lulled by the man's strumming.

The fat old man and the skinny young one that girl had referred to sat off to the right and back a ways, partially hidden in the room's dingy shadows. They sat at a square table, the older one with a young, scantily clad Mexican woman straddling his left knee and whispering into his ear. The old man was giggling and caressing the girl's arms over a sheer, light green wrap that was all she wore except for a faded red corset and black net stockings. The young man was leaning forward in his chair, staring delightfully at the girl on his partner's lap, also giggling like an idiot as he lightly, eagerly stomped his feet.

Colter cleared his throat and hooked his thumb over his shoulder as he said, "You two are wanted outside."

Both men looked at him, their eyes bright from drink. The older man wore buckskins and a deerskin vest, with two Colt Navy revolvers holstered on his hips. He had long-ish, dark brown hair liberally streaked with gray, and a long, horsey face with a thick wedge of a nose.

The young man wore ragged, patched denims and a hickory shirt, with a red bandanna knotted around his neck. A funnel-brimmed Stetson was tipped back off his high, bulging forehead. His close-set eyes and small nose and mouth gave him a ratlike look. He wore a Colt Army wedged into a wide brown belt, and a bowie knife jutted from a beaded sheath strapped to his right thigh.

"Ah, hell," the old man said, scowling at Colter before turning toward his crestfallen partner. "Why doesn't she just dry up and blow away?"

"A curse is what she is," said the young man, bunching his red face, squinting his little eyes furiously, and pointing toward the door behind Colter. "I done told you, Wade — the girl is a curse some old Yaqui witch done hexed us with!"

"Forget her, Harlan," said the older man, returning his attention to the girl on his knee.

Colter wandered over to the bar, noting that the rest of the dark room was empty.

"Sounded like she meant business to me. In fact . . ." He glanced out the window to his right, beyond which the girl was just now stepping off the edge of the windmill's water tank and into the stirrup of a tall, brown-and-white pinto mare. "I think she's pullin' her picket pin at this very moment."

"Ah, shit," said Wade.

"Damn that little cockroach," Harlan said, pounding the table before him. "Just when we was startin' to have fun!"

Colter gave his back to the two men as the oldster voiced his apologies to the *puta* on his hip and scraped his chair back with a baleful sigh, the whore muttering her regret and Harlan groaning miserably. The barman continued strumming his mandolin as he glanced at Colter, one brow arched.

"I'd like a bottle of whiskey," the redhead said. "And I'll take a plate o' them beans, too."

He looked at the big iron kettle bubbling atop the range behind the man. The steam lifting from the pot was rife with the aroma of beans, garlic, and chili peppers. Corn tortillas licked out from beneath the lid of a pan on the warming rack above the pot.

Colter's empty belly chugged.

"No whiskey, senor," said the barman as he rose from his stool and set the mandolin atop the bar, the cat lifting its head and regarding Colter with eyes as expressionless as two gold marbles. "Tequila. Agave."

Colter gave a disgruntled snort. He'd just started getting the whiskey down without his belly bucking like a wild stallion. But maybe the tequila wouldn't be all that different. Possibly not as harsh. He'd never tried it before.

"All right."

The barman had turned lazily away to dish up a plate of steaming beans. He added two tortillas from the pan on the warming rack before setting the plate on the bar, then grabbing a clear, unlabeled bottle off a shelf behind him and setting the bottle on the table beside the plate. He opened his hands in front of his chest as though to catch a ball and said in his heavy Spanish accent, "One dollah, senor."

Colter fished around in his pants, glad he'd been paid a week ago and hadn't had time to spend the twenty-two dollars he'd made for a month of horse-breaking at Camp Grant, and flipped it onto the cottonwood planks. He hauled his rifle over to a table in the room's rear shadows, near a cold wood stove, then returned to the bar. As he picked up his plate, bottle, and glass, he caught the barman inspecting the S branded on his cheek.

Colter looked at the ostentatiously mustached Mexican, and the man quickly averted his gaze, picking up the mandolin and hiking a hip on his stool. The cat was not so kind — it continued to brashly study Colter with unblinking but sullen, possibly disapproving, interest. The redhead turned away from both the man and the cat, made his way back to the table, and slacked into a chair, facing the door and the two front windows, one on either side of it.

Wade and Harlan had gone out, and they were just now stepping drunkenly into their saddles as the strange girl rode out of the yard the way Colter had come into it, hipping around in her saddle to regard her two slothful employees with bitter disdain. He could hear her yelling something at the men in her croaking, raspy voice, but he couldn't make out what it was. Wade and Harlan merely glowered like two schoolboys caught roughhousing at recess, and reluctantly booted their mounts along behind her.

Colter quickly downed half a shot of tequila, not minding the taste as much as he thought he would though it was a little like drinking coal oil mixed with fruit juice, then took a break to lead Northwest over to the water tank. When he returned to the station house, he hunkered back down over his meal, forcing himself to eat slowly despite the seemingly bottomless pit south of his breastbone and enjoying the soft, melodious strumming of the barman.

The rataplan of oncoming riders lured his gaze to the front of the station house. The thudding of hooves grew louder until a puff of tan dust swept into view beyond the window to the left of the door, and two riders drew their trotting horses up in front of the hitch rack beyond the window to the door's right. The riders were soldiers clad in tan or blue kepis or billed forage caps, dark blue tunics, and light blue trousers, some with the same deerskin inseams that Colter wore in his denims, to keep their pants from wearing out as they rode. Three more trotted up behind them, drew rein, and, speaking amongst themselves as the horses snorted and blew, swung down from their McClellan saddles.

Colter nearly dropped his spoon. Renewing his grip on it, still hunkered over his plate, he stared out the window to the right of the door, squinting, trying to get a better look at the soldiers. But the window was obscured with wafting dust that came through to powder the tables near the front of the room, and the men themselves were so coated in the dust that he couldn't make out much except that they were badly sunburned.

Could he be lucky enough that Hobart was part of this group?

His pulse throbbed like snakebites. As the men batted dust from their tunics and pants with their hats, a low hum rising as they spoke amongst themselves, and boots pounded the cottonwood logs of the gallery, Colter glanced at his rifle. Then he dropped his left hand beneath the table, closed two fingers around the walnut grips of his Remington, and gave the pistol a little tug to loosen it.

He lifted his right hand back onto the table and continued to try to casually fork beans into his mouth as the soldiers dunked their heads in the water barrel outside on the gallery. They stayed out there, talking and washing, occasionally chuckling, until the front door widened suddenly and the first of the soldiers came in, setting his hat back on his now-wet head.

His face was cleared of dust. It was as pink as an Arizona sunrise, and it belonged to Lieutenant A. J. McKnight. Colter dropped his eyes quickly but then remembered that the newcomers likely couldn't see him, at least not well, sitting back in the shadows as he was. So he lifted his gaze to scrutinize the other soldiers clomping in, wet hair dripping onto the shoulders and breasts of their dust-powdered tunics.

The two men behind McKnight were a corporal and a sergeant, respectively. They were followed a few seconds later by another corporal. Then a tall man with a dripping red-blond mustache walked in, clamping his hat under one arm while he ran both hands through his thick, wet red-blond hair and saying, "Hey, Calderon, a round of your best tequila for me and the boys!"

"Ah, Lieutenant Hobart!" said the bartender, setting his guitar atop the bar planks and rising, grinning broadly at the last of the soldiers. "What brings you to this god-forsaken country? Apaches, or" — he slid his gaze to the young Mexican whore sitting back in a chair at the table that Wade and Harlan had vacated — "Pilar?"

Colter had looked up suddenly. Excitement and rage, like boiling water, churned in his belly and danced in his knees.

As the whore ran an emery board across her nails with a desultory air, she looked up from beneath her arched black brows to quirk her lips in an alluring smile at the soldiers.

The soldiers all looked at Pilar, grinning.

110

Finally, Hobart turned to the barman, who was splashing tequila into five shot glasses while the cat gained its feet and arched its back disdainfully at the newcomers.

"Unfortunately, neither," said Hobart, reaching out suddenly and swiping the cat off the bar. "Good Lord, man, don't you know those things carry vermin?"

The cat hit the floor behind the bar with a thud and an indignant yowl, then, hissing, tail raised, slinked out from under the bar and on out the half-open front door.

Calderon chuckled and said, "Lieutenant, I must warn you — you have made a nasty enemy in El Fuerte."

Hobart made a face and lifted his shot glass between his thumb and index finger. "El Fuerte needs a bullet, Calderon. I see that cat on your bar again, I'm gonna feed him one between his eyes." He raised his glass to his chuckling companions. *"Saludos!"*

The soldiers tossed back their tequilas. Hobart gestured, and Calderon refilled their shot glasses. "So, if it is not Apaches or Pilar you have come all this way for, *mi amigo,* what is it, if I may be so rude?"

Hobart threw back half his tequila and stretched his lips back from his teeth sheathed by his wet blond goatee, hissing

111

like a cat and shaking his head as though to clear it. "A kid," he rasped. Clearing his throat, he added, "A young, lanky redhead with an ugly 'S' branded into his right cheek. That's who we're after, *mi amigo* Calderon. Been after him for the past couple days. He killed Lieutenant Belden 'cause he wanted his girl, and then he killed his girl because she was about to tell me where he was holed up."

Hobart gestured for another round. "He hasn't come through here, has he?"

Calderon's swarthy face paled as he stared at Hobart.

Still hunkered over his table, Colter Farrow let his fork drop to his tin plate with a loud, ringing clatter.

CHAPTER 10

Hobart, McKnight, and the other three soldiers swung around quickly, as though they were all tied to the same string. Hands dropped to the covered holsters on their hips. Still seated, Colter lifted his Remington from beneath his table, clicking the hammer back. He extended the revolver out over his table and squeezed the trigger.

In the close confines, the explosion echoed like a dynamite blast. Everyone in the room jumped, Calderon cursing in Spanish and stumbling back away from the bar. The whore screamed, bounded out of her chair, and dashed out the door, barefoot. From the corner of his eye, Colter saw her streak past the left front window as she hightailed it around the corner of the station house.

Hobart screamed and crouched as he grabbed his right knee with his right hand, blood oozing out from the shattered knee to saturate his pale blue cavalry slacks. He dropped to both knees and gave another yowl, showing gritted teeth beneath his red-blond mustache, his habitually sneering hazel eyes locked on Colter. His eyes weren't as sneering now as exasperated.

The other men stood dumbstruck, their hands frozen on their holsters from which McKnight had gotten his Colt Army .44 halfway out.

Colter clicked his Remington's hammer back again, loudly. Keeping the pistol aimed at the bar, he scraped his chair back casually, slowly rose, picked up his rifle and the tequila bottle, held the rifle atop his left shoulder with the hand holding the bottle, and stepped out around the table. He stopped about ten feet from the blue-uniformed statues at the bar and Hobart, who sat on the floor farthest down the bar on the right, his right leg and knee extended to one side as he leaned on the opposite hip.

Blood continued to gush from Hobart's wounded knee. His face was crimson, forked veins bulging in his forehead. His eyes were agonized, fearful, incredulous. They brightened with recognition as Colter stepped into the wan light seeping through the windows.

"You son of a bitch!"

McKnight still had his Colt half out of its holster. He blinked in disbelief, then shaped a grim smile. "Kid, you're one crazy son of a bitch if you think you're gonna get away with this."

Colter raised his Remington's barrel. "You fellas ease those pistols out of their holsters, toss 'em over there, on the other side of the room. Do that real slow because I'm just itchin' to ruin another knee."

"You're gonna die, boy," Hobart hissed through his gritted teeth and the damp ends of his mustache. "You're gonna die real slow."

"You, too," Colter commanded the wounded lieutenant. "With your left hand, reach across and ease that Colt out of your holster and toss it over there."

He kept his eyes on the others as, glancing around at each other nervously, they finally complied with Colter's demand. One by one the Colts arced through the air and hit the floor on the other side of the room with heavy thumps. One bounced off a chair and slid up against the far wall. Hobart's was last. In his weakened condition, the wounded lieutenant couldn't throw his as far. It hit the floor halfway across the room and skidded beneath a table.

"You'll never make it, kid," McKnight

said, fear sweat dribbling down his sun-blistered cheeks. "We're meetin' up with a whole platoon. They'll be here soon. Should've been here by now, in fact."

"Good. They can take down that son of a bitch's confession, too." Colter hardened his gaze at Hobart. "Go on, Lieutenant. Tell 'em what happened to Lenore."

"You're crazy."

Colter glanced at McKnight. "If you'll take a closer look at Miss Lenore's bullet wound, you'll see it was delivered by a Colt pistol at close range. Not a rifle. I bet it's ringed with powder and only about twice as big as what a rifle would do."

McKnight slid an edgy look toward Hobart, who met his gaze with a similar one of his own.

"But you probably already know that — don't you, Lieutenant?" Colter looked at the two corporals and the sergeant still staring at him in mute fear. "Hobart killed Miss Lenore because she was foolish enough to tell him she knew what really happened back at Camp Grant, a couple nights back. How they held me so Belden could beat me till my bones rattled. How he died was an accident, sort of. I lashed out with a boot, caught him off balance, and he fell and rapped his head against an open tailgate."

116

Colter slid his gaze back to Hobart. "Tell 'em that's true. Even if they don't believe you, tell 'em."

Hobart's face looked like an overfilled water flask, and above the wet goatee it was as red as an Iowa barn. He shook his head, grinding his jaws, his hazel eyes sparking. "That wasn't how it happened. You killed her 'cause she was gonna sell you out."

Colter narrowed his right eye as he slid his Remington toward Hobart's other leg.

"No–o–o!"

The man's cry was drowned by the Remy's thunder.

Dust puffed from the blue cloth over the man's left knee. Hobart jerked as though he'd been struck by lightning. He threw a wail at the ceiling, then dropped over his left knee, covering it with his left hand and sobbing. "Oh, you son of a bitch!"

"Tell 'em," Colter said quietly. "Or the next one's gonna raise the pitch of your screams about five hundred notches."

Hobart glanced at the others, tears and sweat dripping down his face and into his mustache. "I did it," he said, panting, eyes on Colter's aimed Remy. "I shot her."

The barman, Calderon, was leaning back against the shelves behind him, holding his hands shoulder high, palms out. He made a raspy whistling sound as he stared brightly over the bar at Hobart.

"Good enough," Colter said, starting to move toward the door, keeping his Remington extended at the soldiers and his Henry resting on his shoulder. "I just wanted to hear you say it. I wanted Lenore to hear you say it." Softly, he added, scowling against the knot growing in his throat. "I think she did."

He glanced at the sergeant. "You might mention that to the major, when you boys get back to Camp Grant." At the half-open door, he turned to face the soldiers directly once more. "Fairchild can thank me later for not havin' to go to all the work of buildin' a gallows."

As he stared at Colter, Hobart's eyes jerked wide. His mouth opened, but before he could scream, Colter blew the top of his head against the bar behind him. The other soldiers screamed and jumped, eyes pinched in horror as they glanced down at Lieutenant Hobart flopping and bleeding on the floor.

"You fellas stay put till I'm outta sight," Colter told them. "You so much as poke your head out this door, you'll look like him."

He jerked his pistol toward the now-lifeless Hobart slumped on his side with his brains oozing out the top of his head, then nudged the door open with his heels and backed out onto the gallery. He crossed the gallery and backed down the steps, then strode toward Northwest waiting by the hitchrack, staring at Colter and thrashing his tail uneasily. Colter walked quickly, turning often to make sure the soldiers weren't coming after him. From inside the station house came a low murmur of alarmed voices, but he reckoned the soldiers knew he meant business.

None so much as poked his head out the door.

He shoved his tequila bottle into his saddlebag pouch. Keeping an eye on the station house, he slid the bit through the coyote dun's teeth, tightened the latigo strap, and stepped into the saddle. He swung the horse away from the cabin, looked to the east — the direction from which he'd come — then west.

Dust rose like distant smoke. Beneath the rising cloud was a smudge of blue. Just above the blue was a wavering patch of red and blue, which would likely be the oncoming platoon's pennant-shaped cavalry guidon. Judging by the size of the dust cloud, there were probably around twenty riders galloping toward him.

Colter swung the coyote dun south and booted him into a gallop, heading between a barn and what appeared a stone blacksmith shop. As Northwest clomped through the sage and yucca, Colter spied something hunkered down near the base of the hay barn. Calderon's cat, El Fuerte, swung his head to follow Colter and gave his tail a parting flick. Colter pitched his hat brim to the indignant feline, muttered, "My pleasure, cat," then hunkered low in the saddle, broke out away from the relay station's outbuildings, and galloped straight south across a flat expanse of sandy green desert rolling up gradually toward a rise of distant blue mountains.

He wasn't sure where the line was that separated Arizona from Mexico, but he was heading south, so he was heading for it. And when he came to it he'd cross it and he wouldn't look back.

He figured he'd crossed into Mexico by seven or eight o'clock that night. And, just as he'd vowed, he did not look back. He wasn't sure if the soldiers would follow him across the line, but he had to assume they would. U.S. troops often chased Apaches deep into Mexico, sometimes as far south as the Sierra Madre, but usually with the permission of the Mexican government.

Would they attain that permission to follow him? Most likely. He was wanted for killing several U.S. soldiers and the daughter of a cavalry major, after all, and that probably made him just about as wanted as any bronco Apache. He doubted anyone would believe — or would want to believe — Hobart's gunpoint confession.

He gave a grim smile and reined Northwest to a halt atop a small knoll over which a dusting of stars gleamed so crisply in the dry, cool air of a desert September that they looked close enough to reach up and grab. He, Colter Farrow, a young horse rancher from Colorado's Lunatic Range, was as wanted as an Apache. Hell, maybe he was even more wanted. And here he was in Mexico, once more on the run with soldiers after him, and likely now more bounty hunters than he'd ever imagined.

His chest felt tight with anxiety and uncertainty. He did not know Mexico. He did not know the language. Where would he go, and how, down here, would he ever be able to make a living? He had nineteen dollars in coins rolling around in his pockets and saddlebags, and that would last him a month or two if he lived sparingly, but eventually he'd need money if only for ammo, flour, sugar, and half a bag of Arbuckles'.

If they even sold coffee down here. Did the Mexicans drink it?

He shook his head and sighed. Here he was, practically on death's doorstep, and he was worried about where he'd find coffee in Mexico. He must still be addled from Belden's beating. His ribs hadn't been screaming with every lurch of his horse lately, but he could still feel the fatigue of his injuries deep in his bones, in every fiber of his being.

He needed a long night's rest in a bed.

That half-formed thought was what had stopped him here. He stared southwest, where several wan lights glowed amongst the rolling hills, at the base of a low gray wall of ridges that blocked out the stars along the southern horizon. A town of some size, most likely, as there were too many lights for a stage station or a ranch. He'd find a bed there. He'd done his best these last few hours to cover his tracks, avoiding trails and riding where Northwest's hooves were less likely to leave a print, so he figured he'd bought himself at least a few hours of badly needed rest.

He booted Northwest on down the knoll

and after another half hour, when he was half asleep and could tell by the horse's splay-legged stride that Northwest was nearly asleep himself, the trail rose along a gradual slope, and he could begin to smell the smoke of burning piñon and mesquite on the autumn-chill air. He'd smelled that aroma at Camp Grant, as well. It was the sweetest-smelling perfume, and it seemed to go with an almost eerily quiet, night-cloaked desert landscape and the distant yammering of coyotes.

Lights appeared on both sides of the trail — lamplight dimmed by curtained windows in small, boxlike adobe or mud-brick houses that seemed as one with the rolling hills as the rocks or paloverde trees. As Colter rode on up into the town, a potpourri of smells washed over him — the burning piñon mixed with the ammonia musk of chicken and goat pens and privies, as well as the more inviting aromas of spicy roasted meat.

He rounded a bend and caught a whiff of perfume and tobacco smoke, and he heard the low rumble of conversation mixed with women's laughter. On the left side of the trail that had become the pueblo's main street, he saw a three-story adobe with a gallery on the first floor and balconies on each of the two upper floors. On both balconies and on the gallery, he could make out the silhouettes of men and women smoking and drinking and laughing as they sat or stood, the women casting alluring poses, the lamplight from the windows behind them glistening on their brushed black hair and dangling earrings.

On the far right end of the third-floor balcony, away from two other men and one woman, a pair were fumbling and muttering in a lovers' drunken embrace. The woman was speaking Spanish in scolding tones while she laughed and appeared to be nuzzling the man's neck while at the same time brushing away his hands that kept lifting her ruffled skirt to expose her brown legs clear up to her rump.

Colter turned quickly away and lowered his hat brim down over his forehead, perusing the buildings around him for a quiet place to hole up. He drew back on Northwest's reins and stared down into a window on the left side of the street. Just inside what was apparently a café, beyond a warped glass window, the strange blond girl he'd seen earlier at the stage relay station sat at a table with old, rumpled Wade and the rat-faced younger man, Harlan.

Wade sat across the table from her, to Colter's left. His head was resting on his arms on the table, and he appeared sound asleep. Harlan, facing the window on the far side of the table from Colter, sat straight-backed in his own chair, his eyes closed, head bobbing.

Meanwhile, the strange, little blond girl was hunkered over a paper she'd spread out on the table before her, near a pile of what appeared to be their scrap-laden supper plates. She was jabbing the paper with a pencil, and her lips were moving, which meant she was speaking, though her two male companions didn't appear to be hearing her any better than Colter could.

Just then she looked up, scowled, grabbed a fork, and rapped it violently against the tin cup on the table before Harlan so loudly that Colter could hear the ringing clatter through the window.

Both men jerked awake, Wade lifting his head and running two thick hands down his face, blinking. The girl jutted her chin angrily across the table at the men, berating them both while jabbing her pencil at the paper before her.

Colter gave a wry snort. Not caring enough about why the girl was here to even wonder about it, he nudged the coyote dun ahead, sleepier than he was hungry, just wanting a soft bed to drop his tired body into.

CHAPTER 11

He wandered through a dark stretch of street, hearing a man singing a Spanish song off in the night-cloaked hills beyond the pueblo — a sad song from the tone. A Mexican ballad. Colter reined up when he saw a two-story mud-brick building off to his right, south of the main street, on the far side of a sandy wash along which a slender strand of a stream glistened in the starlight.

Most of the windows on both stories appeared lit, and behind one a shadow jostled. The place seemed too large for a private house in this country — at least, he'd never seen one this size yet — and as he crossed the wash and put Northwest up the opposite side, a wooden sign appeared, limned in starlight, over the broad front porch.

HOTEL DE BABYLON.

Through a front window left of the door, he could see four men playing cards by lamplight, a fire dancing in a hearth against the far left wall. No sounds emanated from the place. Figuring he could get a good night's sleep here, in this quiet hotel at the edge of town, Colter swung down from Northwest's back and looped his reins over the hitch rack. He'd been hearing the balladeer off in the hills, and now the song was growing louder, and he could hear the accompaniment of slow-plodding hooves as the horse and singing rider moved closer.

Colter stood atop the porch and stared in the direction of the balladeer. A drunk Mex heading to town in search of love, no doubt. He'd always heard the folks south of the border were a romantic lot. Fleetingly, he remembered his old Mexican friend, Cimarron Padilla, who'd run a ranch up in Wyoming and on which Colter had worked for a time, before all hell had broken loose up there, as well. Wishing he could feel half as good as the singing rider sounded, he swung around and pushed through the Babylon's front door.

He paused just inside, taking note of the thick red rugs on the floor and the warm fire, a polished oak bar on his right, with rows of pigeonholes and key rings flanking it, along with a back-bar mirror and shelves holding bottles and glasses. A humble place with stark, brick walls made comfortable by the polished bar, the rugs, and the fire. There were a half dozen oak tables arranged around stout ceiling joists, and what appeared an old suit of armor, maybe worn by a long-dead conquistador, standing sentinel against the back wall, to the left of a broad, stone stairs rising toward the second story.

The three cardplayers, dressed in short, fancily stitched jackets, colorful neckerchiefs, and leather pants with broad cuffs hanging around polished black or brown, silver-tipped boots, all turned to regard the newcomer with mute interest. Vaqueros, Colter thought. Mexican cowboys. Steeple-crowned sombreros hung down their backs by braided horsehair thongs.

Colter latched the door against the night chill. A stout man with a tumbleweed thatch of gray-streaked black hair ducked out of a curtained doorway flanking the bar. His arms were filled with split firewood. He glanced at Colter, frowning, then continued on around the bar and crossed the room to the fireplace on the other side.

He said something in Spanish, and the three vaqueros laughed as they swung quick, appraising looks at Colter. The man with the thick hair, dressed in a shabby suit with a wide red necktie swelling out over his broad belly, glanced at Colter, then ambled back over to the bar.

"You didn't understand me," he said in Spanish-accented English.

"No, sir, I didn't."

"I didn't think you would," the man said, breathing heavily from his wood-hauling chore. "Gringos never understand Mexican, as they call our language, down here, while when we are up there" — he canted his head toward the north as though to indicate America — "they expect us to understand American."

Colter didn't know what to say to that, so he said nothing, feeling his cheeks warm uncomfortably. It was a lonely feeling, being in a foreign country alone. Now he thought he understood a little better how Cimarron must have felt, up in Wyoming.

The barman leaned an elbow on the counter and studied Colter with fascination. "You are a branded man, *Rubio.*"

"That's mighty observant of you, partner."

"What if I had something against branded men? Down here, you know, branded men are usually wanted men. Or they are *not* wanted, maybe — by anyone at all. Which are you?" The thick-haired man lifted his thick upper lip away to show the edges of his yellow-brown teeth, his eyes flicking to the Remington holstered for the cross draw on Colter's left hip. "Judging by those blue eyes and the shredded beef someone made of your lips" — he ran a hand across his own mouth — "maybe both, uh?"

Colter's tongue tied in frustration. He was damn tired, but he wasn't so tired he'd take any shit. He'd hole up out in the country again. He'd just started to swing around when the man said, "You want a woman, *Rubio*? Is that what you're here for?"

"I'm here for a good night's sleep."

"What's your name?"

Colter hesitated. The man saw the indecision right away, and that made his lips spread farther away from his teeth.

Defiantly, Colter said, "Colter Farrow."

"In *Mejico* alone, Senor Farrow?"

"Look, partner, I'm not here to chin with you. I just need a room and a stable and food and water for my horse out yonder. If that's too much trouble, I'll light elsewhere."

Behind Colter, one of the vaqueros said something angrily in Spanish. Colter glanced over to see one of the men slowly sliding a Schofield pistol from a black, silver-trimmed leather holster thonged to his left thigh. Colter had begun sliding his own right hand across his belly, toward his

131

Remy, when the man before him closed his hand over Colter's wrist as he turned to the vaqueros and spewed a string of hard Spanish.

The vaquero's face reddening in chagrin, he slid his Schofield back snug in its holster, fastened the keeper thong over the hammer, and returned his hands as well as his eyes to the cards before him. The other two were chuckling.

"A pistolero, muchacho *Rubio*?" asked the thick-haired man with the red necktie. "Or you just fancy yourself one?"

"Me?" Colter feigned an innocent air. "I'm just a saddle tramp lookin' for a bed. And since the ones here cost too much in the way of idle chatter, I'll be —"

The thick-haired man laughed. "That's the trouble with you gringos. You're too serious!" He tapped Colter's arm, then ambled around the bar. "I am Florentine Dominguez, and I make it a point of chewing the ears off all my customers. I am a curious man, as well as a cautious one. And an excellent judge of character. If you were a dangerous man, *Rubio,* you would not be so beat-up. Besides, only a greenhorn muchacho would carry such an old gun into Mexico. Does that thing even work?"

He laughed loudly as he looked down at

Colter's holster, winked condescendingly, then turned and grabbed a key off one of the rings beneath the pigeonholes. "Here is a key. Room eight on the second floor. All the way back. Nice and quiet. Behind the hotel is a stable for your horse. Parched corn and water will cost you five pesos extra."

"I don't have any Mexican *dinero,* Senor Dominguez."

"Why did I know this?" Dominguez sighed. "In that case, one American dollar for both you and your horse. If you decide you'd like some company" — the hotelier shrugged his heavy shoulders — "fifty cents extra will buy you the romp of your wild, young life." He grinned, eyelids drooping.

Colter flipped the man a silver dollar. "I reckon I ain't feelin' too wild tonight. Thanks just the same." He held his hand out for the key, then headed for the front door and his horse.

Behind him, Dominguez said, "When you return, take the outside stairs to the second floor. Your room will be on the right."

Colter pinched his hat brim to the man and closed the door behind him. He took Northwest's reins, mounted up, and walked the horse around to the back of the hotel and the low-slung stable. A privy stood

133

halfway between the hotel and the stable, and from inside came the singing of the balladeer that Colter had heard before. The man wasn't singing as loudly as he'd been, and the song was punctuated with frequent grunts and snorts and several other rumblings that echoed around inside the wooden outhouse.

Colter led Northwest into the barn, where several other horses were stabled, including a big, snorting sorrel Arab with steam curling off its back. The magnificent-looking creature still wore a big black saddle adorned with red and green stitching and gold medallions, the stirrups trimmed with fighting, horn-locked bulls. A pair of stout bandoliers was draped over the horn. The horse was the mount of the privy-riding balladeer, most likely. Another vaquero who spent nearly all his monthly earnings making himself and his horse look good for the senoritas, Colter thought reprovingly.

The Arab and Northwest whinnied their greetings, and then the other horses chimed in, until Colter's ears fairly rang.

"Ah, shut up, for chrissakes. You hosses're gonna wake up every dead Catholic in Sonora!"

When Colter had given Northwest the attention the loyal mount deserved, including a long, thorough rubdown with a scrap of burlap, Colter hiked his saddlebags on his shoulder, took his rifle and scabbard under his arm, and headed on out of the stable and past the outhouse from which no more singing rose, only the grunts of a man finishing business and clanking a belt buckle against a wooden wall.

His feet feeling like lead, his saddle and saddlebags weighing as much as a wagon-load of ore, Colter mounted the creaky wooden stairs that rose up the rear of the adobe hotel. He pushed through the sun-blistered door to find himself in a hall outfitted with a flowered green floor runner and wine red wallpaper trimmed with gilded palm leaves.

A couple of bracket lamps guttered and smoked, casting more shadows than light. The air smelled of coal oil and sweat and perfume as sweet as sugared cherries.

Colter had just found the door to room 6 to the right of the entrance when the latch of a door down the hall, toward the stairs rising from the main saloon hall below, clicked. Hinges squawked. The door was two rooms down from Colter, on the hall's left side — too far away for him to see it clearly in the guttering lamplight, but he thought he could see the reflections of two dark eyes staring out at him.

He stared back, frowning.

The door widened a foot, and a girl with long dark brown hair poked her head out. She said something just above a whisper in Spanish. Colter just stared at her, frowning. She frowned then, too, impatiently, and said louder in broken English — "Is he still here? Did he ride on?"

Colter shook his head, so weary that his knees were nearly buckling. "Sorry, ma'am . . . er, senorita. I don't know who you're talkin' about."

"Santiago Machado!" she hissed. "He sings! I heard him just a . . ."

She let her voice trail off and shuttled her gaze to the outside door behind Colter. The balladeer was singing again, softly, and the singing was punctuated by heavy thumps on the outside stairs. The thumps were so heavy that Colter could feel the floor jounce beneath his boots.

"Oh, him," Colter said. "Yeah, I heard him comin' from a long way off!"

He chuckled and turned toward his door, poking his key in the lock. The girl came up behind him, dressed like some gaudy bird in a pink velvet corset with matching camisole, black stockings, and a silky black wrap that hung off her shoulders and probably didn't weigh as much as a butterfly. She had black feathers in her hair, and they danced like antennae as she shouldered Colter aside and turned the key in his door.

"Quickly!" she hissed, reaching forward to pull him into the room before closing the door painstakingly quietly behind him.

CHAPTER 12

"Look, miss . . . er, senorita . . . I told Mr. Dominguez downstairs that I —"

The pretty, half-dressed whore pressed two fingers to her ruby red lips. *"Shhh!"*

She stared at the door. The thumps on the outside stairs continued, making nearly the entire building shake.

Colter stared at the terrified girl, absently musing that the man on the stairs must have been as big as those ape-men some folks claimed they saw in the western forests of a deep, dark night. If he didn't always behave himself, the girl likely had reason to be afraid. But it wasn't Colter's job to give her sanctuary — not when he'd plopped down a whole dollar for the room and he was dead on his feet.

He wasn't the bouncer of this establishment.

He was about to say as much to the girl when the outside doors opened. The balladeer stopped singing. Colter could hear his breath rasping in and out of strained lungs. It sounded like sandpaper worked against rough wood.

The man took a step, seemed to stagger, dragging what sounded like a spur the size of a cymbal. The girl gasped and clamped a hand over her mouth. Colter turned to the door, incredulous, as a gurgling sounded on the other side. It was followed by swallowing sounds, and then a raspy sigh. The man had taken a drink from a bottle. He snorted.

A rumbling voice said, "Alegria!" His voice boomed and echoed like a cannon, pronouncing the name, "Ally-*gree — ahhh!*"

Colter started, as did the girl, gasping again. Some Spanish followed. The girl placed a hand on Colter's arm as she stared at the door, wide-eyed, digging her fingertips into his skin through his canvas jacket until he could feel the sharpness of her fingernails.

"Alegria!" the man fairly cried once more. And it did indeed sound like a cry, or something very close to a cry. Almost a plaintive, beseeching wail.

"Hell," Colter said, regarding the girl critically. "That jake seems to be gone for you, Miss Alegria."

"*Now* he seems — as you say — *gone.*"

She drew her hair back behind her ear, exposing a long white line angling down the side of her face. "Later, when he starts seeing snakes and javelinas crawling over the walls and ceiling, he'll think I'm a witch and try to cut off my head again. The man is loco!"

"All-ee-gree-ahhhhh!" the man's deep voice thundered, making Colter's tired bones rattle together.

The girl gave a clipped shriek and covered her mouth with both hands.

He yelled something else in Spanish, and then there was the booming crunch of a door being kicked open. He shouted for Alegria a few more times, and then footsteps hammered the stairs, and Colter recognized the voice of Dominguez pleading with Machado while Machado continued raging and demanding Alegria. Meanwhile, the girl sobbed and moved up close behind Colter, wrapping her arms around his waist and pressing her cheek against his back.

"*Por favor,* senor," she pleaded. "Don't let him kill me."

Fatigued and bewildered, Colter stared dumbly at the door. Shortly, four or five more men ran up the stairs, and there ensued what sounded like two grizzly bears fighting in the room from which Alegria had sought sanctuary. "The sheriff and his *diputadoes*!" the girl exclaimed, easing her grip on Colter's pistol belt. He could feel the relief relax the tension in her warm, supple body still pressed against his. He could also feel, despite his fatigue, a warming in his young loins.

Suddenly, the commotion died down. Colter cracked the door to see four men wearing serapes and straw sombreros hauling what appeared a huge, shaggy bear with a gold stud earring and dressed in black leather and a bright red-and-white-striped poncho out of Alegria's room, each carrying a limb. When they'd carried Senor Machado on down the stairs, Dominguez stepped wearily out of the girl's room, smoothing his own shaggy hair back from his temples and looking as though he were about to faint. He saw Colter staring out at him, and spoke softly first in Spanish, forgetting himself, then quickly switched to English.

"The girl — Alegria. Have you seen her?"

Colter stepped back, and the girl poked her head out. She and Dominguez conversed in Spanish for a time, and then the girl pulled her head back into the room and closed the door. Colter looked at her, skeptically.

"They haul him off to jail?" he asked.

"*Sí.*"

"Well, then I reckon you're safe now." Colter opened the door. "Glad I could help, but I'm awful tired, and" — he couldn't help letting his weary gaze rove across the girl's body, the corset pushing up her breasts enticingly — "I could really use some shut-eye."

"I am safe until he breaks out. He always breaks out. Why don't I stay here tonight, Rubio?" She rose on the balls of her feet, slid his hair back from his left cheek, and planted a silky kiss on it. "You can keep me safe."

"I'm awful tired. I doubt I could . . . you know . . . even if I'd paid for it, which I haven't. Besides, there looks to be plenty of other rooms. Ain't there other girls you could hole up with?"

"There are no other girls here at the Babylon. Just me. The others all went to Senora Matilda's down the street. There is more business there. I was going to give you a free one, for helping me, but . . ." She flared her nostrils at him. "If you don't want one, *adelante!*"

She started to step out into the hall. Colter grabbed her arm and pulled her back into the room. He closed the door behind her. "I didn't mean to get your neck in a hump."

She frowned, puzzled by the expression.

"This gonna be all right with Senor Dominguez?" he asked.

She hiked a shoulder, still looking indignant. "The hombres downstairs are more interested in cards . . . and heading over to Senora Matilda's later . . . than me. She has two fat Apache girls, and a blond gringa." She curled her lip in a jealous sneer. "So, why not?"

Unbuttoning his jacket, Colter turned toward the bed, whose brass headboard abutted the wall on his left. This had always been the hardest part for him — undressing in front of a girl. He wished he hadn't lit the lamp.

Truth was he wasn't all that experienced in the ways of love — he'd slept with only a few women, mostly girls — and when he found himself around one, even one he didn't even intend to lie with, he felt shy and awkward. Especially now, with the brand on his cheek. Not too many girls would lie with a man so scarred, and he supposed he had to take his opportunities wherever they appeared. With a few more years on him, he supposed he'd lose out on even the pity pokes.

When he'd tossed his jacket on the floor, he removed his shell belt. The girl moved around to the other side of the bed, removing the gauzy black wrap and sitting on the edge of the bed, her back to Colter, then unlacing the corset and grunting softly with the effort.

Colter kicked out of his boots, peeled off his socks, then removed his jeans. He'd just started sliding his long-handles off his shoulders when he looked up and saw the girl rising, naked, from the edge of the bed. She was a pretty girl in a waifish way, with big brown eyes and thick, curly hair. Her body was smooth and brown, well proportioned, with small, firm breasts with budlike brown nipples. She pulled the bedcovers back, small breasts jostling, then crawled in, fluffed her pillow, and laid her head back on it, looking at him with vague impatience.

He swung around to blow out the lamp.

"Leave it," she said, wrinkling the skin above the bridge of her nose, incredulous. She quirked her mouth corners in a faint smile. "I like to see what I am doing."

Colter shrugged, feigning nonchalance, then quickly crawled beneath the covers, and laid his head back on his pillow. A few minutes before, he'd been so sleepy he thought he'd pass out on his feet. Now he could feel his heart throbbing in his chest. He stared at the ceiling, listening to her breathing beside him, wondering how he should get started and knowing he had to roll toward her soon and do something decisive. He didn't want her to know how inexperienced he was, but he *was* inexperienced, and he was damned nervous though he was also as randy as those stallions in Trace Cassidy's holding corral.

He drew a breath and rolled toward her quickly and flung a leg over hers. She lay beneath him, staring up at him curiously. He lowered his lips to hers, but suddenly she pushed him back down on his side of the bed, and rolled onto her side, giving him a knowing little smile, curling her bottom lip wistfully beneath the upper one.

"What's the matter?" he said. "You change your mind?"

She shook her head. Strands of her curly hair snaked across her smooth brown cheeks. Her brown eyes, flecked with tiny bits of gold, caressed him as she said, "There is no rush, *Rubio.*" She placed a hand on his chest and smiled. "And there is no need to be nervous."

"Hell, I ain't nervous."

"No? Well . . . I guess it is me that is nervous, then. Machado. If we rush, it will be over so soon, and you will fall asleep and leave me alone, listening for his singing and his spurs."

"Dominguez oughta put a bullet in that big bastard, next time he comes around, pestering you."

Her eyes brightened fearfully. "No, no. Machado is the leader of a notorious gang. His gang would avenge his death most severely. And they will likely be in town soon, as they always split up after they rob a bank or a stage, then gather again here in Corazon."

She half closed her eyes, slowly lowered her face to his, and kissed a small scab on his chin. "What is your name, *Rubio*?"

"Colter Farrow."

"Colter Farrow," she whispered, as though testing the words out on her own tongue. With the back of her hand, she slid a lock of his long, straight red hair away from his cheek. "How did that happen?"

"Ah, don't look at that."

"You saw mine," she said, motioning to her own cheek. "How did it happen?"

Annoyance bit him. As well as impatience. "We gonna tell each other our stories now, or we gonna get down to business?"

She frowned reprovingly. "What is your hurry?"

He studied her angry eyes for a moment. "Sorry." He rested his head back against his pillow. "You're right. I am nervous. And if I get all in a hurry, it'll be done before it even gets started, and I reckon I'm nervous about that, too." He blew a raspy whistle at the ceiling. "Jeepers — I sound like an old woman!"

The wrinkles in her forehead smoothed out. "I like that you are nervous."

He rolled his eyes down to regard her seriously. "I just want you to know — this won't be my first time."

Gently, she traced the S on his cheek with the index finger of her right hand, her eyes crossing slightly as she followed her finger with her gaze.

"A law dog up in Colorado gave me that."

"I have never known a lawman any better than the men they lock in their jails."

Colter thought of old Spurr Morgan, the deputy U.S. marshal whom Colter had teamed up with to run his friend Cimarron Padilla's killers down in Wyoming. "Oh, there's a few out there." His eyes acquired a hard, pensive cast. "But not Bill Rondo."

"Did you kill him?"

Colter shook his head. "I left him wishin' he was dead."

"Ahh," Alegria said with a sly smile. "That

is better yet. That is how we do it in Mexico!"

She slid her hand down his chest and he drew a painful breath when she touched his ribs. "That hurts?"

"Some. It's gettin' better now."

"In the morning, I will wrap your ribs with a poultice. An old Mexican remedy. Tornillo beans and mescal. It will feel good on your lips, too." She slid her hand lower and grinned, slitting her eyes, as she whispered alluringly, "For now, though, I will make you feel better down here, uh?"

Colter drew a long, slow breath as she started making him feel better all over.

They made slow, sweet love, like two young lovers just learning, and he lost all trace of his nerves. After nearly two hours, when the lamp had burned out, they fell asleep in each other's arms. They didn't awaken until midmorning.

When they'd made love leisurely once more, Alegria built a fire in the small charcoal brazier in Colter's room and then retrieved a tin of salve and an old cotton sheet from her own room. She lathered the sheet in salve and wrapped the poultice tightly around Colter's bruised ribs. She applied more of the salve to the cuts around his eyes and on his lips. They were lying back in bed, talking like old lovers and sipping coffee laced with Colter's tequila, when Alegria gasped suddenly and turned her head toward the sunlit window.

"What is it?"

"Shhh!"

Then he heard it, too. Outside, someone was singing a Mexican ballad in the same loud, sentimental voice Colter had heard last night. The singing grew louder as the balladeer approached the hotel, spurs ringing.

"Mierda!" Alegria cursed, clamping her hands to her temples, adding thinly, "This morning will be my last."

Chapter 13

Colter said, "I don't think so," and dropped his bare feet to the floor.

Alegria looked at him from between her hands still pressed to her temples, her gold-brown eyes wide with fear. "What are you doing?"

Colter rose, wincing as the bandage tightly wrapped around his middle drew taut against his battered ribs, and bent his knees to retrieve his clothes from the floor. "Don't you worry about Machado, Alegria. I'll go out and powwow with him awhile, see if I can't get the old dog off your trail."

She blinked, then opened her eyes even wider, dropping her hands to her naked brown legs crossed Indian-style beneath her. "What? Are you *mad*?"

"Prob'ly."

Keeping her voice down, as though the giant Mexican border bandit were already outside their door, Alegria said, "Colter, get back over here. We'll hide, and maybe Senor Dominguez will get the sheriff here before Machado finds us!"

Colter grabbed his long-handles and began to gingerly pull them on. "Last night you wanted me to protect you. Now you want me to hide?" He snorted. "Maybe I can stop him before he gets this far."

She blinked again, swallowed as though downing a whole apple, and stared at him aghast. "Maybe you can do what? *Dios mio* — you are mad!" She flopped down in the bed and drew the covers up over her head.

While trying to calm the girl, assuring her everything was going to be all right, and that even big border toughs like Machado would listen to reason if pushed into a corner, Colter casually dressed and wrapped his shell belt and pistol around his waist. He pulled on his duck jacket against the chill of the early-autumn morning, set his hat on his head, and took a last sip of coffee and tequila. He lifted the bedcovers, exposing the girl's left knee. He bent down and kissed it tenderly.

"Thanks for last night. I'll remember it for a long time. Not just the tussle, neither, but the palaver wasn't half bad, neither."

"You are a crazy boy!" she squealed, poking her head out to regard him with exasperation. "*Por favor,* for the last time — get in here with me, and maybe he won't find us!"

Colter set his saddlebags on his shoulder and grabbed his rifle from the wall behind the door. He opened the door and pinched his hat brim to the girl still staring at him with wide-eyed disbelief. "Been a pleasure."

He went out, drawing the door closed behind him. From the other side of the door, he heard her give another exasperated groan. Colter walked down the hall to the top of the stairs. No sounds rose from the saloon hall below. He couldn't hear Machado's singing anymore, either. Maybe the sheriff had already gotten the big bandit back under rein.

Colter went down to find the saloon hall dark, the chairs upended on the tables. Senor Dominguez stood at the window to the right of the door, looking out across the wash fronting the hotel and casting nervous glances back at Colter.

"Best get back upstairs, Red."

"He out there?" Colter walked toward the front of the room. Anger was a cold steel blade slipped just beneath the skin of his lower back. He didn't know Alegria very well, but after last night he'd acquired an affection for the girl. There hadn't been many girls in his life after he'd been so hideously scarred. Lenore had been one, and she was dead. There'd likely be damn few from here on out. Damn few who would understand him or could love him despite the brand on his cheek. The tenderness Alegria had shown him last night had been as genuine as Lenore's friendship had been, and it graveled him that the big outlaw had carved the line on the side of the Mexican girl's pretty face, and that he continued to terrorize her.

"*Sí, sí.* He's stopped to wash his face. Vain son of a bitch."

"How'd he get out of jail so soon?"

"The sheriff must have let him out when he sobered up. No point in trying to hold a man like that. Not with his gang heading for town. The sheriff has a wife and a family. . . ."

"What about Alegria?"

Dominguez glanced over his shoulder at Colter, nodding. "She's a hell of a good moneymaker on the weekends. Without her, I'll have to close my doors, but what can I do? I'll find another one, maybe." He raked a sigh and turned back to the window and fingered his chin pensively.

Colter gave a caustic snort and opened the door. Dominguez glanced at him again, incredulous. "What are you thinking? Get back upstairs, *Rubio*!"

Colter went out, Dominguez calling behind him, "Kid, get back in here!"

Colter stopped on the gallery. Machado was down on his knees in the wash, his big sombrero on the ground beside him as he leaned forward over the trickle of water and splashed it across his face and over his hairy neck. His face was as large as a horse's, and thick, curly dark brown hair fell to his shoulders, framing it. Much of it was thinly braided, the braids wrapped in beads hanging over his ears. He wore a mustache that curved down over the corners of his mouth to his chin, and a gold stud ring glistened in his right ear. His big face was cut and bruised from last night's dustup, a deep, scabbed gash angling over the edge of his left brow.

Colter wondered how the lawmen looked this morning.

Machado wore two big Colt Navy revolvers — one in a holster positioned for the cross draw, another wedged behind his belts over his bulging belly, on the outside of his red-and-white serape. A shoulder holster angled down beneath the flap of his fancily stitched bull-hide vest, also worn over the serape, and Colter could see the handle of a broad knife poking up from the well of his right, high-topped black boot.

Colter let his saddlebags slide down his shoulder and drop to the wooden floor of the gallery. He leaned his rifle against a post, then stepped down off the gallery and walked over to the lip of the wash.

The big, bearlike bandito was cupping water to his bruised temple. He jerked his chin toward the bank upon which Colter stood, frowning, the man's red-rimmed eyes small as dark pebbles in his large, brick red face scored with deep lines around his eye sockets. He said something in Spanish. It sounded like a command. Colter just stared at him stonily.

"Gringo, uh?" Machado said. "Get out of here, kid. You're annoying me. *Vamos!*"

"You're the one who best vamoose, amigo."

The big bandit had dropped his eyes to the stream, but now he looked up again as though at a fly that would not go away. He looked puzzled. "What you say, little scar-face boy?"

"I don't want you comin' around Miss Alegria anymore. I seen what you did to her." Colter bunched his lips and shook his head. He let his glance flick to the three pistols the man was wearing. Machado might be fast, but he was too big to be faster than Colter. Besides, when a man wore that many guns he was usually trying to compensate for something. They gave him confidence when he knew he wasn't as fast or as accurate as some.

Colter felt little fear. Only rage, which he held on a tight rein inside him. He drew deep, regular breaths as he remembered the scar on Alegria's face and the terror in her eyes. He thought of this big man going upstairs now and doing what he would to her, with no one to stop him.

No one except Colter Farrow.

Machado continued to study him with cowlike stupidity. He flicked his dark eyes up and down Colter's lean frame as though he thought his eyes were deceiving him. As though thinking that no one this young and scrawny, with only one old Remington on his hip, could be trying to stare down Machado. The big man's eyes brightened. His face crumpled with laughter. He threw his head back and pointed at Colter and then he laughed even harder, his shoulders quaking, tears streaking his broad cheeks to dampen the ends of his long mustaches.

His laughter diminished to a slow boil. And then it left his face entirely, and his dark eyes bored into Colter's. Heavily, he climbed to his feet, letting his big hands adorned with several gold and silver rings hang straight against his sides. He continued to stare. Then his right hand slashed across his cartridge belt toward the pearl-gripped Colt Navy on his left hip.

Colter jerked as though with a start, his own right hand slashing across his belly. The Remy was out and up faster than it took most men to blink, and the pistol barked three times.

Machado stumbled backward, dragging his *chinging* spurs. The big man had gotten the Colt clear of its holster but was not able to get it half-raised before Colter's Remington spoke again.

Machado screamed and flew back, twisting around and hitting the ground hard in a quivering pile. On his side, he groaned, spasmed, drew a deep breath, and fell still.

Colter was still crouched, feet and arms perpendicular to the wash, making as small a target as possible. His Remington was still extended in his right hand. Smoke curled from the barrel. His senses were still so attuned to danger that when he heard the Babylon's front door scrape open behind him, he wheeled and took aim at the shaggy-headed Dominguez stepping slowly out onto the gallery.

"Hey, hey!" the hotelier said, throwing up his hands. He wore the same soiled red necktie that he'd worn last night.

Colter depressed the Remington's hammer and raised the barrel.

"*Dios mio,* kid," Dominguez said, his voice raspy with disbelief, stepping off the gallery and staring skeptically toward the wash. "You . . . you kill . . . Santiago *Machado*?"

"He drew first." Colter spat into the dust. "Or tried to." He holstered the Remington but kept his hand on the grips when he saw three riders sitting their stalled horses near where this side street intersected with the village's main drag. He let his hand relax. The lead rider was the strange blond tomboy, and the two men flanking her were Wade and Harlan. They were all dressed in wool coats and leather gloves against the chill, and they were trailing a pack mule laden with bulging canvas panniers.

The girl stared skeptically at Colter, as did Wade and Harlan, canting their hatted heads this way and that and flicking their eyes between Colter and the big man lying dead in the draw. Finally, the girl turned her head to say something to the two men behind her, then nudged the heels of her low boots against her horse's flanks, and the three rode on down the street along the side of the draw opposite Colter, their mounts' shod hooves lifting powdery dust. The two men continued to stare at the redheaded shooter, expressionless, maybe a little skeptical, until they'd ridden past him, and then they turned their heads forward and gigged their horses into trots after the girl, Harlan leading the pack mule by a lead rope.

Colter kept his hand on his pistol grips, because several men in serapes or long deerskin coats and sombreros, one in the shopkeeper's attire of a white shirt, wool vest, and armbands, were moving toward him, dragging their feet with caution.

Dominguez stood at the edge of the draw, staring down at Machado, who lay on one hip and shoulder, his thick, long legs scissored. The owner of the Babylon turned his astonished eyes on Colter, letting them flick once to the gun on his left hip.

Then he tossed his head toward the hotel. "Fetch your horse and hightail it, *Rubio*. You might be faster than greased lightning, but you can't take on Machado's entire gang. And that's what you'll have to do if they find you here — with your four bullets in their leader."

"I hope I didn't cause you too much trouble, Senor Dominguez."

Dominguez turned his still-shocked gaze toward Machado. "Hell, *Rubio.* I believe you saved me some. The gang, though — they will be after you."

Colter started walking toward the barn. Dominguez grabbed his arm. "Ride south. I have a brother near the Sierra San Angelo, where Trinity Creek runs into the Rio Yaqui. Ride to him — Ferdinand Dominguez. Tell him I sent you. He will hide you there in return for feeding his chickens and pigs, so he can drink mescal all day and hide from his wife and kids in his silver mine."

"I don't want to get anyone else in trouble."

Dominguez shook his head and clamped Colter on his shoulder. "The gang won't follow you that far — even if they could track you across those rugged wastes. They'll want to avenge Machado, but in the end they want to rob banks more, so they can drink and entertain the *putas* in Monterrey." Again, he clamped Colter's shoulder. "Go!"

Colter strode at an angle across the yard but stopped when he saw Alegria standing on the Babylon's gallery, above the steps. She had a hand on a support post and was staring at Colter with much the same expression as the others. She wore only a sheer pale wrap over a loose burlap tunic. Her legs and feet were bare.

She wrinkled her dark brows. "Pistolero?" she said quietly, dubiously.

Colter drew a breath as he stared back at her, not sure if she was approving or disdainful, but somehow not liking the killer she was seeing in him.

"Adios, Alegria," he said finally, then grabbed his rifle and saddlebags and continued on around the front corner of the hotel.

He strode down the side of the building to the barn.

Behind him he heard voices as a small crowd gathered around the wash. He didn't know much Spanish, but he was picking up enough to understand the shouted query, "Who shot Machado?"

"Rubio de la marca de Satan!" came the reply.

CHAPTER 14

"The redhead with the mark of Satan on his face!" resounded in Colter's head as he rode south throughout the morning.

Here he was again, cast out of another town, blood on his hands. Alone.

When would the horror that his life had become ever end?

When could he hang up the Remington forever?

He rode south only because south was where the bulk of Mexico lay, stretched out before him — an alien land that beckoned him with its vastness and its distance from his own country and the various bounties on his head. Growing loneliness followed him like a pack of hungry wolves. He wondered when he would ever be able to return to his own country. Of course, he might never be able to. Not unless he wanted to live looking over his shoulder every minute of every hour, and sleep with one eye open.

Some men could change their names and live relatively anonymously. Colter didn't have that luxury. The brand on his face — "the mark of Satan" — would scar him forever.

So he rode south throughout the morning and into the afternoon. In the back of his mind was the half-formed idea of taking Dominguez's suggestion of holing up at the hotelier's brother's mine, if he could find the place. If he could be certain that he hadn't been followed by Machado's gang, he might take the man up on his offer. It was lonely out here, and it would likely get lonelier.

He fancied the idea of meeting folks and spending time with them, getting to know them, sitting down to a table with a family. Of course there was the language problem, but he'd have to learn Spanish sooner or later, and maybe this was his opportunity to learn enough not only to get by while he was here, but to have conversations with folks. The farther south he went he'd likely run into fewer and fewer Mexicans who could speak English as Dominguez and Alegria did.

Alegria.

The memory of last night tempered the

hollow feeling in his gut for a time. Gradually, however, remembering the warmth and smoothness of her body, the softness of her kisses, and the sound of her passion as they lay together only made the sky seem vaster, the clay-colored ridges starker and less welcoming, the thickets of catclaw and mesquite around him more threatening.

And then he saw Lenore lying dead beneath Hobart's prancing horse, and he was gripped by a grinding horror and anger.

As though reflecting his mood, clouds closed over the sky, turning the land a charcoal gray. By midafternoon, it had started to rain. Just a mist at first. But then larger drops began to fall hard, and a wind came up of a sudden, growing colder with every sucking, blasting gust.

Lightning that had danced around the far western ridges now flashed nearer, and the accompanying thunder sounded like near cannon fire, making the ground shake and causing Northwest to hesitate and prance in place, nickering his disdain for such weather. Colter rammed his boots against the horse's flanks to keep him moving.

By the time he'd unwrapped his rain slicker from his blanket roll and pulled it on, he was soaked. Continuing to push south, he hoped to outrun the storm. But the sky grew darker. The rain hammered against him — a white curtain slashing sideways and pelting the growing puddles filling every dimple in the clay-colored earth to a creamy froth. Lightning pounded near ridges, touching the wet air with a brimstone tang.

He began looking around for cover, saw a canyon opening between two yawning stone jaws to his right. This was broken country, carved by a maze of rocky arroyos, and Colter leaped down from Northwest's saddle and began leading the jittery horse into the relative shelter of the canyon.

Lightning flashed over his left shoulder. Thunder clapped, sounding like boulders tumbling down the ridges. Ahead, another flash. Colter heard a bullet screech inches past his head. There was another flash ahead and to his left from a niche in the canyon wall. Rock dust flew up on Colter's right. It was followed by the muffled belch of a rifle.

Northwest whinnied and lurched up off his front hooves.

Colter crouched, drew his pistol, silently cursing the dry-gulching bastards.

There was another rifle flash on his left, the bullet tearing into another rock on his right. Dropping to one knee, Colter triggered off two shots toward the shooter firing from the canyon's left wall, and then triggered three more straight up the canyon, unable to see where his bullets struck in the pouring rain. Getting the message that strangers weren't wanted here, he bounded off his knees, jerked Northwest around by his reins, and led the dun off into the cabin-sized boulders farther up the trail.

Banditos, he thought. Holed up out of the rain, and surly as cougars.

When the canyon mouth disappeared behind him, behind the jutting southern wall, he mounted Northwest once more and, hunkered low, the rain sluicing like a mini waterfall from his hat brim, continued up the winding arroyo he'd been following and that was turning into a shallow river swirling with tea-colored water and more and more bits of mud chunks and branches. He looked around for another sanctuary and was crestfallen to see the slick, red-clay arroyo walls rising on both sides of him, until they were nearly six feet high. The thought that he needed to get out of there, as no one but a tinhorn would get caught in an arroyo during a rain squall, had no sooner shunted across his mind than a low rumbling sounded.

The rumbling, like the muffled belching of a discomfited god, seemed to originate from all around him. It grew louder. He glanced down to see that the water was rising and swirling faster and faster. He swung a worried look over his shoulder, and panic was an instant flash within him, taking his breath and making his heart leap and turn somersaults.

A veritable tidal wave of mud brown water was plunging toward him. The flood looked like a brown rug unfurling, the wave gaining on him so quickly that the brown of the froth-limned wave filled his vision. He could see the bubbles and leaves and mesquite leaves and small mud chunks it was hurdling. The cold water slammed over Northwest's rump and against Colter's face, washing through his mouth still hanging wide in shock and dread.

The horse lurched forward and up as the wave lifted him off his hooves, hurling him upstream. Colter heard himself grunt as he was jarred back off the horse and into the cold, dark water, flinging a hand out for the horse's dark brown tail but missing it by at least two feet as the indignantly whinnying dun was plunged downstream and away from him.

Colter was dragged under by the churning currents, sucking half a lungful of water. He surfaced, gasping and choking and glimpsing Northwest's hip to his left. Then he was spun around like a top, feeling himself being hurled with the rest of the debris downstream. He and the horse and the water then began moving faster, as though they were dropping quickly in elevation, maybe into a canyon, and Colter was once more dragged under by unseen hands. Kicking off the rock bottom, skinning his knees on rocky knobs protruding out from the arroyo's bank, he forced his head above the frothy surface and again sucked a deep breath, choking on the water that lodged in his throat and trickled like icy witches' fingers into his lungs.

He vomited water, and as the currents continued to spin him while sweeping him downstream, he flung his arms out toward both banks, hoping to grab a rock or a shrub. He saw a root looping out of the bank on his left. It was coming up fast in a gray-brown blur, dodging and pitching. He kicked toward it, leaned forward, got a hand on it, but before he could close the hand, the rabid dogs of the currents fastened their jaws on his legs and ripped him off downstream.

There was a sudden plunge as the arroyo dropped down. Colter rolled sideways, throwing his arms out for balance as well as in an instinctive effort to grab whatever he could. At the bottom of the drop, the jaws of the dirty cream froth sucked him down once more. When he managed to jerk his head up again, the massive gray fist of a rock wall slid resolutely into his path. Its unyielding bulk slammed against his left side, numbing that arm and shoulder and scrambling his brains, blurring his vision.

He was thrust to the right, now just trying to keep his head above the water. As he was tossed around another bend, he saw an object on his right, and thrust that arm up halfheartedly. Something told him to stiffen the arm a quarter second before it made contact with the object, and he was glad he did, because a second later he found himself hooked around a stout branch protruding from a crack in the rock of the arroyo's ridge.

He vomited, sucked a spoonful of air, retched again.

He'd hit the branch violently, and he felt as though his right shoulder had been partly torn from its socket. Looking down, he saw the water swirling around his waist. His brown leather holster flopped in the current, empty. Somewhere, he'd lost the Remington.

Maybe partly because of the braining he'd

taken by the rock wall, the loss of the old gun was what he was most concerned about. Not his own physical condition, or Northwest's, but that he'd lost the Remington that he'd left home with so long ago. It had become a security blanket of sorts.

"Ah, shit," he heard himself mutter above the water's pulsating thunder as he stared down at the soaked, empty holster.

He hooked his other arm around the branch and hoisted his knees onto it. The rain continued to hammer at him, thick as wind-driven snow. But he could see the top of the bank to his right, only about four feet above. He gained his knees, praying the branch would hold and not send him tumbling into the torrent again. Twisting around, he grabbed the top of a rock jutting a ways out from the bank. From there he was able to scramble off the branch and onto the wall from which he climbed, cursing and grumbling against the renewed ache in his ribs as well as the fresh agony in both shoulders and knees, and onto the top of the ridge.

He collapsed on his back and lay there, raking air in and out of his lungs, squinting against the pelting rain falling out of a sky the color of a bruised plum.

Every bone and nerve throbbed. But he

couldn't lie here. For all he knew the arroyo would continue to flood until it washed over its banks to sweep him away again. Groaning, he climbed to hands and knees, looked around, saw that he was in a narrow canyon with steep ridge walls on both sides of the arroyo.

Northwest . . .

Holding his aching ribs, he limped off, bandy-legged and bent-kneed, along the arroyo, looking around desperately for his horse. In many ways the animal was like an equal partner to him, his only remaining companion, but his main concern now was being stranded out here on foot. On foot and without a gun, he'd be as helpless as a newborn calf without its mother.

He felt nearly as freshly beaten as after his dustup, if you could call it that, with Lieutenants Belden, Hobart, and McKnight. His heart thudded wildly, desperately.

"Northwest?" he called, the roaring torrent beside him and the pounding rain drowning the cry as it left his lips.

He stumbled around a bend in the wall, and stopped suddenly.

"Northwest?" he said, softer now and tempered with relief.

To his left, the arroyo had flattened out, and the walls dropped, so that the water didn't appear to be moving as fast. Ahead, he stared in slack-jawed relief as he watched the horse lunging up a series of low shelves in the arroyo's stone wall, until Northwest gained the top of the bank, the saddle and the rest of Colter's tack hanging down his right side, and gave a splay-legged shake.

"Northwest!" he shouted, and stumbled forward, choking on more water forcing itself up from his lungs.

The horse was badly rattled and it trotted a ways on down the canyon before it turned to face the canyon wall as though seeking protection from the flashing lightning and blasting thunder. Colter slowed his pace and held up his hands, palms out in supplication, as he stole up to the mount who stood with his head nearly touching the wall, shivering and snorting and twitching his ears.

"It's all right, boy. You're safe. Er . . ." He blinked against the rain as he looked around, having no idea how far the flood had carried him or where he and the horse had ended up. ". . . at least you're not drowned."

He looked around, squinting, and saw what looked like a cave mouth a little farther up the canyon. It lay back in a concave depression in the canyon wall — sort of triangular-shaped but much lower on the left than on the right. He took Northwest's reins and after much coaxing, got the horse to follow him over to the cave, which appeared at least from the outside tall enough to shelter both himself and the horse. He stepped cautiously inside, squinting into the dense shadows, half expecting to find some wild animal holed up out of the weather. It was dark, but there was enough gray light seeping in behind him to reveal the two side walls, and the occasional lightning flashes briefly showed him the back wall, which appeared a jumble of strewn rock and gravel, as well.

Colter pulled on Northwest's reins. The horse whinnied shrilly and drew back, lifting his head and flattening his ears. "Come on, horse," Colter urged, pulling on the reins. "You don't wanna stay out here in the rain, do you?"

When he'd finally led the horse into the cave — the ceiling about a foot higher than Northwest's head — he quickly stripped off the tack, which included Colter's rifle and scabbard, thank God. At least he had the Henry. Shivering against the cold arroyo water, teeth clattering, he slipped Northwest's bit and left him ground-tied. He figured the horse had drunk enough water in the arroyo, as Colter had, so he poured out a small pile of damp oats from his saddlebags, then walked over to the mouth of the cave.

He tightly crossed his arms on his chest, trying to drive the cold out. No use. Every muscle in his body felt electrified. There was likely no dry wood anywhere near, so a fire wouldn't be possible.

Deciding he'd just have to gut out the storm right here, soaked to his gills, he sank down against the cave wall. Even shivering, he managed to fall into an aching, miserable kind of sleep. He was half aware of the storm abating, stopping, then starting up again, the wind like a cold breath blowing against him.

A world-rattling thunderclap woke him. Northwest whinnied. For a second, Colter thought the canyon walls were collapsing on top of him. A lightning bolt blasted the bank of the arroyo just outside the cave, and the redhead leaped nearly a foot straight up off his rump.

Brimstone fetor filled his nostrils. The lightning played along his retinas the way he'd once seen it sizzle along the rim of a steel stock tank.

It took him a long time to get back to sleep.

When he did, he dreamed of Alegria's warm bed and of sunlight caressing him. It was a miserable dream, because while he could see the delicious light, he could not feel its warmth — only the chill of a frozen steel blade sandwiching his beaten body.

He woke and lifted his head from his chest. He felt a patch of warmth on his left cheek and shoulder. Looking out of the cave mouth, he blinked against lemon sunlight angling into the canyon from a clear blue sky and penetrating the cave's opening. Delectable warmth from a sun he'd begun to think had burned itself out.

"Oh, Lord," he said, feeling the warmth begin to penetrate the chill that still held him fast. Steam rose from the canyon floor — gauzy yellow snakes rising in the sunlight to gently caress the far canyon wall still purple with the lingering night.

Northwest snorted. Colter turned to look at the horse standing facing him and flicking his ears. Colter had opened his mouth to speak, but something to the far left of the horse caught his eye, and he jerked back against the cave wall with a start, his heart fluttering.

Just enough sunlight tumbled into the cave to reveal a man in a gray hat sitting back in the shadows amongst the rocks, aiming a rifle at Colter's heart.

CHAPTER 15

Colter reached for his rifle leaning against the wall to his right and racked a shell into the chamber so loudly that Northwest lifted his head with a start, snorting. Colter aimed the Henry out from his right hip at the hombre pulling down on him from the cave's heavy purple shadows. He could just make out the man's figure and the rifle in his hands limned with sunlight whose intensity was greatly diminished back there.

He stared at the shooter, his racing pulse gradually slowing. The man wasn't moving. There seemed an unnatural stiffness in the silhouette.

Cautiously, Colter said, "Hey."

The shadow did not move.

Colter got his stiff legs under him and hauled himself to his feet. He strode slowly across the cave floor, angling toward the left rear corner, keeping his Henry aimed at the man-shaped shadow, and stopped. He frowned down at the bleached skull with gaping black mouth and eyes and nose sockets looking both bizarre and ridiculous in an overlarge metal helmet crusted with grit and grime with only a few patches of gray showing through the spiderwebs.

The skeleton, lounging back against the wall with one leg curled beneath it, wore a steel breastplate with a ridge down the front, and metal plates on his thighs. Fibers of some long-moldered clothing clung to its bony shins, and bits of leather from rotted boots clung by threads to its otherwise bare, skeletal feet and ankles.

A wooden arrow, minus feathers, protruded from the ribs just beneath the breastplate, angling down toward the skeleton's left thigh. Also resting on the skeleton's thigh was a short, stocky rifle, most of the ancient wood having flaked away from the badly tarnished barrel, the end of which flared like a funnel. Colter's sluggish, half-frozen brain recalled the word for the ancient Spanish firearm: blunderbuss.

The conquistador must have crawled in here a long, long time ago, after some skirmish with Indians, and died.

Colter continued to stare down at the skeleton, feeling an added chill climbing his spine. The man's right index finger —

merely a slender, jointed bone, was still curled through the blunderbuss's trigger guard. When he'd died, he must have still been expecting an Indian to charge in here after him.

The round eye sockets stared blankly up at Colter. Inside the left one, a small black spider was climbing around. Somehow, the skull seemed to be grinning at him knowingly, jeeringly, and Colter felt a shudder ripple through him.

He stepped back away from the dead man and turned to his horse, who was regarding Colter with a faint look of castigation in his eyes. "Sorry, Northwest," Colter said, holding his rifle in one hand while caressing the dun's long snout with the other. "I reckon that dead hombre's why you didn't want to come in here last night, huh? Just glad I didn't know about him, or I wouldn't have got what little sleep I did."

He grabbed Northwest's reins, leading the horse out of the cave and over to the bank of the arroyo, along which grew several varieties of grasses, all of which looked nourishing for the dun. In the arroyo itself, the flood had diminished to a slow-moving creek, which appeared only two or three feet deep. Oddly, even after all the floodwater he'd swallowed, he was thirsty. Northwest probably was, too, but Colter didn't want to risk leading the mount down the slippery back, fearing he'd stumble and fall. Swinging around, he started back to the cave to fetch a cooking pot he could fill with water, and stopped abruptly, staring at the ridge wall.

The cave in which Colter and Northwest had spent the night was not the only cave in the ridge wall. There was another one about twenty yards to the left of it, and more beyond, with more above in tiers, sort of like rooms in a sprawling hotel, with ledges fronting their recessed mouths. Colter stepped back and raised a shaky hand to point as he counted the caves, stopping when he got to twelve because he couldn't see beyond the slight bend in the cliff face about fifty yards to his left.

Some of the caves were fronted by dilapidated ladders made of poles and what appeared to be hemp or rawhide, and rising to the next tier above. Some of the ladders lay on the ledges, crumbling. As Colter scrutinized the cliff face, he realized that it wasn't the actual face of the cliff at all. What he was looking at was a veritable mountain of piled adobe blocks forming a large building of sorts constructed against the cliff, the caves being individual rooms — what one might call apartments. Colter had seen similar Indian ruins in canyons near Camp Grant in Arizona, and there were even a few near the Lunatic Range in south-central Colorado. He'd heard about one near Durango that was almost as large as the city of Denver, and would put this one to shame.

Colter looked across the arroyo, to the other side of the canyon beyond a swirling, sunlit fog. Set back against that cliff wall were more of the same manmade caves built into a giant building made of large adobe blocks. Some of the cave mouths had collapsed, and almost all the ladders over there were gone. Birds wheeled in and out of the black gaps, squealing in the rookery for breakfast, their wings flashing in the warming morning sunlight.

"I'll be damned," Colter said, running his damp sleeve across his mouth, vaguely enjoying the sunlight bathing him. "Never know what you're gonna run into, do you? Just lucky this canyon wasn't filled with banditos."

As the other one had been. . . .

He went back into the cave, or apartment, or whatever the hell you'd call it, and felt another swath of chicken flesh rise over him when he raked his eyes across the dead conquistador and his oddly shaped blunderbuss again. He grabbed his soogan and dug around in his saddlebags, pulling out the tin pot he usually boiled beans in. He unrolled his blankets, draped them over a shrub to dry in the sun, then carried the pot down to the arroyo and filled it.

He let the mud and grit settle to the bottom, then took a long drink of the cold water, refilled the pot, and brought it up to where Northwest cropped the grass contentedly, giving his tail frequent satisfied flicks and snorting. Colter set the pot on a low rock near the horse and looked around, giving the canyon a thorough survey, looking for any sign of trouble.

Deeming himself and Northwest alone, he kicked out of his boots and then shucked out of his clothes and the poultice that Alegria had wrapped him in. He laid his duds and boots out where the sun could dry them. Naked from head to toe, he lay down on the damp clay that the sun had already warmed, and loosed a sigh of contentment as the sun began baking the chill from his bones.

He ground his shoulders and buttocks into the warm earth and groaned again. Before he knew it, he was asleep.

The heat woke him when the sun was high in the sky and burning through his eyelids.

He got up, feeling only a tenderness in all the places in which the floodwaters had bruised him. His ribs still ached almost as badly as before, and he wished he had another poultice, but the dry air and sun would have to fix him.

His clothes were dry. So were his blankets. He hoped he could find some dry wood, as well, because he intended to build a fire and keep one burning for warmth and cooking, though all the food in his saddlebags was likely waterlogged and fouled and inedible. When he'd gathered all the dry and semi-dry wood he could find, he'd go out and try to shoot a rabbit or a quail or two, though he didn't like the idea of popping a cap out here and giving his position away. He doubted Machado's men would have followed him through such a storm, or that soldiers from Camp Grant would have penetrated this far into Mexico, but while he did not fear the grave, he wouldn't mind reaching his twentieth birthday.

Since he'd been born, he might as well live as long as he could.

Somehow, despite the "Mark of Satan" on his cheek, he still hoped to have a normal life someday, though he had a vague, unsettling notion that such hope was a child's fairy tale.

Armed with only his rifle, which he took the time to disassemble and clean, and missing his lost Remington, he walked back along the arroyo in the direction from which he and Northwest had been so unceremoniously carried. He didn't have to walk far before he saw several *javelinas* grubbing around a mesquite near a feeder creek to the main arroyo, snorting up beans that had likely been ripped off the tree by the storm. There were three of the wild pigs. Salivating at the imagined smell and taste of the roasted meat — he and Tappin had practically lived off the wild boars at Camp Grant — he got down and crawled until he was snug between a paloverde and a cracked boulder that had leaf-speckled rainwater still puddled on its surface. He dropped a small but plump pig with one shot, grinding his teeth against the echoing of the report's angry crack around the ridges. The echoes seemed to take an hour to die, though it was probably only about five seconds.

Too long in this dangerous country.

Colter hustled over to the dead but quivering *javelina* and, with the knife he kept in his boot, deftly dressed and quartered the pig, leaving the innards steaming beneath the paloverde. He carried one-quarter of the meat back to his camp on his shoulder, grunting against the strain on his battered body. Riding Northwest out to retrieve the rest, he wrapped the meat in its own hide and lashed the bundle behind his saddle with rope. He returned to camp, stowed the meat in the cool cave, away from the flies, and got to work building a fire just inside the cavern with the flint and steel he always kept on hand, sulfur matches often being scarce and unreliable.

For tinder, he used a long-abandoned bird's nest found in one of the other caves. He pulled the tightly woven nest apart and fed the fledgling flame a few strands of dried grass and animal fur at a time, until the one flame became two, then three, and the fire began to consume the rest of the nest in a rush. He added the driest and smallest bits of wood. When the fire was on its way, he added some of the larger stuff and piled the rest of the branches close to the ring so it would dry out faster.

He spent the rest of the afternoon gathering more wood, not caring if it was dry or not. It would dry out fast in the sun by the fire, as he intended to keep the fire going all night and maybe even all day tomorrow. He needed to stay warm, and he needed to rest and heal after his drift down the arroyo. And Northwest could use a few days' cropping the wild grasses.

Besides, he had nothing else to do or anywhere else to go.

He built a spit from the green branches of a willow and roasted a quarter of the pig, leaving the rest of the meat for later. He ate ravenously, chewing the meat off the spit and cleaning the rib bones until they shone in the firelight. He had no coffee, as it had all washed away in the arroyo, but the tequila bottle he'd wrapped in several spare shirts had been spared. Washing the pork down with tequila, and feeling a warm glow wash over him as he sat by the fire in the cave entrance, he watched the sun go down and the stars spread out and sparkle over the canyon.

He no longer minded the presence of the dead conquistador. In fact, he'd started to feel comforted by the dead man's company and, after a few shots of strong drink, found himself calling him Hector. "Look at that, Hector," he said, sitting back against the cave wall, the fire snapping and crackling before him as he gave his gaze to the sky. "Shooting star! I wonder how far away. . . ."

He slept soundly, warmly, waking only to build up the fire. He kept one ear open for sounds of interlopers, but all he heard were coyotes and, once, the distant screech of a hunting mountain lion.

The next morning he led Northwest down the arroyo a ways, in the direction from which they'd come, to a game trail that led down into the wash and where the grass grew lush. He hobbled the horse in the grass and then walked along the canyon, hoping to maybe find some quail eggs for breakfast, and was surprised and relieved when his Remington appeared, embedded in the thick, still-damp clay of the wash's bottom. He scooped up the old, mud-caked gun, took it back to his camp, where he roasted more of the *javelina,* and set to work taking apart the pistol and cleaning all the parts. Now if he could find his hat, which he'd also lost in the flooded arroyo. He'd have to find another one soon or the Mexican sun would fry him.

He'd just finished his breakfast as well as loading the Remy with fresh, dry cartridges when from down-canyon to his left, Northwest gave a warning whinny.

Colter scrambled to his feet, kicked dirt on the fire, and, despondent that the world was shouldering into this quiet sanctuary, cast a nervous glance up-canyon. Biting out a quiet curse, he rolled the Remington's oiled cylinder across his forearm.

CHAPTER 16

Colter kicked more dirt on the fire, covering all the logs and dousing the smoke. Holstering the Remy, he bolted on out of the cave and dashed up the arroyo, scrambling down the bank to where Northwest stood in the tawny, fetlock-high grass, switching his tail and staring up the canyon.

Colter couldn't see anything in that direction, but the horse must have smelled or heard something. The redhead quickly unhobbled the mount and led him up the bank and back to the cave and deep inside. The horse flicked its ears once more at the dead conquistador but otherwise paid the skeleton little heed.

Northwest had grown as accustomed to their dead companion as Colter had.

Colter forced the horse to lie down — not a difficult maneuver since it was one that Colter had trained the horse on, and one they practiced frequently. It was all part and parcel of trying to stay ahead of the bounty hunters.

When he had the horse lying flat on his left side, Colter grabbed his Henry from the cave wall and crabbed up toward the front, stopping about six feet from the mouth. He lifted his head just high enough that he could see the wet arroyo and its following of willows and dun-brown brush and rocks that stretched toward a bench at the base of the opposite ridge.

Staying low, he caressed the Henry's hammer with his thumb and watched and waited. After a few minutes, he heard the slow clomps of shod horses moving toward him. Voices rose, then, too — men conversing in Spanish, the voices growing louder, as did the thuds of the hooves. Colter kept his head lifted just far enough above the cave floor to see the arroyo.

A horse appeared — a rangy steeldust — on his left, following the trail that wound along the arroyo bottom. Two more horses followed, and then two more, with two more appearing several seconds later — all bearing Mexicans clad in dove-gray uniforms and shabby straw sombreros with what appeared eagle insignias stitched into the brims. The men were either mustached or bearded; they were all well armed with pistols and Springfield carbines. The lead rider — a tall man with a gray mustache and goatee setting off the copper red of his angular face — wore brass captain's bars on the shoulders of his gray jacket.

Colter felt his jaws ache from tension. These men were members of the Mexican Rural Police Force. He'd never seen them but he'd heard of them from the men back at Camp Grant. They always had to deal with the *rurales* whenever American soldiers rode into Mexico on the trail of Apaches or cattle rustlers, and from what Colter had heard, they were a surly lot — at least when dealing with gringos. Many were also no more law-abiding than the outlaws they hunted on their own side of the border.

Colter kept his body pressed flat against the ground, his chin raised about eight inches. The gray-mustached captain rode on past the cave, looking around at both canyon walls. The others followed, talking conversationally amongst themselves. An eighth rider came into view, riding alone. He had an arm thrown back behind him, and as he continued riding toward the cave, Colter saw that he was holding a lead line. The other end of the line rope was connected to the bridle of a brown-and-white pinto on which a young girl rode. A young blond in a dark gray dress and shabby wool coat, with a bullet-crowned hat pulled low on her freckled forehead.

Colter stared, the corners of his eyes creasing with interest, his thumb no longer caressing the Henry's hammer.

He slowly turned his head from left to right, his eyes on the girl astride the slow-moving pinto. He knew right away he was looking at the strange blonde he'd seen before, in the company of Wade and Harlan, because, especially in Mexico, she was a distinctive-looking little gal. Her expression beneath the narrow brim of her hat was grave, glum. And she had every right to be, as her hands were cuffed before her and tied to her saddle horn. Colter also saw that her right ankle was tied to its stirrup.

The blond was a prisoner of the *rurales.*

Colter thought that maybe Wade and Harlan would also ride into view, but so far he saw no sign of the two men. Riding at the head of the pack, the captain stopped his steeldust gelding about forty yards up the canyon, to Colter's right. The tall man hipped around in his saddle, tossing his head around and speaking loudly as he surveyed the ancient Indian ruins closing around him.

The others slowed their own mounts and

looked around nervously, as well. Colter thought that someone had smelled his fire smoke, but then the *rurale* captain rammed the spurs strapped to his high-topped, mule-eared boots against his steeldust's flanks, and the horse lurched ahead as though shot out of a cannon. The others followed suit, the last man pulling the blonde's pinto along behind, the blonde's head jerking back as the horse broke into a gallop.

Colter lifted his head farther above the cave floor, following the *rurales* with his eyes, his brows ridged in befuddlement. When they were almost out of sight, the blond girl bringing up the rear, he climbed to his feet and pressed his shoulder against the right cave wall at the opening, edging his gaze around to follow the group as they galloped on out of sight down-canyon.

A trap? Had they known he was here — maybe smelled the smoke or seen his and Northwest's tracks that were plainly etched at the arroyo's bottom and all over this side of the canyon? Maybe they'd only slipped away, fearful of a bushwhack, to swing back later and take him by surprise.

He waited. The breeze ruffled the grass along the arroyo, and shadows slid around rocks and shrubs.

Finally, he had a feeling the *rurales* had

left for good. Being that they were a super-stitious lot, maybe the ruins had spooked them. Concern for his own welfare edged toward the strange blond girl. He'd heard the *rurales* often imprisoned *norteameri-canos* on some trumped-up charge, and the taken gringos were never heard from again. Rumor had it that the *rurales* took part in cross-border slave trading, a booming busi-ness in southern Sonora and Chihuahua, with all the silver and gold mines studding the mountains.

Colter doubted the little blonde would make a good rock breaker. And he also doubted she was so hardened a criminal that she deserved incarceration in Mexico. Abruptly, he dropped a brake on such concerns. She was none of his business. He was having enough trouble keeping his own ass out of jail. . . .

Quickly, knowing he couldn't comfortably spend another night here in the canyon, he gathered his gear and the *javelina* meat and saddled Northwest. He slid his rifle into the saddle boot, then led the horse out of the cave and mounted up. He had no idea where he was. All he knew was that bandi-tos had occupied a canyon to the northeast, somewhere back the way he'd come before the flood had swept him away, and that the *rurales* had drifted southwest.

After a quick pondering of the situation, he decided he'd follow the *rurales'* tracks for a time, then swing off their trail and head wherever the four winds blew him. Doubtless, he'd never find his way to Dominguez's brother's silver mine now, even if he got his bearings back.

He nudged Northwest ahead, following the edge of the arroyo for a hundred yards before dropping into the wash via a game path, and then followed the *rurales'* tracks for one slow, guarded mile. Checking Northwest down, he stared off in the direction the gang had drifted, and, relatively certain they were gone, with no intention of circling back, he reined Northwest sharply south, through a break in the canyon wall, and heeled the horse into a spanking trot. As he rode, and though he tried hard to close it out of his mind, the remembered image of the blond girl's depressed, fearful face hovered behind his retinas.

He knew it wasn't like her to look so glum. He'd seen her taking the proverbial stick to her two male companions. For her to look so beaten down and fearful now meant she was up to her freckles in Mexican muck.

And likely a long ways from home.

Goddamn it, Colter, get your mind off the

girl's problems. You're swimming in a whole barnyard of horse shit yourself!

He continued riding, eyes aimed straight out over Northwest's head, but a half hour later, he was swinging back out of the break between canyons and booting Northwest back onto the *rurales'* trail, cursing all the while.

Five hours later, hot and tired and his ribs squealing under his shirt, he put Northwest up to a towering ponderosa pine and heaved himself, groaning like an old man, out of the saddle. He stood with his back against his saddle fender, drawing deep breaths to ease the fatigue as well as all the aches and pains in his body. A cool breeze smelling of pine resin slid against him, drying the front of his sweaty wool shirt. It lifted an end of his red neckerchief, tickling his ear and making him remember that blessed night he'd spent with Alegria, which seemed a hundred years ago now.

Ah, but the cool air felt good after chasing the *rurales* and the strange blond girl across a hot, dry, rocky waste, then up into the low reaches of a high mountain range that had stood like a giant anvil against the southeastern horizon. As he'd climbed, remaining about a quarter mile behind the men he was shadowing, in case the captain had sent an outrider to check their back trail, he was glad to see shimmering streams and pines and fir forests, and slopes stippled with mule deer.

All his troubles had seemed to come on the hot desert. Maybe up here in the cool, fragrant air, his luck would change and he'd be able to rescue the blonde from her captors without getting both himself and the girl killed.

Now he tied Northwest's reins to a branch of the pine tree and slid his Henry from the saddle boot. Slowly, quietly, he levered a fresh cartridge into the chamber and started up the steep slope to his right, his boots slipping in the slide rock and gravel. He gained the dome of cracked granite that crested the slope, then crawled the last few feet to the top. He crawled between two ancient stone bubbles, one with a spindly cedar twisting up from a crack, and peered into the canyon on the other side.

The sun had gone down several minutes ago, so the opposite, pine-clad slope was cloaked in gray-purple shadows. He could still make out the dove-gray uniforms of the *rurales* milling about in the trees near the base of the slope, where two men were securing horses to a long picket rope strung between several trees. Through the pines,

Colter could see a broad dome of rock much like the one he was hunkered on, capping the opposite slope. At the base of the dome, there appeared several narrow caves, and around these caves, the orange flames of a fire danced.

Occasionally, the silhouette of a *rurale* passed before the fire. He could glimpse other shadows arranging gear around the flames, likely breaking out coffeepots and other cooking utensils and grub. As Colter remained low, studying the *rurales'* camp and pondering how he was going to get the girl out of there, he saw her moving down the slope amongst the columnar pines, stooping to gather fallen branches. It wasn't an easy maneuver for the girl, as the *rurales* had looped a rope around her neck. The opposite end of the rope was tied around a large pine knot with several short branches jutting off it.

Obviously, the stump was their backwoods version of a ball and chain. He could hear a few of them chuckling from up around the fire, while the two men picketing the horses were calling to the others from the base of the slope, laughing, enjoying themselves.

The girl did not react to the jeers of her abusers. She merely continued to scour the slope for firewood, crouching, building up the load in her arms. When she had several good-sized logs and a few smaller ones tucked under her chin, she turned and began walking toward the fire, slouching beneath the weight of her load and having to stop and jerk the stump free when it got caught up behind another log or a tree.

She made it back to the fire and dropped the wood beside the dancing flames. The captain was sitting by the fire, his knees drawn up. It was hard for Colter to tell from this distance and in the dimming light, but the man appeared to be washing from a bowl in his lap, a towel draped over his shoulder. The air was still enough that Colter could hear the girl speaking as she faced the captain. She jerked around quickly, angrily, and then she fell hard with a little shriek and rolled a few feet down the slope.

At first, Colter couldn't make out what had happened. But then he saw that the captain had extended his left leg to trip the girl. Now he raised his knee again and, laughing loudly, continued to splash water on his face. The girl lay on the slope for a time, shoulders slumped in defeat. Finally, she got up and, pulling the stump along behind her, headed back down the slope in her search of more firewood.

Despite his having tracked her with her *rurale* captors, Colter had reserved the right to turn away if he saw that rescuing her would be too risky. There was no point in getting himself killed for a strange little girl he didn't even know. Now, however, he pursed his lips and nodded as he stared across the narrow canyon at the captain.

"All right, little miss," he said. "All right."

He glanced at the sky, judging there was about forty-five minutes of daylight left. Then he crawled back down the slope to wait for good dark. And for hell to pop.

CHAPTER 17

Colter fed and watered Northwest, hobbling him near the pine tree so the horse could freely graze. He removed his spurs from his boots and draped them over his saddle horn. Making sure that both his Remington and Henry were loaded, drawing the loading tube out from under the rifle's barrel, then shoving it back in and locking it, the redhead gave the coyote dun a parting pat on the neck and stole off down the canyon, making his way through the darkness relieved only by starlight.

He wished he could have made a more thorough reconnaissance of the *rurales'* camp before dark. As it was, he pretty much had to hope that the luck of the Mexican gods was with him, and that he could make his way around behind the *rurale* camp without being shot by a picket. And that there was a way up and over that caprock from the backside. His intention was to sneak up on the camp from that direction, find out where the girl was, and free her in whatever way he could come up with on the spur of the moment.

Dangerous. But he'd been in dangerous places before. Danger had become such a way of life, he wondered if he'd ever be able to enjoy a settled life if he found one.

The farther he tramped away from his horse, the quieter and more slowly he walked. He followed the canyon around to what he figured was the backside of the one the *rurales* were camped on, and started to climb. Here, he moved even more carefully, more slowly, setting his boots down softly. The crunch of gravel might give him away to any pickets about, and surely the *rurale* captain had posted a guard or two.

Keeping his eyes and ears skinned, Colter continued to climb the steep ridge, hunkered low, holding his rifle in his right hand, using his left to push off rock and boulders, and for balance. He knew now why the old deputy U.S. marshal he'd gotten to know in Wyoming — Spurr Morgan — had preferred moccasins over cowhide boots. They were a hell of a lot quieter. Try as Colter might, he could not keep his boots from grinding gravel ever so faintly.

It was the boot-grind of another, though,

that stopped him in his tracks.

The sound had come from above a rock ledge on his right. He dropped instantly to a knee. A stone rolled off the ledge and onto the ground about six feet in front of Colter. The starlight shone on it faintly. Colter pricked his ears, squeezing the rifle in his hands.

He did not hear another footfall. But as he knelt there, as patient as an Apache, he caught a whiff of tobacco smoke. He lifted his chin, sniffing the still air. The smoke was drifting down from nearly straight above him and, judging by how the smoke peppered his nostrils, not more than a few yards away.

Colter crept slowly forward, crouched beneath the ledge. He leaned his hatless head out away from the ledge and peered up over the mantel-like slab of rounded rock. A man's silhouette stood above him, tall against the starlit sky. The man, his back facing Colter and dressed in a dove gray uniform, held a carbine with a lanyard in his left hand. His right arm was bent forward, and a gauzy stream of smoke slithered into the air around his head.

Colter caught another whiff of the eye-stinging tobacco smoke.

Colter leaned his rifle against a boulder,

lifted his denim pant leg above his right boot, and slipped his wooden-handled skinning knife out of the sheath he'd sewn into the well. He'd just drawn his pant leg down over his boot and tightened his hand around the knife when he heard a boot crunch gravel behind him.

A warning bell tolled loudly in his ears.

He started to swing his head around but stopped when he heard the gut-wrenching click of a gun hammer, felt something cold, hard, and round pressed against the back of his neck. He suppressed a shudder.

A soft, deep Spanish voice said something behind him. The Mexicans down here spoke much faster than Cimarron and his Hunkpapa daughter, Rose, had spoken Spanish to him up in Wyoming, and all he could only make out were the words "move" and "little bastard."

Colter's mouth went dry. His heart fluttered. He gripped the knife in his right hand, mind racing, knowing he had to make a fast move or he'd die. Just then the man behind him spoke more loudly, directing his harsh words upslope.

Ah, shit, Colter thought. Too late. He heard the man who'd been smoking above the ledge walk toward him, and in the corner of his right eye, he saw the man's gray silhouette on the ledge above him, staring down at him, holding his rifle across his chest, the cigarette smoldering between his lips. The two *rurales* spoke for a time, arguing, the one with his pistol pressed to the back of Colter's neck berating the other one for letting a "muchacho" sneak up on him.

Then the one behind Colter jerked the Remy from Colter's holster and spoke loudly in Colter's ear, "Drop that knife, or I carve you up with it!" Or something close.

Colter opened his hand. The knife clattered to the gravel at his boots — a grating, sickening sound that filled the redhead's gut with sour bile. He was totally unarmed. A boot hammered into his back, and he fell belly-down. The *rurale* held him down with his boot while he leaned down and, pressing the gun against the back of Colter's neck with one hand, patted him down with the other. Finding no other weapons, the *rurale* grabbed his rifle and told him to get up.

Colter climbed to his feet. The *rurale* asked him what he was doing here. Colter started to answer in English that he'd gotten lost in the dark — it was all he could come with on short notice — but the man gave an impatient grunt, cutting him off. Apparently, he didn't understand English. He told the other man to stay where he was, then shoved Colter forward with his own rifle. *"Vamos!"*

Colter started forward.

"Parada!"

Colter stopped. The man grabbed his shoulder and swung him around to half face him. The *rurale* was about Colter's height, but broad, with shaggy mutton-chops framing his pockmarked face. He stared at the brand on Colter's cheek, then grinned and prodded him again with the Henry.

"Adelante!"

Colter walked forward, sweat dribbling down his back. What a fool he was! All he'd gotten for his trouble was most likely a bullet. If he was lucky. If he wasn't so lucky, he'd soon likely be breaking rocks somewhere in southern Sonora and start dying slowly from exhaustion or consumption.

The *rurale* prodded him over the breast of the mountain and then down the other side, a game path twisting amongst the rocks vaguely limned by starlight. Colter glanced behind him. He needed to make a play for the Henry, but the *rurale* was staying too far back. By the time Colter could swing around, the man would punch a .44 slug through his heart with his own rifle.

Defeat and shame burned in Colter's ears. He'd let the son of a bitch walk right up behind him. . . .

He gave up on trying for the rifle when firelight appeared on his right, the throbbing glow silhouetting the still, columnar pines. The small group of *rurales* was lounging around the flames, some leaning back against saddles or sitting on rocks. They were smoking and sipping from tin cups, talking, two playing cards spread out on the ground between them. The captain was facing the fire, his back to Colter, the firelight glistening on the two gold bars on his tunic shoulders.

The blond girl sat a ways from the fire, back to a tree, hands behind her back. She was dirty and sunburned, and her hair was badly mussed, like a tumbleweed around her head. One eye was swollen, and the right corner of her mouth was split. She blinked at Colter, her eyes dull. If she recognized him, her eyes didn't betray it.

The stocky man behind Colter called to the fire. The tall captain turned around, his gray mustache and goatee looking pale against his dark, angular face. A short cigarette jutted from one corner of his mouth. In his left hand he held a steaming tin cup. His other hand dropped automatically to the pistol thonged on his right thigh.

Colter stopped, as did the man behind

him, telling the captain about the gringo he'd found sneaking around atop the mountain.

The captain canted his head to one side, squinting, as he strode out away from the fire and stopped in front of Colter. *"Habla español?"*

Colter shook his head.

"What are you doing out here?" the captain asked.

The other men were watching Colter expectantly, some nervously. One sergeant had grabbed his rifle and stood, jerking his head around as though looking for others stalking their camp from the darkness beyond the fire.

Colter had formulated a story — the only one that made any sense at all. "I prospect out here with my pa. I got caught out in the darkness. My horse fell, broke his leg. Had to put him down."

"What were you doing, lurking around on the back of this mountain?"

"I saw the firelight from the other side, was makin' my way to your camp here." Colter gave a halfhearted grin as he regarded the big black coffeepot steaming to one side of the fire. "Sure could go for a cup o' that mud." He wasn't bullshitting about that.

"Or perhaps you intended to steal one of our horses."

Inwardly, Colter cursed. He hadn't thought of that possible interpretation of his story.

He shook his head and started to speak, but the captain turned to one of the other men around the fire and barked an order in Spanish. When one of the men jumped to his feet, his teeth showing white as he grinned, the captain turned back to Colter and translated: "Take this thief down the mountain a ways, where his screams won't disturb me, and beat him to death."

"Hold on, now!" Colter said, lurching forward. "I told ya, I was just . . ."

He let his voice trail off. The captain had swung around, giving Colter his broad back, and was casually kneeling for the coffeepot. A brusque hand grabbed Colter's shirt collar from behind, and he was jerked around so suddenly that his boots got tangled, and he rolled several yards down the slope, his battered ribs coming alive again, as did the aches in both tormented shoulders. He rolled off his right shoulder and looked up.

The stocky man who had his Henry was striding toward him, while the *rurale* whom the captain had summoned from the fire was walking toward Colter, as well, looping his suspenders up over his shoulders. Colter noticed the man wasn't wearing a gun. He was hatless. Long hair fell from a nearly bald pate, and he had a small cross tattooed into his chin.

The stocky man, compressing his lips and narrowing his eyes, brought a boot back and was about to swing it forward when Colter scrambled to his feet, trying to ignore the wailing of his ribs, and backed away crouching, trying to avoid the kick. The tattooed man chuckled. The stocky man wagged the Henry's barrel at Colter. The redhead turned away and started walking down the slope through the pines, the firelight's reflection dwindling as he moved down the hill.

His blood jetted hot through his veins, and thoughts hammered through his skull. His eyes darted around, looking for an escape route. If he broke into a run, were these men good enough shots to bring him down before he could disappear into the darkness?

"That's far enough," said the tattooed man in broken English, when Colter gained the bottom of the slope. The horses picketed to his right nickered and thumped the ground softly with their hooves.

The tattooed gent snapped his suspenders

with his thumbs and strolled casually toward Colter, a grim smile etched on his broad face shadowed with beard stubble. The other man turned to lean Colter's rifle against a broad fir tree. Colter knew he couldn't run and get away. Neither could he fight these two with any hope of winning.

Power born of raw terror throbbed in him. He looked around, scuttled to one side, and grabbed a brick-sized rock. Before he even knew what he was doing, he was bolting forward, swinging the hand holding the rock back behind his right shoulder. The tattooed man's eyes snapped wide in surprise, and he'd just opened his mouth to yell when Colter hammered the rock soundly across the man's left temple.

The tattooed man twisted around and back and hit the ground hard and lay there, unmoving. Blood dribbled from the gash in his crushed temple.

Colter looked at the other man, who'd just leaned the Henry against the fir and had started toward Colter. Now he stopped and regarded the tattooed gent's still form incredulously. Colter bolted off his heels, intending to catch the stocky man off guard, as well, but then the man swung his head toward him. The man's eyes were bright with anger, and his mustached lips curled in a sneer.

Colter stood a few yards away from him, facing him, crouching, balled fists raised chest-high, hoping against hope that the stocky gent would not call out for the others. So far, so good. He just stood glaring at Colter, incredulous and embarrassed, too proud to ask for help.

Good. Colter probably couldn't take him, as the man outweighed him by a good fifty pounds, but he'd upped his chances considerably. As with the other gent, who looked dead, he'd have to use his lightness and quickness to best advantage.

The man walked casually toward him, lips pursed, chest rising and falling slowly as he breathed through his nose. Colter raised his fists and sidestepped, crouching, weaving — wasn't that what the bare-knuckle fighters did to help avoid blows? He didn't avoid the stocky gent's first punch, however. The next came just as fast, catching Colter off guard, hooking the nub of his scarred cheek.

The pounding impact threw him straight back to land on his butt with a grunt, dust and pine needles blowing up around him. He felt blood trickle down his cheek as he watched the stocky man, who was smiling now, close on him. When the man was four feet away, Colter threw his shoulders back and kicked up with his right boot, driving the pointed toe squarely into the stocky gent's crotch.

The man's face swelled and he growled like an enraged grizzly as he crouched forward and clamped one hand over his burning balls. Colter shook the cobwebs from behind his eyes and heaved himself to his feet. But the man was on him almost instantly, bulling Colter onto his back so hard that he heard his teeth clatter.

The bigger man was sluggish from the blow to his oysters, and Colter managed to grind his heels into the ground and heave the man over on his back. Colter straddled him, got his hands on the man's neck and began grinding both his thumbs into his throat. The stocky man's broad face swelled, turned red. He growled and groaned and, hardening his jaws and closing his eyes, raised his arms up between Colter's and thrust his fists sharply to both sides.

The blow broke Colter's stranglehold. The stocky gent smashed his right fist into Colter's chin. Colter grunted and flew back and to one side, hitting the ground on his shoulder.

Knowing that he had to keep moving or die, he gained his heels and saw the Henry leaning against the tree not six feet away. He ran for it. The stocky man grabbed his right boot. Colter hit the ground hard on his chin. He cursed shrilly. Stars burst inside his head.

Colter jerked his ankle free, rose to hands and knees, and crawled madly toward the fir. He grabbed his rifle, twisted around on his butt while swinging the rifle around and jacking a cartridge into the chamber. The stocky gent was crawling toward him, a knife in his hand, a savage snarl on his spittle-flecked lips.

Blam! Blam! Blam!

The Henry's reports sounded like dynamite explosions in the silent night. Each of the three bullets blew dust from the stocky *rurale*'s tunic, in a straight line across his chest. He loosed one final growl, his big face crumpling with misery, and flew backward to hit the ground on his back and shoulders, head smacking a rock resoundingly.

CHAPTER 18

Colter paused, letting the last echo finish rocketing around the ridges. When it died, he ejected the spent cartridge, hearing it cling off a rock behind him, and levered a fresh shell into the chamber. The *rurales'* horses were nickering and pulling at their picket line. He swung around to face the dark slope. The fire flickered about seventy yards away, the trees silhouetted before it.

He could hear no voices from that direction. None of the *rurales* appeared to be heading toward him. Not yet. He backed up to the dead stocky *rurale,* stooped down, and pulled his Remington from behind the man's cartridge belt. He also slipped a big bowie knife from a sheath on the man's belt, and stuck that into the sheath in his own boot well. The horn-gripped knife was an improvement over his own skinning knife.

He continued to stare at the flickering firelight up the slope through the trees as he quickly moved around behind the horses, passing the small remuda, then climbing the slope a good seventy yards from where he and the two dead *rurales* had descended it. He climbed quickly, his knees like jelly, his heart hammering in his ears.

Someone shouted in Spanish, the raspy voice echoing. It was the captain's voice.

When Colter figured he was halfway to the fire, he hunkered behind a deadfall log, his breath raking like sand in and out of his tired lungs, and looked over the top of the log to survey the area around the fire.

All the *rurales* were on their feet, spread out and holding rifles as they peered down the slope toward the dead men and the snorting, nickering horses. The captain shouted to the two dead men, and then he gestured for the others to continue down the slope, saying something that Colter couldn't hear and wouldn't have understood even if he had heard. While the others headed on down the slope, spread out amongst the trees, the captain stood about ten yards downslope from the fire, turning his head slowly from left to right and back again. His right shoulder faced Colter. His profile shone umber in the firelight, his jaw dimpling with tension.

Colter rose and backed away from the log,

then, keeping an eye on the captain, continued climbing the slope. Ahead, he saw the tree to which the blond girl was tied. She sat before it as she had before, with an air of extreme defeat though Colter could only see her profile in silhouette.

Slowly, he continued upslope, breathing through his mouth, squeezing the cocked Henry in his hands. Quietly, he dropped down behind the tree the girl was tied to, then shouldered around the trunk and clamped his right hand over her mouth. He felt her mouth come open, felt her little teeth against his palm, and he heard her gasp, but his hand stifled the scream. He showed her his face, rested his rifle against his knee, and pressed two fingers to his lips.

Her eyes were bright and round with fear as she studied him.

Gradually, her terror was replaced with confusion. Colter tapped his fingers to his lips, and she nodded. Colter lowered his fingers, then glanced over his shoulder at the captain, who stood where he'd stood before, staring down the slope.

Suddenly, an alarmed shout rose from below. The other *rurales* had found the bodies. Quickly, Colter jerked up his pants leg, removed the big bowie from the sheath, and sawed through the girl's ropes. She continued to stare at him apprehensively, her eyes darting between him and the captain. But she said nothing.

The captain was angrily shouting orders. Colter could hear the other *rurales* scrambling around at the base of the bluff.

Colter slid the knife back into his boot and put his face up close to the girl's ear. "Real quietlike, run straight back across this slope and hide. If I can, I'll bring a horse."

She nodded and began running, holding her skirts above her ankles. Colter had just started to turn toward the captain when a gun flashed and popped.

The slug *spanged* into the fir trunk to Colter's left. The redhead wheeled and fired the Henry from his hip. When three explosions had cut open the night, the third followed by a shrill scream, the captain was on his back on the ground, moving his arms and legs like a turtle trying to right itself.

He shouted hoarsely, summoning his men, and Colter aimed and fired one last shot at the man, drilling a silencing round through the captain's right temple. Instantly, he wheeled and ran down the slope roughly the same way he'd climbed it. He could hear the others running back up, yelling, boots crunching brush and gravel.

Rifles barked. Bullets sizzled around

Colter, plunked into trees and rocks. He saw several murky, gray-clad figures on his left, stopped, dropped to a knee, and emptied his rifle, the Henry's muzzle flashing wickedly, powder smoke wafting around his head.

In the relative silence following his barrage, and as he pressed his back to a pine while he quickly plucked fresh cartridges from his shell belt and slid them down the rifle's loading tube, several men groaned. He could still hear a couple moving around more cautiously now, small branches breaking beneath their boots as they tried to work around Colter.

The redhead sat on his butt against the tree. He slid the sixteenth cartridge into the Henry's loader and quietly levered a round into the chamber.

A rifle flashed and barked from the other side of the tree and right. The slug hammered the tree, spraying bark. Colter turned, snaked his Henry around the bole, saw a strip of gray in the forest beyond him and which was vaguely illuminated by the fire's amber light, and fired two more rounds.

Silence.

There was a raspy sigh, the thump of a knee hitting the ground. A man gasped.

Colter could still see the murky patch of gray, drew a bead on it, and fired.

There was the thump of a heavy body falling, and the crack of the branch it had fallen on.

Colter pulled his head back behind the tree. From somewhere straight out beyond him rose the footfalls of a single man, maybe two, running away across the slope. Raspy, anxious breaths sounded faintly.

Colter continued to hunker on one knee behind the tree, looking around and listening. When he continued to hear only silence save the occasional cracks and pops of the dying fire up the slope on his left, he rose slowly, stepped quietly out from behind the tree, and made his way down the slope to the *rurales'* fidgeting horses. He picked one out of the string — the pinto gelding he'd seen the girl riding before, then turned the others free. As they galloped off into the night, he found the *rurales'* tack piled in nearby shrubs and began saddling the pinto with the first saddle he found.

Footfalls sounded from upslope. He'd just set a big-skirted, double-rigged Mexican saddle on the gelding's back, and now he swung around to grab his rifle.

"It's me," said a girl's voice. "Don't shoot."

He looked toward the slope, saw the slender figure moving down through the pines, striding confidently and swinging her arms. Her coat was open, showing a cartridge bandolier wrapped twice around her slender waist. A Colt Army revolver jutted up from the bandolier, over her flat belly clad in a shabby plaid flannel shirt. Colter stared at the girl skeptically as she walked up to him and ran a hand down the pinto's neck, cooing softly to soothe the beast's jangled nerves.

"He's mine."

"I know." He glanced at the pistol jutting above her bandolier. "Where'd you get that?"

"Off one o' them Mescins." She shook her head resolutely. "Never again will I go unarmed in Mexico." She slid her glance from the horse to Colter. "That was some shootin'."

"Thanks."

"Get 'em all?"

"I don't know. I think one or two run off."

"Figures. You a gunslinger?"

"When I need to be." Colter reached under the pinto's belly to tighten the latigo straps. "Where're your pards?"

"Dead." The blonde jerked her chin toward the slope. "Them bean eaters killed 'em deader'n hell when they run us down. Only reason they didn't kill me is 'cause the captain thought he could make some money off me. He said Wade and Harlan were worthless. Can't say as I disagree, God bless 'em."

"Probably figured they could use you in the southern mines."

"Or whorehouses."

Colter snapped a surprised look at her, and bit back a chuckle. Her little face pinched angrily. "What're you lookin' at?"

He buckled the latigo, then started shortening the left stirrup. "What's your name, little miss?"

"It sure ain't Little Miss. I declare, I hate bein' called that. You like bein' called 'Skinny Red'? My name's Bethel Strange."

Colter couldn't hold back a chuckle at the appropriateness of the girl's name. "No kiddin'?"

"What's yours?"

Colter went around the pinto to adjust the opposite stirrup. "Colter Farrow."

Bethel Strange followed him around the horse and stood close, frowning at him, as she asked, "Why'd you do this — risk your life for mine?"

He slid the stirrup up the side of the horse, then buckled it secure. "I don't really

know, little Mi . . . I mean, Miss Bethel."
He studied her closely, dubiously. "Ain't
you scared?"

"Of course I'm scared," she said, walking
around to the other side of the horse. "But
I never seen how cryin' and carryin' on
changed anything. Help me up here, will
you, Colter?"

Colter went around and helped her into
the saddle. She grabbed the big silver-
capped horn with both hands. Even with
the big hog leg in her belt, she didn't seem
to weigh much more than a fifty-pound sack
of grain. He climbed up behind her and
took the reins. "Hold tight, Miss Bethel.
We'll go back and pick up my own horse,
then find us a place to camp."

"You alone out here, Colter?" she asked
as he put the pinto around the base of the
mountain, glancing around to make sure no
surviving *rurales* were trying to flank him.

"I sure am," he said with a sigh.

"Me, too."

They said nothing more, knowing the danger of allowing others to know they were
out here, as they rode back and retrieved
Colter's horse and then headed westward,
putting as much ground between them and
the *rurale* camp as they could.

They rode for nearly an hour in the star-speckled night, velvet black ridges humping up around them. They dropped down onto the shoulder of whatever sierra they'd been in, and, so tired he could hardly move, Colter reined up on the bank of a narrow, rushing stream. Bethel did likewise, and Colter helped her out of the fancy saddle.

The strange blond girl obviously knew how to care for a horse, and knew the value of doing so even when she was so fatigued she could hardly stand. She unsaddled the pinto, then thoroughly rubbed the horse down before leading it to the stream for water. Both she and Colter hobbled their horses in the grass along the creek and then made a fireless camp.

Neither he nor Bethel had thought of appropriating a bedroll from the *rurales,* so Bethel had none. Colter arranged his own blankets at the base of a stone escarpment, then grabbed his saddle and rifle. "You can sleep in my soogan tonight, Bethel. I'll be fine in the grass."

"I won't take your bed, Colter."

"You don't have a choice." Colter shouldered his rifle and saddle and headed down to the creek, where he found a soft bed in some jimson weed. The water was not so loud that he could not keep an ear skinned as he slept, waking every hour or so to lift his head from his saddle and to look around. Northwest stood nearby, like a sentinel, while the pinto lay on its side a little farther downstream.

Colter wished he hadn't left any of the *rurales* alive. He doubted they'd follow him of their own accord, but not knowing made him jumpy. Of course, Machado's men might also be trailing him, not to mention U.S. soldiers from Camp Grant, which made it wise to sleep with one ear pricked and one eye skinned, anyway. That was something he'd likely have to do for the rest of his life, which, by all recent signs, wouldn't be all that long.

He didn't much care.

He woke again at the first flush of dawn. Birds chirped all around him. Northwest lay down, flat on his side in contentment. Bethel lay a few yards from the stream, at the base of the stone escarpment. She was curled up in a tight ball in his soogan, sound asleep, her blond hair made tawny by the sun tangled about her head. Deciding they could both use as well as afford another hour or so of shut-eye, Colter laid his head back down on his saddle and let himself slide back into a restful though shallow slumber.

Maybe it wasn't so shallow. The hot sun on his face woke him. He lifted his head, blinking, looking around. Both horses stood with feed sacks draped over their ears. The sun was well up though the dew had not yet left the grass. Colter looked toward the escarpment. His blankets were rolled and tied in a neat bundle where Bethel had slept.

He stood, stretching, feeling a little chastened by how late he'd slept, as well as how deeply, and looked around until he saw the blond girl sitting up on a shoulder of the scarp. She sat in a niche in the rocks, silhouetted against the buttery eastern sky. She had a book or something open before her, and she seemed to be intently studying it, occasionally looking up to stare off to the south.

Colter grabbed his saddle and bridle and went over to the base of the scarp. He set his gear down, gathered firewood, formed a stone ring, and built a small fire. Soon, he had some of the *javelina* spitted, the juices sizzling in the flames. He went off and drained his bladder, then returned to the fire, kneeling to tend the meat.

Bethel came down the rocks, leaping from one rock to another and holding what appeared to be a Bible in one hand. Between her open coat flaps, Colter could see the bandolier from which her big Colt jutted.

"Thought you was dead," she said as she approached the fire.

Colter's ear tips warmed. "I heard you the whole time. Kept my eyes slitted." He glanced at her and grinned. "You couldn't tell, could you?"

She smiled as she sat down on a big rock, the toes of her brown boots dangling a few inches above the ground, and looked off. "No, I sure couldn't."

Colter sat back on his rump, raised his knees, and wrapped his arms around them. "I know it's none of my business, but I'm going to ask it anyway. What're you doin' down here, Bethel? In Mexico, I mean. Who were Wade and Harlan? Kin?"

She was studying the roasting meat. "That sure smells good." She looked at Colter. "You got any coffee? Them bean eaters wouldn't give me any. Hardly any water at all, neither. When I got up, I 'bout drank the stream dry."

"No coffee. Just water and meat'll have to do us for breakfast." Colter studied her as she looked off to the south. "All right — don't tell me if you don't want to. But wherever you came from, you best go back. Mexico is no place for a little girl alone."

She narrowed her frosty blue eyes at him

beneath a shelf of straight-cut bangs the tawny yellow of ripe wheat. "I'm twelve years old."

Colter chuckled.

"How old are you?" she asked defiantly.

"Older'n you."

"Not by much, I'd fathom."

"I'm nineteen."

She looked off sharply, sneering. "Shit."

Colter jerked another surprised look at her. "Who taught you to swear like that?"

"My pa, I reckon."

"Well, you run back to him, and you an' him can swear together in the safety of your own home." Colter pulled a chunk of meat from the spit, set it on a tin plate, and handed it to her. "Here ya go. Breakfast. Eat as much of it that's done, and throw the rest back on the fire."

Bethel set the plate and the smoking meat on her lap. She touched the meat, then jerked her hands away, cursing. Colter chuckled as she gingerly pulled the meat apart with her fingers. He took a chunk of the meat himself, leaned back against his saddle, and began to eat the succulent wild pork, using his hands. He saw no reason to break out his forks and have to clean them when his fingers would do. The meat filled the hollow place deep inside him. He felt his blood begin to flow, waking him up and steeling him against what would likely be another long day of directionless riding and looking over his shoulder.

After a time, Bethel said as she ate, "My pa's down here somewhere. That's what I'm doing here. Lookin' for him." She paused, looking down at her plate and her greasy fingers, chewing. Her eyes were sad, anxious when she lifted her gaze to Colter. "Think he might be in trouble. A whole heap."

CHAPTER 19

"What kinda trouble?" Colter asked the girl. He wouldn't normally be so forward, but it wasn't likely she'd shoot him. He doubted she could hold that big Colt steady with both her little hands.

She took another bite of the lightly charred pork, then set the rest down on her plate. Squinting an eye at Colter, she said, "Can you keep a secret?"

Colter glanced around. "Who am I gonna tell it to?"

"My pa came down here to sell guns to some *revolucionarios* around Hermosillo."

Colter continued eating. "Who is your pa?"

"The notorious gunslinger and road agent Jed Strange." Bethel looked at him as though he should know the name.

Colter shrugged.

"He was written up by Mr. Ned Buntline, a time or two."

"Musta been a while ago."

"Before I was born. Pa's got a few years behind now. He married up with Ma in Tucson a couple years before I was born. After I was born, he promised Ma he'd walk the straight and narrow. He was a deputy sheriff for a time, and even rode shotgun for a stage line. Till a couple months ago, he was the night marshal of Tucson. He hated it, thought it was beneath him."

"Your ma still in Tucson?"

Bethel shook her head. "Ma's dead. Had a cancer inside her. The doctor tried to cut it out, but she didn't make it. That was a year ago, just before Pa left for Mexico. Said he'd come back rich, build us a new house, maybe. The one we got's a rat-infested dump."

"And you come down here to pull him away from them gun runners?"

"I don't think he's with the gun runners no more."

Colter frowned as he swallowed the last mouthful of meat and clawed up a couple of handfuls of dirt and sand to clean his hands with. He let the dirt sift back down to the ground as he said, "How do you know that?"

Bethel picked up the Bible sitting on the rock beside her. She pulled a folded scrap of lined notepaper out of it and held it up, the breeze nudging it. "This come in the mail just before I started down here. It's a treasure map. Pa drew it himself."

"Treasure, huh? What'd he say about it?"

"Nothin'. Pa can read a little but he can't write. He can draw pretty good, though. When I was sittin' up on them rocks yonder, I could see some of the landmarks he put on this here paper."

"What do you suppose he wanted you to do with it?"

"I don't know. Maybe nothin'. Maybe he just wanted to have a safe copy in case he lost his."

Colter stood and took the girl's empty plate. "He left you alone in Tucson?"

"Nah. My aunt Kate's been livin' with me, Ma, and Pa for a long while. She don't know I come. I left a note and slipped away, hired Wade and Harlan to guide me into Mexico. They worked for the stage line in Tucson, and knew Pa. Wade rode with Pa once. I saved money up from working in a sewing shop and sellin' eggs, and I plundered the box Pa kept his savings in beneath the stairs. Figured it was worth spendin' his money to get him back. Besides, I showed Wade and Harlan this here map, told 'em they'd get a percentage of whatever gold Pa found, if they helped me find him."

Colter gave a rueful chuff. "They tumbled for it?"

Bethel scrunched her eyes up, angry. "Tumbled for what? I'm an honest woman, not a snake charmer. They took the gamble 'cause they was friends of Pa's. Besides, they were both on the run from federal marshals on an old charge, and had come to town lookin' to Pa to help 'em get out of it. Pa did his time in Yuma, and he's in good now with the deputy U.S. marshal out of Prescott."

Colter gave another rueful chuff and headed with the two plates for the river. He'd never heard such a silly idea — a twelve-year-old girl allowing herself to be led down here by a couple of raggedy-heeled bandits who had nothing better to do than take a wild gamble on a treasure scribbled out by some cork-headed old outlaw named Jed Strange. Old Jed had probably heard some wild story of treasure buried by Spanish pirates or conquistadores or maybe those Indians who once lived in these parts — the Aztecs — and had run off in search of the fabled cache.

"Colter?"

He heard her running up behind him. As he knelt at the edge of the stream and dunked the plates in the water, she stood just off his right shoulder, lightly lacing her fingers together and regarding him with vague suspicion. "I was thinkin'," she said haltingly.

"Oh? What were you thinkin' about?"

"I was thinkin' I could let you buy chips in my and Pa's game, if . . ." She let her voice trail off and turned her troubled gaze to the stream.

Colter raised the clean plates from the stream and waved them in the air to dry them. He glanced at her, waiting.

"If I knew you wasn't an outlaw or nothin' like that," she said, regarding him nervously.

Colter chuckled and draped a hand over a knee. "What makes you think I'd want chips in your game, Miss Bethel? I got enough problems of my own without taking yours on, too."

"Because it's most likely Spanish treasure!"

Colter chuckled again, rose, and headed back to his saddlebags. "I'm young, and I made a lot of mistakes, but that's one I won't make." She was right on his heels. She'd opened her mouth to give him a burning retort when he held up a hand, cutting her off. "That said, Bethel, I would help you find your old man, because I know what

it's like, not havin' one. Heck, I lost two."
He shook his head and sighed as he returned
the tin plates to his saddlebag pouch.

"You said you *would* help me find him,
like you ain't gonna."

He buckled the pouch's strap and nodded. "I would, but I'd likely get you in a
heap more trouble than you're already in."

Bethel kicked a rock. "You are an outlaw.
I could kinda tell by the way you beefed
that big Mex in the gulch outside the Babylon. Not to mention that scar on your cheek.
Some secret sign, is it? Helps you get in and
out of hideouts? Every ranny in your gang
got one?"

"No, nothin' like that," Colter said, tossing his saddlebags over his shoulder and
grabbing his saddle. He stared to the northeast, where blue-clad riders were filing
down a trail and into a canyon the stream
ran through. "See those blue bellies there?"

Bethel turned to follow his gaze. "What're
blue bellies doin' this far south?"

"They're after me." Colter had spied the
riders a few minutes ago. Now he hefted
the saddle on his right shoulder and headed
over to where the horses grazed by the
stream. "Grab your saddle, Bethel. We got
some dust to lift — if you're gonna ride with
me, that is. I suggest you cut and run your

own direction."

"Well, shit!" The girl scrambled over and began to lift the heavy Mexican saddle, grunting with the effort and cutting frantic glances toward where the last of the blue uniforms was disappearing into the canyon. "I don't have a direction. I was hopin' you could help me find one. You can probably follow this map better than I can!"

"Come on, then." Colter tossed his gear down and ran back into the camp for his own saddle and bedroll. "We'll lose the soldiers, then get you headed straight . . . and on your own."

"Colter?"

He shouldered his own saddle and then grabbed hers out of her hands as she struggled to carry it, and strode quickly back to the horses. "What?"

"What'd you do?"

"Nothin'." Colter tossed his saddle onto Northwest's back and glanced at Bethel, who stared at him uncertainly. "I know — that's what they all say."

When he had his horse saddled and his rifle slid snug in its boot, he lifted the big Mexican saddle onto the pinto's back. Bethel unhobbled both horses and stowed the hobbles in Colter's saddlebags. He tossed her up onto her horse, stepped up onto Northwest's back, and cast a look behind him. He couldn't see the soldiers, as they were riding along the canyon bottom, which was deeper up toward the mountains, but he figured they were a couple of hundred yards away and moving toward him fast.

"Let's go, Bethel!"

"I just hope it ain't a hangin' offense, Colter!"

"It is, Bethel!"

He couldn't hear the strange little blond girl's reply amidst the thudding of Northwest's hooves and those of the pinto, but he could imagine it was as salty-tongued as most everything else she said. Colter put the horse downstream, heading southeast over the hogback foothills stippled in Spanish bayonet and cat-law and barrel cactus and several other kinds of cactus, with here and there a gnarled cedar or juniper. It was rocky country, and both horses galloped a serpentine course around the brush and rocks and over the hogbacks that swelled like ocean waves.

Beyond lay another low mountain range. Another lay to the south, with a slight gap between them. Colter aimed Northwest toward the gap and glanced over his shoulder. Bethel rode just off Northwest's right hip, hunkered low over the horse's neck, her hat brim blown flat against her forehead, batting the heels of her black boots against the pinto's flanks. She'd obviously ridden before, and for that he was glad. He'd have hated to ride double with someone even as light as she out here, as Northwest had all he could handle negotiating the rough country with just Colter on his back.

Several times Colter glanced behind him. He couldn't see the soldiers, but he could see their dust. The dust cloud wasn't growing, so they weren't gaining on him and Bethel, but they were staying glued to their trail.

About an hour after they'd left the stream, Colter found a shallow, broad-bottomed, gravel-floored canyon that formed the gap between the two barrancas. Here, amongst the rocks, he might be able to lose his shadowers.

He and Bethel followed the canyon for a mile as it twisted around through a maze of devil's country, with ancient bones sticking out of the sides of the banks around them, and here and there a dead coyote or buzzard-eaten deer carcass. He found a narrow opening in the right canyon wall, reined Northwest to a stop, and dismounted to peer inside.

The crack in the sandstone appeared just wide enough to get a horse through, and it led back out of sight around a bend, well lit by the sky above. Colter might be leading him and Bethel into a trap, but it was the best chance he'd seen so far of losing the soldiers. Quickly, he grabbed Northwest's reins. Bethel was just now riding up behind him, her eyes bright with anxiety, but she otherwise appeared to be holding up well. The girl was little more than a hunk of rawhide and a shock of bleached blond hair, but a fire blazed in her heart.

"In here!"

"Where? That *crack* there?"

Colter whipped a look at the defiant child. "You got any better ideas?"

"I ain't on friendly terms with tight places."

"Time to shake hands, Bethel," Colter snapped back at her as he led Northwest into the crack.

The coyote dun balked, too. Colter had to pull hard on the reins, and when the horse saw it had no choice in the matter, it stopped chopping its hooves around in the rocks and allowed Colter to lead it through the narrow gap, both sides of the opening scraping the stirrups and almost tearing off Colter's saddlebags. When he had Northwest about twenty yards up the defile, the redhead ran back out into the canyon, where Bethel was cursing as she tried to lead the obstinate pinto into the corridor.

"I'll take him," Colter said, grabbing the reins.

"He don't like it any more than I do."

When Colter got both the pinto and Bethel into the gap, he led both horses as far as he could, until piled boulders blocked his path. He settled the animals down while Bethel poured water from a canteen into her hat and set it down in front of the pinto.

Colter said, "Try to keep 'em quiet."

He walked back to the opening and peered along the canyon the way he and Bethel had come. About ten minutes later, he heard the clatter of shods hooves on stone and stepped back away from the opening. He glanced up the corridor, could see Bethel holding her hand over the pinto's snout to keep the mount quiet as she stared back anxiously toward Colter. He pressed a finger to his lips and shoved his back against the side of the narrow feeder canyon, positioned so that he could watch the broader canyon with one eye.

He counted his heartbeats until he saw the first riders move into sight. As he'd expected, Lieutenant A. J. McKnight led the group, riding side by side with a beefy, bearded man in buckskins and with two sheathed rifles lashed to his saddle. The buckskin-clad gent had a face as red and eroded as a sandstone wall, and he wore a broad-brimmed, low-crowned sombrero over flinty eyes he raked along the ground before his zebra dun.

He was Saul Brickson, scout leader at Camp Grant — a Civil War veteran who'd also fought Red Cloud up in Wyoming and Dakota Territory. Some said he could track a snake across a solid lava bed, but Colter had his doubts. Whenever he'd seen Brickson at Camp Grant, he was drunk and bragging of his exploits up on the Plains and of his sexual prowess with the Lakota maidens.

Colter hoped the man was, indeed, all bluster. In a minute, he'd likely find out.

The hooves clomped and clacked on the rocks as four more soldiers, riding Indian-file behind McKnight and Brickson, passed the defile's opening, each man appearing for half a second in front of the canyon before passing on, their faces pink from the sun, blue tunics sweat-darkened, copper dust wafting around the party like wood smoke. Colter kept his back pressed against the uneven stone wall, every sore muscle drawn taut with tension. Gradually, as the horses clomped away into silence, leaving only a few shreds of dust waving in the sunlit air behind them, Colter felt his jaws relax.

Fortunately, as Colter had figured, Brickson had spent himself on the sutler's tanglefoot. Unfortunately, Colter hadn't figured on a tracker, but he should have. And he was even more fortunate that McKnight's party wasn't being led by one of the three Apaches employed at Grant. If so, he'd likely either be shot or hauled away in chains. On the other hand, the soldiers probably would have taken Bethel back to the border and seen that she made it safely back to Tucson. . . .

Colter jogged back to Bethel and the horses. "Time to light a shuck!"

He grabbed the pinto's reins and backed it out of the defile and onto the rocky canyon bed. He hoisted Bethel onto the pinto's back, then retrieved Northwest and stepped into the saddle. They rode a mile back the way they'd come, then followed a game trail up out of the canyon, kicked their horses into lopes, and headed straight south across a rolling stretch of desert. When they'd crested a low ridge, with a breath-sucking stretch of craggy peaks surrounding them, one sierra after another foreshortening into the southern distance, all the way to the Sierra Madres most likely, they checked their tired mounts down.

Colter glanced back toward the canyon. Amidst the vastness stippled with low ridges and capped with a vaulting sky, he could spy no dreaded mares' tails of rising dust.

He and Bethel had likely lost their pursuers for now.

"You mighta been safer with them," he said, lifting his canteen, uncorking it, and handing it over to her.

She took it and drank, not saying anything. When she'd finished, she wiped her hand across her mouth and returned his gaze.

"They'd take you home, most like, Bethel."

"I ain't goin' home, Colter. I'm stayin' with you."

Colter shook his head, shifted in his saddle, and cast another cautious look behind him. "That wouldn't be smart. Wouldn't be safe, you takin' a chance gettin' caught with me." He looked at Bethel again. "They think I killed a girl." He was trying to frighten her now. The best thing for her was to ride off and find McKnight and Brickson. "They think I shot her just north of the border."

The remembered image of Lenore lying

dead before Hobart's prancing bay turned his guts sour.

The information didn't seem to faze Bethel. She pooched her lips and hiked a shoulder. "Folks think a lot o' things. I know all that by heart. Try havin' an outlaw for a father . . . and a fallen angel for a ma."

Colter hitched a brow.

"Ma was a whore workin' the Red Dog Saloon in El Paso when Pa met her. She ain't done that for years, but she's soiled by it. Leastways, she was. Just as Pa's soiled by his past, runnin' with curly wolves in Texas and down here in Mexico. Oh, I forgive 'em both. Ma and me — we went to church every Sunday though the other folks, including the Reverend Mathew Hollis, looked at us like we was nothin' more than scorpions tryin' to find a way into their button boots. But we went anyway, and we held our heads up. 'Cause it don't matter what other folks think. It's only what we think about ourselves that counts."

Bethel paused, and Colter felt himself shrink a little against the grave scrutiny in her gray-blue eyes that owned a depth far older than her years. "I know you for a killer, Colter. 'Cause I seen you shoot men dead. But there weren't a one that weren't deservin' of the bullets you gave 'em. I can't imagine you ever gunnin' a man . . . or a girl . . . in cold blood."

"What about my outlaw scar?"

"Hell, it ain't no outlaw scar. I never really thought it was."

"Just the same, we best fork trails here."

She nodded slightly and stared south across the vast Mexican desert — one sierra after another.

"Where you goin', Colter?"

"I reckon I'll head west."

"Well, Pa's south. According to his map, there's a string of little villages all leading up to a mountain range he drew a dragon over."

"Los Montanas Del Dragones," Colter said. "The Dragon Range. I heard of it. Not a fit place for a girl alone. That's where the Chiricahua Apaches go when they need to rest up from raidin' farther north. In the Dragons and in the Sierra Madres."

She looked at him and kept her voice flat, eyes hard, as she said, "Ride with me there?" Then she quirked her mouth in a little smile. "I bet them 'Paches'd run away when they seen your outlaw scar."

Colter stared straight west. As he did, Bethel stared south. A warm wind blew, lifting a dust devil that pranced around them for a time before dying. Colter's loneliness weighed heavy on his shoulders, so that he felt himself slumping beneath it. The vast land was hard and barren, the distant ridges unwelcoming. As far as he could see in all directions, nothing moved.

He glanced at Bethel. She sat straight-backed in her saddle. The breeze touched her blond hair. Her eyes were pensive, speculative, but without emotion as she stared across all the sunbaked, foreign country she'd have to cross alone.

To find a father who, Colter knew, might very well be dead, his bones scattered by coyotes and mountain lions. Colter thought about his own natural father, dead of a sickness that swept the Lunatics when he was six, and of the man who adopted him and raised him as his own — Trace Cassidy, whom Bill Rondo had shot full of holes and sent back to his ranch, crucified to the bed of his own wagon.

Colter turned the coyote dun south, touched his heels to Northwest's flanks, and started down the hill. "What the hell?"

CHAPTER 20

They rode into a village about an hour after dark, following a winding cart path up the shoulder of a mountain. Stock pens and low, pale adobes slid up on both sides of the trail, as much a part of the landscape as the rocks and cactus. A thumbnail moon rose over a black, craggy peak ahead of them, in the southeast, limning the surrounding dark-shrouded desert in ghostly, shimmering silver.

As Colter and Bethel continued into the town, which, according to the map tucked away in Bethel's Bible, was called Travesia de Jacinta, the strains of guitars and mandolins sounded. Oil pots glowed along both sides of the street, and torches here and there revealed the facades of low adobe shanties and men and brightly though scantily clad women laughing and drinking.

Somewhere, a dog was barking. The barks echoed off the ridges and formed a backdrop to the din emanating from a few lit, congested areas along the otherwise dark street.

To Colter's right, a gun blasted loudly. He could see the sudden flash inside an adobe, briefly silhouetting several human figures clad in serapes and sombreros.

"Hell!" Bethel said with a start, riding off Northwest's right hip.

Inside the adobe, a man groaned loudly. There was the raucous scrape of a table across a wooden floor. The adobe fell silent except for the thud of boots and the chime of spurs. A man groaned again, louder, and then a figure pushed through the adobe's front doorway, the door propped open by a rock.

He stumbled across a narrow porch, a pistol in his right hand. He triggered the pistol into the porch, flames stabbing down. Colter's old Remington was instantly in his hand and tracking the big Mexican as he stumbled into the street and dropped to his knees about ten feet from where Bethel sat her dancing pinto, sawing back on the reins.

The man lifted his head, sombrero falling down his back, and gave a wail that for an instant drowned out the dog's barks and echoed loudly around the town and surrounding ridges. He looked down at his belly, pressing both hands against the glistening wound, then sagged slowly forward until his forehead hit the ground.

Behind him, more boots slowly pounded the adobe's wooden floor as men moved out to see about the wounded man.

"Come on." Colter depressed the Remy's hammer and returned the gun to its holster as they continued along the street.

A few minutes later they found a big wooden livery barn on the right side of the street, almost directly across from a two-story adobe with several arched windows and doorways and with a second-story balcony. HOTEL was painted across the top of the second-floor wall, vaguely revealed by two oil pots burning on the street fronting the place and the two white-clad figures lounging on the front veranda.

Colter and Bethel rode their horses up the livery barn's wooden ramp. Inside they found a shriveled, old, sandal-and-pajama-clad man whom, for a few coins each from Bethel and Colter, somberly led the horses off into the shadows cast by a single, low lantern, nodding and muttering. Bethel knew some Spanish, so she'd done all the talking, what little there was, and as she and Colter tramped down the ramp, Colter burdened with his saddlebags and rifle, he said, "He gonna rub 'em down and feed 'em proper?"

"Said he would. You never know for sure about anything here."

"Hell, I'd just as soon care for my own horse."

"And insult that old-timer?" Bethel shook her head. "That ain't how you get along down here, Colter. If you don't wanna wake up with your throat cut, you'd best let me do the talkin' from now on."

"You do have a way with words." Colter looked up and down the street lit here and there by flares and lamplit windows. Normally, he would have bedded down in the barn with his horse, but Bethel could use a bed for a night. It would likely be her last for a while. He glanced at the hotel on the other side of the street. "Come on. I'll get us a coupla rooms."

"Ah, hell, you don't have to do that. I can sleep in the barn or find me a creek with some nice, soft grass. Trail supplies and payin' Harlan an' Vincent a pretrip retainer left me light."

"My ass is sore. Come on."

He swung around, crossed the street, and climbed the steps of the hotel's veranda. The two lounging men fell silent and watched them from beneath their broad-brimmed hats, both holding cigarettes in their fingers. Their hats kept the light from their faces, though it touched lightly on the sides of their eyes. Bethel pinched her hat brim cordially to the men, who sat like statues holding their smoldering cigarettes, and Colter followed her inside the hotel.

The small lobby was appointed with dilapidated leather furniture, a gilt-frame mirror, and a broad oak desk at the back. The walls were papered in dark blue with silver leaves. A middle-aged man with gray hair and a black mustache plucked coins from Colter's proffered open palm, Bethel chastising him gently when he apparently took one too many before grabbing a lantern and leading them up a narrow stone stairway to the second story.

The man stuck a key in a lock and opened the door, the hinges squawking loudly in the musty dimness, the lantern offering the only light except for that emanating from under a couple of other doors. When he'd lit a lamp on the room's only dresser, the gray-haired man gestured for Bethel to enter, then looked at Colter, who frowned. "Which one is mine?"

"We'll share this one," Bethel said.

"I got enough for us each to have a room."

"I don't want you spendin' more money

than you have to. This room's got two beds though he's only chargin' us for one." She gave a devilish little half smile. "Since we're brother an' sister an' all . . . and down on our luck."

Colter sighed and followed her into the room. Muttering to himself, the gray-haired man drew the door closed, and his slippered feet scuffed away down the hall. Colter dropped his saddlebags on the floor, leaned his rifle against the wall, sat on the edge of the bed abutting the cracked left wall decorated with a garish oil painting of two white horses standing before an elaborate hacienda surrounded by large, green trees, and doffed his hat. A spider was spinning its web down the front of the painting, almost reaching the horses.

He leaned forward, elbows on his knees, and scrubbed his hands through his long, tangled hair. His aches and pains bit him bone-deep, and he realized that he was so tired he didn't think he had the energy to take his jacket and clothes off and crawl under the blankets.

With effort, he shrugged out of his coat and tossed it on the floor. As Bethel poured water into the tin bowl on the washstand that stood below the room's single window, he rummaged around in his saddlebags for his tequila bottle and burlap-wrapped bundle of cooked pork.

"Hungry?"

Bethel toweled her face and neck off and sagged down on the edge of her bed. "How much you got there?"

"Enough for two."

Colter held the bundle out to her, and she took a chunk and began picking it apart with her fingers. She still had her coat on. Her face was clean of trail dust, and it fairly glowed red from the scrubbing. Wisps of damp hair clung to her cheeks. In a few years, she'd make a pretty girl — not beautiful but pretty — though likely a bossy one, Colter ruefully, silently opined. Might get a little plump, too, though she sure could use some tallow on her bones now.

He took a slug of the tequila and coughed as it followed a bite of pork into his belly. Handing the bottle out to Bethel, he said, "Snort?"

"I don't drink, thanks." Her voice owned an uppity tone, and she did not favor him with a glance. "And by the sound of it, you don't, neither. Why start now? It's the ruin of otherwise upstanding men."

Colter shoved the last of the pork into his mouth, tossed the burlap onto the floor, and leaned back against the wall, facing the window, the bed's single pillow padding the small of his back. He raised a knee, wagged it, and took another pull from the bottle. "It makes me feel good." It, did, too — a soothing balm, sort of like the wild mint his mother had used as a poultice for open wounds and the stinging, itching rash of poison oak — all the way to his toes.

Bethel frowned like an old lady as she continued to stuff small bits of pork into her mouth, keeping her eyes on her hands. "Well, don't get drunk over there and think about tryin' nothin' with me, Colter Farrow. Or I'll be forced to use my hog leg on you and wishin' I'd made you fork over good money for a second room."

Colter choked on another swallow of tequila. Some of it came up his nose. He coughed, rubbed his forearm across his mouth.

She looked at him, annoyed. "What's so funny?"

"Sorry, Bethel." He chuckled again, coughed again, closed his eyes, and shook his head.

"What — you don't think I could get even a drunk man's blood up?"

Holding his bottle on his thigh, Colter leaned back against the wall again, the tequila making him want to have some fun with the overly serious girl. "Oh, I reckon if he was drunk enough." He closed one eye as he appraised the amount of tequila left in the bottle. "I don't reckon I got enough busthead left for that."

She continued to stare at him angrily. "Some boys have come callin' for me, you know."

"You don't say."

"What's so surprising about that?"

Colter chuckled, glancing at her sitting across from him, on the edge of her bed, still wearing her coat and the big Army pistol jutting up from her cartridge belt. "Hell, you're all skin and bones and a stringy tangle of yellow hair."

She glared at him, bunching her thin lips and narrowing her blue eyes. "You take that back!"

"Not only that," Colter said, glancing once more at the pistol, "but you come armed for bear! What man in his right mind would risk life and limb, sparkin' you?"

He threw his head back as the laughter rippled out of him, making his eyes water. The release was almost as intoxicating as the tequila. Bethel didn't find it all that cathartic, however. She jumped up from her bed and clouded up like a late-summer monsoon squall. She balled her fists at her sides.

"Take it back, or you'll pay."

Colter couldn't stop laughing in spite of his beginning to realize he'd taken the joke too far. She hurled herself onto him with such violence he dropped the bottle. He reached for her arms, but in his laughing, drunken state, the blond wildcat was too much for him. Besides, he didn't want to hurt her inadvertently, so he rolled toward the wall and tried to bury his head in his pillow.

"Don't think I don't know how to fight," she said. "Because I do!"

"Prob'ly better than me," Colter said, giving a howl when she rammed her bony knee into his back and then grabbed his left arm. Her strength took him off guard, and suddenly she had his arm curled behind his back and was twisting it up toward the back of his head so that his already-sore shoulder barked in protest.

Laughing as he was, and this sudden display of improbable strength causing him to laugh harder, he found himself nearly as helpless as he'd been against Belden, Hobart, and McKnight.

"Holy shit," Colter cried. "Where'd you learn that move?"

"I had a older stepbrother till he was run over by a stagecoach!" Bethel said, pinching her voice with menace as she added, "You gonna take it back or do I have to dislocate your wing?"

"I take it back!"

"Honest? Or you just yella?"

"Both!"

She gave the injured wing another twist. Pain lanced through his shoulder and collarbone and into his jaw. Then she released it and sank back on her heels at the edge of his bed. He gave another yowl as the blood ran back into his shoulder, reigniting the tender nerves. Rolling onto his back and holding the wrist of his injured arm, heated up by the tussle and feeling a dull hammering in his head from the tequila, he saw her staring down at him, pensive.

"Did I hurt you?"

Colter grimaced as he straightened his arm. "I reckon I'll live." He looked her up and down, seeing her in a whole new light. She might not have weighed much, but she was two shovelfuls of gravel with a ladleful of rattlesnake venom thrown in. "I'm gonna have to have you teach me that sometime."

"It's my secret weapon against boys who bedevil me." She paused, glanced at the dark window, nibbling her lower lip, then looked at him once more. "You got you a girl somewhere?"

His mind flashed back to the girl he'd once known — the chestnut-haired Marianna Claymore — back in the Lunatics. He and she likely would have been married by now, maybe even had a baby on the way, if Bill Rondo hadn't killed Trace Cassidy, and Colter's stepmother, Ruth, hadn't given him the task of avenging his stepfather's killer. That had set off an explosive chain of events that had led to his branding and his crippling Bill Rondo, and to him on the run with this strange little girl in Mexico.

He shook his head. "No."

She looked at him coolly down across her fair, lightly freckled, wind- and sunburned cheeks. "Well, don't go lookin' around here."

Slowly, she climbed down off the bed and removed her coat. She hung it on a peg by the door, then quickly unlaced her boots, kicked them off, and crawled under the ratty covers of her bed, pulling the wool blanket up to her chin. Colter leaned over to scoop the tequila bottle off the floor. Most of the tanglefoot had run out, but there was a swallow left. That was all he needed. He'd had enough of the who-hit-john. Suddenly, he felt as serious as he'd been humored only a few minutes ago. And he felt bad for having goaded her on.

"I'm too old for you, Bethel," he said, scuttling lower in the bed and resting his head back against the pillow.

"Pa's twelve years older'n my ma. I'm just sayin' if you thought I was anything more than a dumb little girl, there wouldn't be nothin' so silly about it."

"You ain't no dumb little girl, Bethel. Hell, you're tougher'n I am." Colter glowered at the black window, feeling the cool, foreign night seep in through the rippled glass and leech the life out of him. He could still hear the mandolins and the guitars from the street below, and while they might have been happy sounds to some, they only made him feel cut off and alone.

And now he'd drunk too much and made fun of this good girl who liked him.

"You gotta be tough," she said, "to wear that brand on your face. That pistol of yours proves it, too."

"I wear that brand because I got no choice. And the pistol doesn't mean a damn thing. I'm just fast because there's something in me that makes me want to keep goin'. Why . . . and what for . . . I don't know."

They were both silent for a time. Then

Colter said, "Oh, well," and got up and stumbled over to the dresser. He leaned over the lamp to blow out the flame.

"Wait."

He looked at her. She was back looking like a little girl again, one whom someone had tucked into her humble bed.

"Can you leave it on?" she asked.

Colter nodded. "Sure. Ain't you gonna get undressed?"

"Don't be craven."

"Well, I am."

She closed her eyes tightly as Colter removed his gun and shell belt and then shucked everything off but his balbriggans. He crawled under the thin sheet and wool blanket that moths had chewed on and rolled onto his side. He was almost asleep when Bethel said softly, "Colter?"

He turned to her. "Yep?"

"You think my pa, Jed Strange, is dead?"

"I honestly don't know, Bethel. If he's alive, we'll find him. I promise."

"Thank you."

"You got it."

"I hope I didn't hurt you too bad."

"I'd appreciate it if you'd just forget about that now, Bethel. It's one thing having the stuffin' beat out of me by men bigger an' more experienced than I am, but it's a

259

whole other bailiwick havin' a lit . . . havin'
a girl makin' me yell 'give.' "

Bethel laughed.

They slept.

CHAPTER 21

From his and Bethel's second-story window, Colter studied the street in the predawn darkness.

Bethel snored softly behind him, fully clothed under the blankets and lying flat on her belly, cheek against her pillow. He'd risen a few minutes ago, washed and dressed quietly, and decided to let Bethel sleep while he scrounged up breakfast for them both.

The street was pearl gray. It had rained softly during the night, and a few small puddles shone in the dung-littered trace curving between rows of wood and mud-brick business buildings. A few drunks slumped on boardwalks. A shopkeeper in a crisp white shirt and black pants and sandals was sweeping off the gallery fronting his small pink adobe shop. A dog slumped in the shop's open doorway.

Otherwise, nothing moved down there. If the soldiers led by Brickson and McKnight had followed him and Bethel into town last night, they were nowhere to be seen now. Colter would check out the town thoroughly before exposing Bethel to a possible threat, however.

He grabbed his rifle from where it leaned against the wall near the head of his bed, set it on his shoulder, and then quietly opened the door. He had no way of locking the door from outside without locking Bethel in, so he left the key inside. She had her pistol lying on the bed beside her; anyone who might try to get to her while Colter was gone would likely wish he hadn't.

He went out, shut the door behind him, and descended the wooden steps to the lobby and went on outside to the vacant veranda. The fresh, damp air was perfumed with the smell of sage and cedar. Colter looked up and down the street. There were no pockets of horses that might belong to McKnight's men, no recent shod hoofprints in the muddy street fronting the hotel.

Colter's cautious tension eased, but he kept his eyes peeled as he stepped off the veranda and headed northeast along the main street. He stopped suddenly, squeezing the neck of the rifle perched on his shoulder. But he left the Henry where it was, frowning at a narrow gap between two buildings about twenty yards ahead and on the left side of the street.

He'd seen a fleeting glimpse of blue. Or thought he had. Maybe he'd only thought he'd seen it because he was on the scout for the blue of an American army tunic. Nothing there now. More slowly than before, and pivoting at his hips to look carefully around him, Colter continued forward.

Ahead, the street broadened into a bowl shape surrounded by humble wooden or brick structures, with a few cottonwoods and some kind of nut trees gently rattling their leaves that grew silver as the sun climbed. Smoke rose from a wooden building on the other side of the plaza, in the center of which a few trees and a fountain sat, both still darkly wet from last night's brief rain. A weak stream of water dribbled up from the fountain, the base of which was a cracked statue of Madre Maria. A stone bench sat before it, and mossy rocks lined the patch of grass and the trees.

Colter headed for the small, lime green adobe from which the aromas of roasting meat and coffee emanated. As he walked, he swung his head around, scrutinizing the thick shadows sheathing the buildings around him, and a small corral on the right in which three mules stood still as statues, one staring over the top cottonwood rail at Colter. A freight wagon with a drooping tongue fronted the corral. White-and-red chickens clucked and pecked in the dust around the wagon for seeds.

Smoke billowed up from a brick chimney of the green adobe, and from inside, behind a brush-roofed ramada, a baby fussed. As Colter approached the building, he could hear meat sizzling on a griddle, and the coffee smells grew thicker, making his mouth water and his stomach rumble. A sign over the ramada announced CAFÉ DEL LUCILLA. A man sat in a wicker chair on the ramada — an unshaven peasant in dirty white pajamas, sandals, and a sash, holding a stone mug in a large, dark, callused hand with the tip of one finger missing and the nail curling over the stump. He regarded Colter gravely, and did not return Colter's greeting as the redhead slowly crossed the ramada, cast one more edgy glance over his shoulder, then passed through the wooden bead curtain that served as a door.

Inside, Colter found a plump, pretty woman in her thirties frying goat meat and making tortillas on a large black range while bouncing a small child on her hip. There was a lunch counter and three wooden tables, and spicy-smelling *ristras* hung from ceiling beams. Colter managed to convey to the woman that he wanted to take two burros and a jug of coffee away with him, and then he went outside to stand by the silent peasant man on the gallery, one arm on a ceiling joist, staring into the eerily quiet plaza before him.

A few shadows moved amongst the shops around the plaza — shopkeepers unshuttering their windows or sweeping or moving merchandise onto their front boardwalks. One of the mules in the corral to Colter's left brayed raucously. Another mule chimed in. Colter turned toward the corral and lowered his Henry, but, glancing at the peasant man who stared in the same direction, he did not raise the barrel.

But he slowly, quietly, levered a cartridge into the chamber, then off-cocked the hammer with his thumb.

A mule brayed once more and then they all fell silent.

On the other side of the plaza, behind a large, wooden building that appeared to be a warehouse of some kind, blackbirds lifted from a broad oak and screeched off into the morning's misty shadows, wings flashing.

"Senor, su alimento esta lista."

Colter jerked his head around to see the pretty, plump woman standing in the open doorway behind him, holding out a small burlap bag in one hand, a corked stone jug in the other.

"*Cuanto?*" he asked, holding out some American coins in the palm of his left hand.

She picked out two bits, then gave Colter the food sack and the coffee jug. He held the sack in his left hand and cradled the jug between his elbow and his side, thanked the woman, and turned to face the plaza. As he did, the peasant man rose quickly from his wicker chair and followed the woman inside the café, drawing the wooden door closed on the beaded curtain.

Colter looked around once more. The men who'd been milling around their shops around the plaza had disappeared. The sun had risen, angling a buttery gold light over the eastern ridges, which was the direction that Colter headed now, dropping slowly down the gallery steps and angling across the plaza. His boots made a grinding sound in the sand and gravel, spurs *chinging* softly.

The only other sounds were the distant, intermittent thuds of someone splitting wood to the north. No dogs barked. No birds chirped.

But then a squirrel suddenly chittered across the plaza on Colter's right. In the periphery of his vision he saw a deep blue

266

shadow slide out from a front corner of a dilapidated wood-frame building. When he turned, he saw the rifle barrel leveling on him from beneath the brim of a tan kepi.

Colter lunged forward, dropping the food sack and the stone jug and lighting on a knee as he raised the Henry and clicked the hammer back with his thumb. Smoke puffed from the barrel of the Spencer carbine the soldier was aiming at him. At the same time, Colter triggered his Henry. The simultaneous barks rocketed around the plaza, the soldier's bullet hammering into the stone fountain to Colter's left. Colter's slug tore through the soldier's brisket and drove him back and out of sight, the rifle rising suddenly, then falling.

Another rifle barked. Colter saw the smoke and flames stabbing from another barrel forty yards to the left of the man he'd just drilled. The slug curled the air off Colter's right cheek.

He ejected the smoking cartridge from his Henry's breech, seated fresh, aimed, and fired two shots quickly, one slug tearing into the gallery post the soldier was standing beside, the second one boring through his face and causing his head to jerk back as though he'd been punched hard in the chin.

Only a half second after the second

shooter had fired, more rifles belched around the plaza, kicking up dust and gravel around Colter's boots, chewing into trees, and loudly hammering the stone fountain statue. Colter pivoted to his left, diving, and hit the ground behind the fountain, sliding his Henry up from under his right side as he quickly levered another round and glanced toward the plaza's west end.

He could see dust puffs in several places on the other side of the plaza and knew that there was at least one more shooter at the south end, near the place from which the first soldier had slung lead. One of this man's bullets clipped a rowel on Colter's left spur, making it ring.

He returned fire quickly at the three smoke puffs wafting near the corral, in which the mules were buck-kicking and braying wickedly. One man in buckskins — the scout, Brickson, most likely — was firing from beneath the wagon. Colter fired at the scout, his slug kicking dirt up into the man's bearded face, then twisted around to empty his rifle at the shooter slinging lead at him from the other end of the plaza.

That soldier had been trying to run up on Colter, and the redhead landed a lucky shot to the man's knee, evoking a scream. The soldier fell and rolled, clutching his right kneecap and losing his hat and rifle. Colter winced, dropping his own rifle as a bullet slammed into his upper left arm. Sucking a sharp breath through his teeth, he shucked his Remington from the cross-draw holster. He tried to get a shot off, but the other three men fronting him were pounding the ground before him with one slug after another, spraying his face with grit and dirt.

Through the dust, he saw Brickson lift his bearded head beneath the wagon. Another man in soldier blues — tall and lanky and sporting a black goatee and muttonchops, probably A. J. McKnight — leaped from the roof of the wood-frame building beside the café, to a woodpile, and from there to the ground.

Colter raised the Remy and fired, his slug slamming into the rain barrel the man had just ducked behind. At the same time, Brickson shouted something Colter couldn't make out, and the scout's carbine sprouted smoke and flames. The slug barked against the fountain's pedestal statue, tearing several nasty rock shards from Madre Maria's outstretched arm. One of the sharp rock slivers tore into Colter's left cheek, just beneath his eye.

He cursed. McKnight yelled, "Get the son of a bitch!"

Colter brushed blood from his cheek and extended his Remy but held fire when hooves drummed wildly to his right, and a pistol popped from that direction, as well. Colter turned, deep lines of incredulity carving into his forehead. A horseback rider was galloping toward him, leading Northwest. Stringy blond hair flopped on Bethel's shoulders clad in her dark wool coat as she whipped her pinto's reins with one hand, which also held Northwest's reins, and fired her Colt Army with the other.

Crouched low in her saddle, she was screaming and cursing like a drunken parlor girl.

Brickson had just started climbing out from beneath the wagon, but now he cursed and grabbed his right temple as he flung himself back under the dray. The other men shouted and continued firing as Bethel pounded toward Colter, within forty yards now and thundering toward him like a Missouri cyclone.

"Come on, Colter!" the girl screamed. "Let's fog some sage!"

Colt emptied his pistol, raking out, "Get outta here, Bethel!"

When his Remy's hammer clicked on an empty chamber, he heaved himself to his feet. Bethel slowed the pinto but not by much.

Colter shouted, "You're gonna get your fool hide drilled!" before reaching for Northwest's saddle horn and, while the galloping horse nearly tore his arm from its socket, hauling himself into the saddle as several more bullets sliced the air around him.

Bethel looked back at him, her face screened by her windblown hair. "Here!"

She flung his reins out, and he grabbed the twin uncoiling black snakes out of the air. Crouching low, he rammed his spurs into Northwest's flanks and bounded straight across the plaza behind the crazy girl straddling the lunging pinto.

Bullets blew up dust behind and around them and hammered a couple of small adobe casas as they threaded a break between them. Once out of town, Colter took the lead and they galloped south over the rolling hills. They splashed across a stream and mounted a low escarpment stretching out from a sandstone ridge. Colter turned Northwest to the right and checked the horse down in a hollow amongst the rocks.

He slipped out of the saddle and glared back at Bethel. "You're damn lucky you didn't get yourself killed, pullin' a fool stunt

like that. Who the hell you think you are —
Calamity Jane?"

The haranguing didn't seem to faze the
girl. She looked back over her shoulder,
then turned to Colter, dropping her eyes to
his upper left arm. "You hit?"

Colter had suppressed the ache of the bullet's hot slice across his arm. As he walked
past Bethel, he said grumpily, "Stay here
and keep down."

He walked back up the scarp, dropped to
his knees about five feet from the crest, and
crawled the rest of the way, glancing down
the other side and back the way they'd
come. Bethel climbed the scarp and
dropped down beside him. She unknotted
his neckerchief, squinting her eyes as she
worked, her cheeks flushed from exertion.

"Don't you listen to anything anybody
tells you?" he asked her.

"You ain't the boss o' me, Colter Farrow."

"I feel sorry for the poor son of a bitch
who has that job." Colter stared at her in
exasperation. As she removed the neckerchief and wrapped it tightly, adeptly around
his arm, he added, "You sure you didn't run
your pa off? Maybe he don't want you to
find him."

"You keep that pulled tight," she ordered,
glancing at the neckerchief wrapped around

his bloody arm, "or you're liable to bleed to death. She looked at him, and a pleased light entered her eyes. Her mouth corners rose. She leaned forward and pecked his cheek.

Startled as well as exasperated, he jerked his head back. "What was that for?"

"For bein' scared for me."

He just stared at her. Movement along their back trail caught his eye, and he pulled Bethel down low beside him. "Maybe it's time you start bein' scared for yourself. More trouble's on the way!"

CHAPTER 22

Colter pressed his cheek against the side of the knoll, holding Bethel down beside him with one hand. He held his Henry against his chest with his other hand, and now, as the thuds of oncoming riders grew louder from the north, he clamped his knees around the rifle's rear stock and slowly levered a cartridge into the chamber.

Bethel turned her face toward him, her eyes nervous, expectant.

The riders came on until Colter could hear their tack squawking and their fast-moving horses raking air in and out of their lungs.

He gave the girl a hard, commanding look. "You do what I tell you, now, and stay put."

He heaved himself up suddenly and scrambled to the top of the knoll, planting his boots a little more than shoulder-width apart and holding the cocked Henry up high across his chest. Four riders galloped toward him from the north and curving to his right as they cantered up the steep, rocky slope — three men in cavalry blues, and Brickson in his buckskins and wearing a bloody white bandage around his forehead, beneath his brown felt sombrero. All four jerked their heads toward him, squinting against the dust and bright sunlight.

"Hey!" yelled the soldier wearing sergeant's chevrons and riding behind the dark, hawk-faced A. J. McKnight. The soldier swung up the carbine he'd been holding across his saddlebows, but before he could press the stock against his shoulder, Colter swung up his own rifle and blew the sergeant off his McClelland saddle.

The man hit the dusty, rocky trail with a crunch of cracking bones and a shrill grunt, causing more dust to rise.

The other three men had checked their horses down. The riderless horse bounded past them up the slope, ears back, stirrups flapping like wings. McKnight glared at Colter. So did Brickson and the third man, a corporal with thin red muttonchops and belligerent gray eyes set deep beneath sandy brows. The sun was peeling the skin off all three unshaven faces.

Loudly, Colter ejected the spent cartridge, sent it tumbling back down the slope behind him, and rammed a fresh bullet in the breech. His nostrils flared as he glared back at the three men, his gaze finally settling on McKnight.

"You fellas are real hoople-heads, comin' as far as you have just to die."

McKnight's right eye twitched beneath the brim of his tan kepi. "You think so, do you, killer?"

Colter offered no response but a grim half smile. That seemed to make his three shadowers even tenser. They all held carbines half up, not quite level with Colter. The corporal's Spencer shook in his hands clad in yellow gloves with gauntlets. Dust dribbled down his brown, red-mottled right cheek.

The sun beat down. Cicadas hummed.

The breeze blew the riders' dust back and forth.

McKnight balled his cheeks and narrowed his eyes as he snapped his carbine to his shoulder.

Colter's rifle belched. McKnight's own shot sailed wild. He screamed as Colter's slug punched him off the far side of his horse and into the rocks. A wink later, both the corporal and Brickson were down, as well, Brickson managing to pop a pill around Colter's boots before he flew down the side of his paint with a shredded heart. He got his left boot hung up in his stirrup, and his terrified horse galloped on up the slope, bouncing the wailing scout along behind it.

The horse's thudding hooves and the dying scout's shrill pleas dwindled.

Colter stared down the slope at McKnight and the corporal, both lying twisted and bloody amongst the clay-colored rocks. He thumbed fresh cartridges down his Henry's loading tube and glanced back at Bethel. She lay flat, looking up at him, her expression not so much frightened anymore as fateful. Maybe a little befuddled at the ease with which this lanky young man with the long red hair and lightly freckled though savagely scarred face could so easily kill.

She'd understand if she'd been through what he had, he thought. Through it all starting with Trace's grisly murder and then Bill Rondo's glowing branding iron shoved toward his face. In the seconds before it had been rammed into Colter's cheek, the smoking iron had smelled like a hot stove. The smell of his own charred flesh would have made him vomit if he hadn't passed out from the burning, unbearable agony.

He looked around cautiously, making sure no one had been attracted by the gunfire, then tramped down the hill, kicking both bodies over to make doubly sure that McKnight and the corporal were dead. Both men's eyes were glassy and sightless, and their wounds were mortal if not instantly killing. Colter leaned his rifle against a rock, chased down both cavalry remounts, and unsaddled them before giving them both water from their riders' canteens and spanking them free. Like him, they'd have to find their way alone.

He took coffee, hardtack, and jerky from the men's saddlebags, and a blanket roll for Bethel. He hadn't owned a hat since the flooded arroyo had taken his, so he confiscated McKnight's, which he found amongst the rocks, and set it on his head. He liked the broad brim even though the sweat moistening the inner band, and the crust of salt around the brim, belonged to a man he hated even in death.

It was an apt trophy.

He adjusted the hat and turned to see Bethel standing near the corporal. She looked around grimly at the blood-smeared rocks and the twisted carcasses, the breeze sliding her bangs around beneath her hat, lifting the tails of her shirt.

Colter tossed the bedroll to her.

"Thanks," she said.

"Don't mention it."

"I like your hat."

"I do, too. Maybe I shoulda joined the cavalry."

He started up the slope to retrieve their horses. She followed him, asking, "How many more hombres you got behind you, Colter?"

"That's a damn good question, Bethel." He grabbed Northwest's reins and stepped into the leather.

For the next five days, they followed a rugged trail, indicated by the map, into the lower reaches of the Los Montanas del Dragones — a giant dinosaur spine of cracked and twisted stone cliffs, monoliths, and pinnacles that appeared to have been punched upward from deep in the earth's churning bowels many aeons ago. Then as now it had been a violent time, Colter thought, as he and Bethel followed the crooked trail ever higher amongst the rocks in which nothing at all seemed to grow, and where the water holes were few and far between.

Here and there pictographs painted by a long-vanished people showed themselves in the sides of boulders — faded, primitive accounts of stick men stalking or killing stick animals. What must have been dinosaur bones shone like chips of ancient china in many rock walls lining the trail. Diamondbacks shaded themselves along the circuitous, sometimes perilous trace, instantly quivering, coiling, and rattling as the riders passed.

Here and there stone shrines to various saints, adorned with wilted and crumbling parched flowers, spotted the trail.

In the early afternoon of their sixth day in the Dragon Range, they rode into a broad canyon where several adobes hunched in the high-altitude sun. The trail that had led them here was well worn by wide-shod wheels, and now Colter saw a large wooden barn and corral on the trail's left side, under a towering lip of sandstone.

Several large freight wagons sat in the scrub near the barn, tongues drooping. Around the barn were several other buildings, some used, some appearing abandoned, scrub grown up around them. One was obviously a blacksmith shop, because a large, charred man in a leather apron was loudly hammering an anvil just inside the open front doors while chickens and two goats pecked in the yard before him.

He had a silver-framed, fancily scrolled Colt revolving rifle leaning against one of the open barn doors, and he eyed Colter and Bethel warily beneath the brim of his low-crowned sombrero as they continued into the yard.

To the left of the trail, a large adobe with pillars holding up a tile gallery roof hunched beneath a dusty sycamore. Five Arabian horses with fancy Mexican saddles and trimmings stood tied to the wooden hitch rack fronting the place.

A frightening outfit, Colter thought. With a saloon so the mule-skinners and anyone else could cut the trail dust. A sign above the large adobe announced SALON DE JUAN DOMINGO GUTIERREZ.

"I don't dance with the devil and I don't patronize saloons, Colter," Bethel said.

"That's real upstanding, Bethel. It truly is." Colter angled Northwest toward the hitch rack. "But neither one of us has had anything to eat but rattlesnake for the past five meals. Me — I'm gonna go in and see if I can get a big plate of huevos rancheros and a steak."

She frowned, pensive. "That don't sound half bad."

Colter chuckled as he stepped down from the saddle. He looped his reins over the hitch rack, and Bethel did the same, mounting the gallery steps behind him. He moved through the arched doorway, a stout oak door thrown back and propped open with a chair to his left, and instinctively stepped to one side, so the door didn't backlight him.

The place was far humbler inside than outside, as there was an earthen floor and a dozen or so crude wooden tables outfitted with rickety, hide-bottom chairs. There was a long, crude bar on the left, with a rattle-snake floating in a five-gallon glass jug, above a white bed of pickled eggs. Colter scowled, sick of the chewy, nearly tasteless meat he and Bethel had been living on. Shelves behind the bar were crowded with cloudy, clear bottles of several sizes, and there was a big crock on the bar's far left, with a gourd handle hanging down from the lip.

Behind the bar was a large black range, the several pots and pans sizzling atop it being tended by a portly old woman in a shapeless dress, her salt-and-pepper hair secured in a tight bun behind her head. The succulent smells of spicy meat emanating from the range nearly rocked Colter back on his heels. A one-eyed man sat on a stool near the crock, fanning himself with a yellowed newspaper. Long, gray-brown hair hung down from the sides of his head while the top of his head was an ugly mass of knotted scar tissue.

The victim of a scalping, Colter knew. He'd seen the grisly display many times before. In fact, one of the men who'd ridden for Trace Cassidy had sported such a scar inflicted by the Sioux on the Dakota Plains. Roy Gallantly had always said he'd fared some better than Custer, who'd lost a helluva lot more than his topknot.

Toward the back of the room, four men were playing some kind of craps game. They appeared to be throwing small bones around their table with a wooden cup, grunting and sighing and speaking in hushed voices as they flipped coins after each bone toss. They were big, savage-faced men dressed nearly all in leather, with sombreros of different shapes resting on their heads. One had an extra chair pulled up beside him, and on the chair rested a sawed-off, double-barreled coach gun with a leather lanyard.

Most likely banditos. Border cutthroats. They had glasses and two clear bottles on their table, one empty, one cloudy with some kind of Mexican tanglefoot that would likely peel the rim off a wheel.

They regarded Colter and Bethel wryly, the one with his back to the newcomers twisting around in his chair and raking his gaze across the two with grunting interest before turning forward and shrugging his shoulders. Colter walked over to the bar. The one-eyed man regarded him and Bethel dully, as though a branded young gringo and a blond young gringa walking into his saloon were a common occurrence.

Colter doffed his hat, brushed it against his pant leg. "Can we get a couple plates of huevos rancheros and steak?"

The portly woman turned toward him briefly, then continued stirring whatever she had sizzling in an iron skillet. The one-eyed man furrowed the brow over his one good eye — the other was milky and half-hidden by its drooping lid — and shook his head. "No. No." He continued shaking his head. Glancing at the range, he said something that Colter couldn't understand but which Bethel seemed to pick up. She looked at Colter and nodded.

"Good enough," she said, tentatively. "We'll just get us a table, then."

While the man called over to the woman, Bethel canted her head toward the room, and then she and Colter walked over to a table on the other side of a ceiling joist from the four craps players and sank into hide-bottom chairs, Colter giving his back to the bar, the banditos to his left, the door to his right, beyond Bethel.

Colter tossed his hat onto the table. Bethel removed her own hat, ran her fingers through her sweat-damp blond hair, which fell straight to her shoulders, then tossed her own hat onto the table with a sigh.

She looked around with a sour look on her sunburned face. "Hope Mama's not lookin' down on me. She wouldn't approve."

"Would she want you to starve?"

"No, but she'd think Pa'd been a bad influence on me in the year since we planted her. She warned me to keep my hat straight, and that Pa needed a strong rudder, and I was it."

"Seems a heavy yoke for a twelve-year-old."

"I got the shoulders for it."

The one-eyed man came over with two clear, mineral-stained glasses and a small bottle filled with clear liquid. *"Pulque,"* he said, and splashed some of the liquid into each glass, setting them before Colter and Bethel.

"The devil's elixir," she said when he shuffled off behind the bar, primly sliding her glass away from her. "No, thank you."

"All the more for me," Colter said, sniffing his glass. The coffin varnish smelled about the same as tequila to him.

"You drink that, you'll be seein' purple bears and pink snakes."

"Don't mind if I do." Colter sipped the pulque, swished it around in his mouth, and swallowed it. The liquid was stronger than tequila, but when he stopped feeling as though it had peeled off his tonsils and washed them into his left boot, and he was able to draw a breath again, a warm, dreamy feeling sank over him. The light angling through the arched windows was soft and buttery. He wanted to cool his heels in this dingy, aromatic place and drink the Mexican panther piss all afternoon.

"Go easy on that stuff," Bethel warned. "That one sip's got you grinnin' like a schoolboy after his first poke."

"Dang." Colter stared into his glass. "I didn't even realize I was grinnin'."

The woman hauled several sizzling plates over to the bone-throwing banditos. A few minutes later, she carried half a dozen sizzling, steaming plates and bowls over to Colter and Bethel's table and plopped them all down in the middle. The one-eyed man outfitted them with plates, crude wooden forks, and a bowl of corn tortillas.

Colter and Bethel stared down at the food.

The man started to turn away and follow the woman back behind the bar, but he stopped and regarded the two *norteamericanos* skeptically. *"Como esto,"* he said, and ripped one of the steaming tortillas in half.

He took a spoon and smeared some goopy green sauce onto the tortilla, following it up with a plop of peppers, onions, and tomatoes from another bowl. To that he added what smelled and appeared like small chunks of goat meat. Onto the goat meat he smeared a goodly portion of what could only have been — try as Colter might to convince himself otherwise — fried insects.

Beetles, to be more precise.

Fried in bits of green leaves and red chili peppers.

The man dropped the pie-shaped tortilla onto Bethel's plate. *"Entienda?"* he said, slapping his hands to his thighs, then turning and walking away.

Bethel stared down at her plate for a long time, then glanced up at Colter, showing her little white teeth through a grimace. "Them what I think they are?"

"I can make out their little heads and their little feet, so I reckon they are. Nothin' goes to waste in Mexico. Go ahead and give 'em a try. I'll wait a couple minutes, and if you don't start floppin' around on the floor, I'll throw in, too."

"Very funny." She glanced over at the one-eyed man and then at the woman, both of whom had retaken their respective positions, the man watching her and Colter expectantly. Not wanting to offend the man, she reluctantly picked up the tortilla with both her hands and held it in front of her mouth, eyeing it distastefully. "That rattlesnake's beginning to look a whole lot more appetizing 'bout now. Well, here goes."

She bit into the tortilla and chewed, her eyes gradually brightening. She swallowed the morsel, hiked a shoulder, and shoved the rest into her mouth. "It ain't a bloody T-bone, but I reckon it'll do."

Colter ripped a tortilla apart and fixed his the way the one-eyed man had shown him and, seeing that Bethel appeared to be thoroughly enjoying her own meal now, quickly bit into it. He'd expected the fried beetles to crunch more than they did. They did not taste bad at all — in fact, they tasted spicy-hot and salty and they went well with the goat meat and the green goop. Colter ate his first bit quickly and then made another, larger burrito, washing every other spicy bite down with the soothing pulque.

As hungry as they were, it still took Colter and Bethel nearly twenty minutes to finish the hearty meal and to swab out the remains at the bottom of the empty bowls with the last bits of tortilla. Colter swallowed the last bite and sank back in his chair, stuffed, his head light from the drink.

He looked across the table at Bethel. He didn't like the look on her face as she stared beyond him, toward where the four cutthroats had been eating loudly and hungrily but from where now only silence issued.

Silence except for the creak of leather and the squawk of a chair as though a man were rising from it. Colter saw something arc toward him from his left, and he gave an instinctive start, reaching for his Remington, as a rawhide pouch landed on his empty plate with a jingling thud. He kept the pistol in its holster, squeezing the worn walnut handle, as he stared down at the lumpy pouch on his plate.

Bethel frowned down at the pouch, then slid her cautious gaze to the men to Colter's left. Colter looked that way, too.

One of the men grunted, sated by food, and a spur *chinged* as he moved away from his chair and ambled leisurely toward Colter and Bethel's table, the flared bottoms of his scratched leather charro slacks buffeting around his high-heeled, black boots.

The cutthroat stopped across from Colter. A very tall man, only about a head shorter than Santiago Machado had been, he had broad jaws covered in a two-day growth of spiked black stubble, and two chins though he was not otherwise fat. His mustaches were long and silky. His dark eyes were dull beneath the brim of his gray sombrero, red-stitched with the outlines of naked senoritas.

Colter lowered his eyes and squeezed his hand harder around his pistol's grips as he saw two pistols — an impressive Colt Peacemaker and an older-model Schofield — wedged behind the man's wide brown belt, and the bowielike knife with a wooden handle curved in the shape of a curvaceous naked woman sheathed under his left arm. He kept the gun where it was, as the big cutthroat didn't seem to be in a hurry to go for his own.

He jerked his chin toward the hide sack he'd tossed onto Colter's plate. "For the girl. Mexican gold. A hundred of your American dollars' worth."

He slid his dark eyes toward Bethel, who looked as though she'd swallowed an entire lemon and shrank back in her chair.

CHAPTER 23

Colter kept his hand on his Remington but tried to smile, trying to pass off the offer as a joke, as he said, "Oh, the girl ain't for sale. Wouldn't be worth that much even if she was."

He chuckled.

Bethel hardened her jaws at him.

The big man stared mutely down at Colter and the girl. An eerie silence had fallen over the place. Colter could hear the big man breathing raspily through his nose, his broad shoulders rising and falling behind his red-and-black calico shirt and leather jacket adorned with tooled silver ornaments.

Colter stared up at him, feeling an ache growing in the back of his neck. Bethel stared fearfully up at the cutthroat, as well. Finally, the man's face broke into a broad smile, and he showed nearly an entire set of crooked, broken teeth as he laughed, jerking his shoulders. He slid his gaze toward his friends, who also broke into laughter.

They all laughed hard, thoroughly enjoying themselves. Tears dribbled down the big cutthroat's cheek, and he placed his big hands on the edge of the table, leaning forward and shaking his head as he laughed.

Colter laughed, then, too, hoping that he and Bethel were only being the target of some odd Mexican joke, and that the big man wasn't really trying to buy her for a hundred dollars in Mexican gold.

"Amigo," he said finally, still laughing, tears dampening his beard stubble, "we offer you a hundred dollars." He flung a hand toward Bethel. "That is better than one dollar a pound!"

He and the others laughed even harder.

"You can forget it, amigo," Bethel snapped at him loudly, her face reddening with rage. "I ain't Colter's to sell, and even if I was . . ." Bethel let her voice trail off as her gaze dropped to the big cutthroat's belt and the two bristling pistols. She frowned. "Hey, where'd you get that hog leg?"

For an instant, he appeared befuddled. Then he followed her gaze down to the Peacemaker wedged behind his belt. "Huh? This?"

Bethel said louder, "Where'd you get it?"

He slipped the gun from behind his belt,

twirled the fancy, silver-chased, factory-scrolled, pearl-handled piece on his finger, grinning.

Bethel slid her chair back and stood tensely, her wide eyes riveted on the pistol in the bandito's hand. Her face had paled, and now she swallowed, lips trembling. "That's my father's gun, you son of a bitch!"

"Que?" the cutthroat said, still twirling the gun, showing off.

Bethel grabbed her own Colt Army from behind the cartridge belt encircling her slender waist and extended it in both hands toward the cutthroat's belly.

"Bethel," Colter said, sliding his own chair back from the table and slipping his Remy from its holster, shuttling his frantic gaze between the big cutthroat before him and the three others, who'd just now started reaching for their own weapons. They froze, one half out of his chair, as Colter aimed the Remy at them, loudly clicking the hammer back.

The big cutthroat did not look worried. He stopped twirling the impressive Peacemaker, but he grinned jeeringly at Bethel, who was aiming her Colt at him, her hands shaking visibly.

"That's my father's gun!" she fairly screamed, narrowing her eyes. "What'd you do to my father, you big bastard?"

The cutthroat held the Colt against his chest. He leaned mockingly, defiantly toward Bethel and suddenly shaped a slack expression, sticking out his tongue, and swiped the index finger of his left hand across his throat. Straightening, he guffawed and glanced over at his cutthroat pards. The others laughed tensely, sliding their eyes between the big bandito and Colter's cocked Remington.

Bethel screamed and squeezed her eyes closed. The Colt in her hands thundered and bounced. The loud report caused the woman behind the counter to shout and drop a pan. Dust sifted from the rafters over Colter's head.

The big bandito took two stumbling steps backward, his laughter instantly dying, as did his mocking, toothy grin. He stared at Bethel as though she'd said something he hadn't been able to understand. And then his eyes lowered to the smoking Colt in her trembling hands. His expression became one of disbelieving exasperation as he continued to drop his gaze to the blood leaking out of the ragged, round hole in his calico shirt, two inches below the hide tobacco pouch hanging by a rawhide thong.

He made a gurgling sound. He appeared

to try to lift his head, but his strength was gone. His knees buckled. Blue-black blood welled from the hole in his shirt, thick as tar. As he dropped straight down to the floor, his head banged against the end of Colter and Bethel's table, bouncing, his hair flying wildly, before he sagged sideways onto the hardpacked earthen floor.

One of the other three banditos bolted out of his chair, reaching for the Smith & Wesson jutting from his shoulder holster and shouting, *"Mate a esa pequeña puta!"*

Colter shot the man in the chest.

As the other swung toward him, also reaching for iron and shouting loudly in Spanish, Colter flung himself across the table and into Bethel, still standing there, staring down in shock at the dead bandito. She hit the floor beneath Colter, groaning, and Colter used his right boot to haul the table down in front of them for a shield as two bullets plowed through it and bored into the floor dangerously close to both him and the girl.

"Stay down!" Colter shouted at Bethel, ratcheting the Remy's hammer back.

He placed one hand on the floor to brace himself as he lifted his head and snaked his Colt over the top of the table, wincing as bullets ripped slivers from the edge of the table and sprayed them into his face. He picked out one man just as the man's pistol blossomed smoke and flames, and fired the Remy. The man screamed. The others were stumbling around, half drunk and shooting wildly, and in a matter of seconds, Colter had emptied his pistol.

Silence.

All three of the other cutthroats were down. Two were groaning. Powder smoke hung in thick clouds over the dingy room.

Colter looked at Bethel, who lay on her side and was just now lowering her arms from her head, her cheeks pale, eyes haunted by the prospect of her father's demise at the savage hands of these four killers. Quickly, Colter flicked open his Remy's loading gate and shook out the spent brass, replacing them with new from his cartridge belt. He thumbed the gate closed and heaved himself to his feet, clicking the pistol's hammer back and aiming in the general direction of the three banditos piled up around their over-turned table.

One of the men sighed and fell still as Colter approached. Another heaved himself onto hands and knees and reached for his pistol lying on the floor a few feet away. Colter put a bullet through the back of the man's shaggy head, then turned to inspect the third man, who lay on his back beneath an overturned chair, blood bubbling up from his chest as well as his mouth, matting his long beard, his eyes staring sightlessly up at the low ceiling.

Colter spied movement through the smoke and swung around to see the portly woman and the one-eyed man rising from behind the bar, both scowling warily, angrily. The woman bunched her face in anger and cut into a Spanish tirade directed at Colter, waving her arms at the mess and pointing and making *bang-bang* sounds.

Colter looked around, saw a sack spilling gold coins on the floor beneath the banditos' table. He scooped the coins back into it, drew the drawstring closed, and tossed it to the woman, who caught it in both hands against her ample bosom with a grunt.

"There you go," Colter said, walking toward Bethel. "That oughta cover the damage."

The woman fell silent as she set the pouch on the bar, and she and the old man began counting the coins. Bethel was on her hands and knees beside the bandito she'd drilled. She held the fancy, pearl-gripped Peacemaker in both her hands in front of her face. As Colter approached, she lifted her face to his. Her eyes were brightly tear-glazed.

"This is my father's gun," she said softly, showing Colter the big popper. "They took it from him."

"How do you know it's his? Colt probably made a hundred guns in that style."

She turned the gun around and showed him the brass plate at the bottom of the pearl grips. Into the brass had been etched the initials JS.

Colter said gently, "That don't mean he's dead, Bethel."

"They couldn't have gotten this gun off old Jed Strange unless they killed him," she said, looking down at the gun once more, as though it were her father's spirit she held in her hands.

Sandals scuffed and Colter turned to see the one-eyed man walking toward them. His one eye owned a grave cast as he stopped before Colter and Bethel. In English so broken that Colter just barely made it out, the man said, "The man who owned this gun — he is your *papa, chiquita*?"

Bethel sniffed and straightened, still holding the pistol in both her small hands. *"Sí."*

The one-eyed man gestured toward the front of the room, then shuffled out the door and under the ramada. Colter and Bethel followed him out. "The man who owned that gun." The one-eyed man gestured toward a dark, serrated ridge looming like a distant, massive storm to the southwest, which was the general direction that Colter and Bethel had been traveling. "He is buried there. Two days' ride." He pointed his right foot. "*Paseo de la Rana*. How do you say?" He paused, thinking hard, and snapped his fingers. "Frog Ridge."

"At the foot of it?" Colter asked.

"*Sí.*" He nodded twice. "Two days' ride."

"Who buried him there?" Bethel asked.

"I did, little one." The one-eyed man jabbed his thumb against his chest. "I found him. Dead along the trail, near his wagon. Gringo prospector. He was here two, maybe three days before. I ride down to Soledad for supplies, find him . . . bury him. I mark his grave with a cross."

The one-eyed man's sole eye sadly, regretfully regarded Bethel. She stared off, dry-eyed now, steeling herself against the pain that threatened to overwhelm her, and nodded. "*Muchas gracias, senor.*"

The one-eyed man glanced at Colter, shrugged fatefully, then shuffled back inside the roadhouse. Colter looked at Bethel, feeling a large rock growing larger and harder in his gut. He stepped forward, awkwardly set a hand on the girl's shoulder, feeling helpless against her sorrow.

She shrugged it off, ducked beneath the hitch rack, and grabbed her pinto's reins. "I came all this way to find him, so I reckon I'll find him. Follow his last ride. Say a few words over him."

Colter ducked under the hitch rack and laced his fingers together, making a step for the girl. She stepped into his hands, grabbed the horn, and heaved herself into the saddle. She began neck-reining the horse away from the rack, giving her gaze to the blue ridge in the southwestern distance. "It'll likely just embarrass him, but I don't wanna go home without seein' where he's buried, recitin' the Lord's Prayer over him."

"I know it don't mean much, but I am sorry, Bethel. I was really hopin' we'd find him alive."

She turned to him now, and a single tear rolled down from her otherwise dry right eye. "You didn't think we would, though, did you?"

Colter just looked at her.

She sniffed and sleeved the tear away. Her voice pinched into a faint screech as she batted her heels against the pinto's ribs. "Me, neither."

She galloped off across the yard, toward a trail branching south. Colter mounted Northwest and headed after her, deeper and deeper into the rugged, rocky sierra. When the freight trail dead-ended in a small village built against the side of a mountain wall, they paused only to fill their canteens from the village's single, covered well before continuing along a fainter wagon path that the boy who tended the well assured them would take them to *Paseo de la Rana*. It was the same trail, it seemed, that would lead them eventually to the dragon drawn on Jed Strange's map.

Though now it appeared there was little reason to push that deep into the unforgiving sierra, a maze of dangerously deep canyons and towering gothic cliffs.

That night they made camp in a shallow wash surrounded by steep, boulder-strewn slopes. Colter managed to snare a jackrabbit just before the sun went down — he didn't want to risk attracting attention with a rifle shot — and spitted it over the small fire that Bethel built from the wood she gathered.

While the meat cooked and the stars sharpened in the darkening sky above the jagged, black velvet ridges around them, Bethel laid out the bedroll she'd confiscated from one of the soldiers Colter had shot and lay back against her saddle, hands entwined behind her head, staring at the sky.

"Meat's done," Colter told her, dragging out a couple of plates from his saddlebags.

"Ain't hungry."

Colter didn't push her. He didn't blame her for not being hungry. He hadn't eaten for days after his blood father and then his foster father had died. Pulling the hot meat off the rabbit bone with his fingers, he ate and sipped the coffee he'd brewed from the Arbuckles' he'd also confiscated from the dead soldiers.

When he'd finished, he cleaned his hands on his trousers and poured another cup of coffee, hearing the coyotes starting to yammer on the ridges around him. He glanced across the fire. Bethel lay as she had before, both her eyes open and staring into the firmament.

He set the coffee back on a rock near the crackling flames and leaned against his saddle, holding the smoking cup in his hands. He wished he could think of comforting words to share with the girl, but none would come, and he didn't want to pretend he knew anything more about assuaging her pain than he did. Which was nothing. All he knew was that time would dull the ache though it would never obliterate it, but that would be little comfort for her now.

"Colter," she said after a time, turning to face him from the other side of the fire. "You got anyone back to your home in them Lunatic Mountains?"

Colter sipped his coffee. "My foster ma's there — Ruth — and David and Little May." Marianna was there, as well, though two years older since he'd left and most likely married to someone else by now. He didn't mention Marianna, however, because there was no point in twisting that knife in his gut.

"You ever thought about goin' back to 'em?"

Colter shook his head. "I'd just lead bounty hunters right up to their front door, if I did. Oh, it'd be nice to see 'em all again, but I can't for a long time. Maybe someday."

Bethel turned her face back to the sky. After a long time, when Colter's cup was nearly empty, she turned back to him once more. "You get lonely?"

"Always."

"It never goes away?"

"Oh, it fades after a fashion. But it never goes away for good." He saw no point in lying to her. It was a tough road she had ahead, without her father and mother.

Expecting it to be easy only made it tougher. "At least, you got your aunt."

"It's not the same."

"No, it ain't."

He finished his coffee and stomped off with his rifle to have a look around their camp. When he was sure they were alone, he checked on the horses hobbled in some nearby scrub, then returned to camp and picked up his saddle and bedroll and carried them over to Bethel's side of the fire. He set his saddle down beside hers and spread out his blankets in front of it.

He removed his pistol and shell belt and coiled the belt around his saddle horn. Lying down beside Bethel, he rested his head back against his saddle and nudged his hip up close to the girl's. She rolled toward him, her eyes bright now, tears clinging to her lashes. She threw an arm across his belly and rested her head atop his shoulder. He wrapped his own arm around her, gave her a comforting squeeze, and pressed his lips to her temple.

Bethel sighed raggedly. She closed her eyes. Gradually, her breaths grew deep and even.

Colter fell asleep then, too.

CHAPTER 24

Anyone stumbling across Jed Strange's grave would most likely have mistaken it for a natural buckling of stones and rocks between a spindly mesquite and a large barrel cactus marked with several gaping holes carved by birds. The grave was set about fifteen yards back of the faint, seldom-used cart trail, and the crude wooden cross that the one-eyed man had erected at its head had been knocked over by the wind or some passing creature.

The grave lay in a broad, sloping valley on the shoulder of a mountain on which virtually nothing but the single mesquite and barrel cactus lived, with two pillars of rock jutting from the crest of the slope to the right of the grave, and a jagged fist of cracked basalt rising toward an even higher, sheerer ridge on its left.

It was a rugged moonscape of sand, gravel, and solid rock torn and blasted by time and weather.

Bethel had searched hard for the small, wiry bits of wildflowers that she now placed atop the mounded stones that marked her father's final resting place. She knelt there for a time, her head bowed, while Colter stood on the trail with the horses, in a trapezoid of shade offered by a wagon-sized boulder. Finally, Bethel rose, straightened the crude cross with heavy stones, then stood beside it, staring down at the grave once more and muttering a prayer the words of which Colter couldn't hear above the sifting breeze.

Northwest lifted his head suddenly, nickered, and worked his nostrils in agitation. Colter studied the horse, frowning. "What is it, boy?"

The horse stomped and turned his head slightly back to sniff the building breeze. Colter tied both horses to a knob of rock jutting out from the boulder, then walked off the trail opposite the grave. Thirty yards from the trail, a deep valley opened, its floor about a hundred and fifty feet below where Colter now stood, casting his gaze around the tan and gray landscape, the breeze bending the brim of the tan kepi he'd taken off McKnight's corpse.

He squatted suddenly, detecting movement down along the canyon bottom, on the same trail that he and Bethel had taken before they'd ascended the mesa they were now on. Squinting, he made out five or six riders. From this distance, he couldn't tell much about them except that they were dark-skinned, all had black hair held back with colorful bandannas, and they also wore bright, probably calico shirts.

Apaches, possibly Yaqui. Either way, if they were following Colter and Bethel's trail, he and the girl were in trouble.

He straightened and walked back toward the horses. Bethel was walking back onto the trail, staring toward him, her own eyes becoming wary when she saw the fear in his own. "What is it?"

"Injuns."

"You think they're after us?"

Colter helped the girl onto her horse. "No way to tell. One thing I do know," he said as Bethel settled herself in her saddle, "is we can't go back the way we came. We're gonna have to keep followin' this trail and hope we can shake 'em."

Colter stepped into his saddle and looked at Bethel sitting beside him, her face still pale from shock and sorrow beneath her tan. "You get enough time with your pa?"

She nodded bravely. "I said good-bye."

She swiped a sleeve of her wool shirt across her cheek.

Colter tapped his spurs against Northwest's flanks, and the horse lunged off its back hooves, barreling into a gallop up the gravelly slope, tracing a meandering course amongst the rocks and boulders. They crested the slope and galloped down the other side and into more of the same kind of harsh, barren, up-and-down country they'd been traveling since they'd started into the Los Montanas del Dragones.

They rode as hard as they dared over the treacherous terrain for a good hour before checking their mounts down to rest them. Colter slipped out of the saddle and tossed his reins to Bethel. "Stay here while I have a look behind us."

He slid his Henry from its boot, racked a round into the chamber, off-cocked the hammer, and hiked back up the hill they'd just descended. At the top, he dropped down amongst some rocks and stared into the broad, angling ravine below, and chewed his upper lip. Far off down the ravine, the riders came toward him, winding around the rocks and sparse tufts of catclaw that littered the wash's floor. The wind was picking up, and occasional curtains of wind-blown dust obscured his view of the Indians.

But as soon as the dust dwindled, there they were again, clinging to Colter and Bethel's trail like hungry, stubborn coyotes.

Colter cursed loudly, squinting against a gust of windblown grit. The jerk of his head saved his life as an arrow whistled past his face to hammer into the rock beside him. He swung his head left. Just then a shrill war cry filled his ears as an Apache bolted toward him from behind a rock, flinging down his bow and swiping the stone-bladed war hatchet from the red sash encircling his waist. Propelling himself off a low rock, he dove toward Colter, who managed to get his rifle raised, hammer fully cocked, and trigger tripped.

The rifle thundered.

The Apache's cry grew shriller as the bullet took the shirtless brave through his lower belly. The hatchet thudded to the ground. Colter threw himself sideways, and the Apache bounced off his right shoulder to pile up in the rocks, groaning and frantically reaching for the hatchet. He'd just grabbed it when Colter, shoving his back up against a boulder, quickly pumped a fresh round and shot the brave through his breastbone.

As the brave dropped the hatchet once more and staggered backward as though drunk, Colter turned to see three more dark-skinned figures running toward him down the sandy slope, all three running in a side-skip motion, the fringes of their high-topped moccasins jouncing, as they nocked arrows to their bows. Colter pumped the Henry again, aimed, and fired three rounds toward the oncoming Indians, plunking one bullet through one brave's thigh. As that brave yowled and dropped, rolling, the others dove behind rocks. They were all yowling like enraged mountain lions.

Colter bolted to his feet. There were likely more Apaches where those four had come from. He didn't think he'd ever run so hard in his life, holding the rifle in both hands across his chest, pumping his knees, and leaping rocks as he descended the hill toward where Bethel waited with the fidgeting horses, a look of bald terror in her eyes.

He'd never fought Indians before. And, after hearing the soldiers' stories at Camp Grant, he'd never wanted to. Fighting the dark-skinned aborigines was just as the cavalry boys had described it — like tangling with a rabid cougar in a one-room, locked cabin.

Wide-eyed and even paler than before, Bethel tossed him his reins, then leaped onto a rock from which she stepped into the fancy saddle of her pinto. Colter hurled himself without aid of his stirrup onto Northwest's back. Hearing the shrill, animal-like wails behind him as the Apaches came after him, he rammed his spurs hard into Northwest's flanks. Horse and rider lunged down the trail with ground-chewing speed though Colter wished he could fly.

As he rode over the hills, plunging into the troughs between them, he slowed only to turn around natural formations and to cross shallow but steep-sided washes. Occasionally, he looked over his shoulder to make sure he hadn't lost Bethel, who rode nearly cheek to cheek with the lunging pinto, the brim of her old hat pasted against her forehead by the wind.

They'd ridden hard for fifteen minutes when Colter's ears filled with an eerie chugging sound. It sounded like a freight train about to run him down. He looked around to see a thick brown buffeting curtain hurdling toward him from a vast tableland opening down the long slope on his right.

The wind moaned like an agonized giant, lifting dust around Colter and Bethel. Bethel screamed and shielded her face with her arm, holding the pinto's reins in her other hand. Northwest rose off his front hooves and whinnied, terrified by what sounded like a million demons screeching around him.

Colter grabbed his hat before it could blow away, tugging it down firmly on his head, then slipped out of his saddle.

"Hold tight!" he shouted against the bellowing wind. He grabbed Bethel's reins out of her hands and, pulling his hat down over his eyes against the stinging grit, headed for a rock formation rising on his left. He had to get himself, Bethel, and the horses into some sort of shelter — out of the wind and away from the Apaches.

Bethel held her head in her arms as Colter led both balking mounts along the cliff wall. After what seemed like hours, he found an opening in the wall, and pulled both mounts into it, instantly finding some release from the pelting bullets of wind-whipped sand.

He lifted his hat brim and looked around, finding himself in a vestibule of sorts with sheer, eroded rock walls rising two or three hundred feet straight above him, forming funnels and flues and pinnacles of crumbling rock streaked with bird dung and various mineral layers. The sky far beyond was a streaming banner of windblown sand.

Just beyond him, a corridor angled darkly into the mountain. Maybe, in there somewhere, Colter could find a cave in which he and Bethel and the horses could wait out the storm . . . and hope the Apaches lost interest and hightailed it out of the weather.

He tied the pinto's ribbons to Northwest's tail and led the coyote dun deeper into the dark, narrow fissure, the wind's keening now sounding eerily distant though cool drafts sifted sand on him from above. After he'd walked for fifteen or so minutes, he stopped where the right wall drew back several feet, forming a natural alcove. If the Apaches came, it wouldn't be hard to hold them off down the narrow corridor, where there was little cover. They couldn't want him and the girl badly enough to sacrifice themselves to .44 rounds slung at them down a narrow stone hall.

They might, however, wait outside, knowing that their quarry had to leave the mountain sooner or later. But that was a bridge Colter would cross when he came to it. For now, he'd secured shelter.

He reached up and pulled Bethel out of her saddle. She was basted in sand and seed flecks and bits of plants that the wind had carried a long way to pelt them both with. He realized now, out of the wind, that his own face and eyes were caked with the stuff. Grabbing his canteen off his saddle, he poured water over his face, blinking his eyes to clean them. They stung, tears rolling down his cheeks.

"Here," he told Bethel, lifting her chin with one hand and pouring water on her face with the other.

She blinked and blew, shaking her head and blowing the sand from her nose and mouth. While she bent over, spitting, Colter swabbed out the eyes and noses of both horses, using nearly half the canteen. They'd need to replace their dwindling water supply soon.

He shoved the cork back into the canteen's mouth, hung the canteen over his saddle horn, and walked over to where Bethel knelt beside her weary, frightened horse, sort of leaning back against the mount and looking fatigued as she scrubbed her face and the back of her neck with a red bandanna.

"You all right?"

She lowered the neckerchief and stared back along the corridor. "You think them redskins are gonna follow us?"

"I'm gonna walk back a ways, check it out. Sit down over there, take a breather." Colter jerked his head toward the depression in the cliff wall, where a single, flat-topped boulder stood. "I'll be back in a few minutes. If you see anything from the opposite direction, fire a shot in the air. I'll come runnin'."

Wearily, Bethel stepped between the two dusty horses and sagged down on the boulder, scuttling her rump back toward the wall, extending her legs straight out in front of her, and half reclining. She set her hat on her thigh, rested her hands in her lap, and stared straight out across the corridor.

Her cheeks were chafed pink from the scrubbing she'd given them, but the paleness shone behind the flush. She looked exhausted. Beaten down in a way Colter hadn't seen her before. It unsettled him. Throughout the entire journey, she'd been tough as rock salt. Now, having learned of her father's death, she looked as if the sap had drained out of her. He hoped that her determination to push forward hadn't bled away, as well. Her flat, wary eyes were not a good sign.

He pulled his canteen down from his saddle and offered it to her. "Have a drink. Take a long one."

"I'm all right," she said, not looking at him but continuing to stare straight across the corridor.

He set the canteen down against her leg. "In case you change your mind."

He looked at her once more, and worry

for the girl turned like a worm in his belly. She couldn't travel anymore today. They'd have to stay here, as long as the place wasn't soon swarming with Apaches. . . .

Turning reluctantly away from Bethel, Colter slid his Henry from its sheath and walked back along the corridor. Ahead of him the wan sun washing down from far above painted the walls a dull red. Through occasional shafts of saffron light, dust sifted like small tan snowflakes.

Slowly, he made his way back to where he and Bethel had entered the corridor, relief swelling in him when he saw no sign that the Apaches had followed him. A peek outside, squinting against the sandstorm, gave him no indication that they were trying to enter. Promising, but odd. Had they simply given up on their quarry? From the stories Colter had heard about the Indians, he hadn't thought they'd let something as insignificant as a little wind and sand deter them.

He waited fifteen or twenty minutes. For whatever reason, the Apaches didn't try to enter the corridor. Feeling lighter, less weary, Colter turned around and, keeping a vigilant eye on his back trail, tramped back to where he'd left Bethel and the horses.

Only, Bethel wasn't where he'd left her.

The flat-topped rock was vacant. His canteen, too, was gone. Both horses were wide-eyed and shuffling around nervously.

Colter raised his rifle in both hands, racking a shell into the chamber. "Bethel?"

The echo of his voice was the only response.

He called again. Again, only the echo replied.

His heart thudded and his hat began to feel too tight for his head. Damn strange for the girl to light out on her own. When he'd left her atop the boulder, she'd been so sapped she could hardly hold her head up.

Squeezing the rifle in his sweating, gloved hands, he continued on past the horses, making his way farther into the mountain. He could see no footprints in the stone floor, but she'd had to have come this way. There were only two routes leading off from the alcove, and he'd already covered one of them.

He'd walked maybe sixty yards down the twisting, turning corridor, when the close walls fell back away from him and he walked out in a broad canyon flooded with daylight. Along both sides of the canyon were ruins like those he'd seen several days ago farther north — tiers of cavelike dwellings that had been built long ago by a long-vanished people.

Birds winged around the canyon, flashing in the sunlight. There was only a strong breeze down here though he could hear the rushing of the wind far above, where the jutting canyon walls touched the tan-blue sky.

Colter started walking forward. He opened his mouth to call for Bethel and closed it suddenly, frowning. He'd heard something. It came again, from far out across the canyon floor. Someone was singing. Loudly singing.

Gooseflesh rose along Colter's back. His sweating hands inside his gloves turned as cold as stones.

The man was singing a sad Spanish ballad at the tops of his lungs.

Colter had heard the voice before, the night he'd given Alegria sanctuary from the Balladeer.

Colter took one more hesitant step forward, trying to detect where the voice was coming from, muttering, "Who in God's name . . . ?"

A spur trilled behind him. He froze midstride. Something hard smashed against the back of his head. The tan dust and rocks sprang up to hammer his face an instant before everything went black.

CHAPTER 25

The same voice that Colter had heard just before the world had died sounded again, echoing in the deep, dark canyon of his unconsciousness. The familiar sound called him up through the muck. As it grew louder, he could feel someone lightly slapping his face.

He opened his eyes, squinting against the sunlight pushing around behind the big sombrero-clad head hovering in the air about eight inches from his own. He winced at the tequila stench of the man's breath, and blinked several times against the impossibility of the bearded, heavy-jawed face he was staring at.

The Balladeer.

The black hair hanging down from his sombrero was braided and trimmed with beads. It curled around the gold stud in his right ear. The man grinned, showing his teeth inside his beard. His nose was like a broad, crooked wedge, his small eyes like coals. His nose was brick red, while his cheeks owned the color and texture of seasoned saddle leather. Fine red lines etched the whites of his eyes, which were more yellow than white, and gunmetal-colored pouches hung beneath the drink-bleary orbs.

"*El Rojo* — it's you!"

Colter stared in mute horror, feeling as though he were genuinely staring at a ghost freshly risen from the grave. Maybe all the crazy stories he'd heard about the strange goings-on in Mexico were true. His tone was more shocked than angry. "I killed you, you son of a bitch."

He tried to move his arms and legs. It was no good. He looked down the length of his lanky body to see that his ankles were tied to wooden stakes driven into the ground. Glancing up to each side, he saw that his wrists had been given the same treatment. He lay on the ground near the stream he'd seen before and which angled through the floor of the canyon, spread-eagle on his back, like a bug pinned to a wall.

He could hear water gurgling and churning to his left, only a few feet away. A river or stream . . .

Around him stood seven or eight Mexicans bristling with pistols and rifles, the bandoliers crisscrossing their chests flashing in the afternoon sunlight. Saddled horses stood around them, grazing the lush green grass lining the stream. Colter was vaguely aware that the wind's rushing atop the canyon walls had dwindled to a soft whisper.

The Balladeer's grin broadened, revealing a silver eyetooth. He placed his hand on Colter's face once more, pinching his chin between his thumb and hand, and jerked it from side to side. "You *tried* to kill me, *El Rojo!*" He laughed loudly, spit bubbles oozing between his tobacco-crusted teth. "The Balladeer — he's a tough *bastardo* to kill!"

The Mexican giant straightened until his full seven feet angled a thick, long shadow over Colter. The Balladeer grabbed the bottom of his red-and-white-striped serape and lifted the filthy garment to his chin. On his chest he wore a steel breastplate like that which Colter had seen on the dead conquistador. The plate hung from the Balladeer's neck by a stout rawhide thong. Three pale, round dents shone in the dark blue metal — all three bullet marks forming a triangle covering an area of the plate over the Balladeer's heart no larger than a ten-dollar gold piece.

Colter lowered his head in defeat and

rolled his eyes around once more, jerking at the ropes holding his arms and legs fast. "What'd you do with Bethel, damn you?"

"What?" the Balladeer said. "Who?"

"You know who." Colter gritted his teeth. "You touch a hair on her head, and . . ."

He let his voice trail off. The big Mexican stared down at him, appearing genuinely befuddled. Again, Colter looked around. Bethel was nowhere near.

"Oh," the Balladeer said, nodding finally. He held his hand out, palm down, at the level of his belly. "The *rubio* muchacha? *Sí, sí.* I was going to ask you the same thing, *El Rojo.*" He bent his knees and shoved his face up close to Colter's once more, the raw, rancid smell of tequila making the redhead's eyes water. "And about the map."

Colter stared at the man. He glanced at the others, who returned his look, eager interest in their eyes. For the moment, Colter placed his concern for Bethel's whereabouts and safety on a back burner. How had the Balladeer learned about Bethel's treasure map — if that was the map he was referring to. And what other map was there?

"I don't know what you're talkin' about."

The big Mexican didn't buy it. Neither did the others. A man in a green felt sombrero and eye patch gritted his teeth and growled like an angry cur, balling his fists at his sides.

The Balladeer stared at Colter, feigning an expression of grave disappointment. He shook his head. "You cannot fool me, *El Rojo*. I know the girl is Senor Strange's daughter. *Mi amigos* who knew Strange in Tucson saw her there with him. He must have sent her the map, and she came down here to find her ole pa-pa. She had to have the map — because you two could not possibly have followed the trail you've been following without it. The one that led you here."

The Balladeer smiled shrewdly.

Colter tried to buy himself some time. His skull throbbed from the braining he'd taken from the man who'd snuck up behind him. "How do you know Strange?"

"Never mind how I know that double-crossing bastard." Machado leaned down and poked his right index finger three times hard into Colter's flat belly. "You tell me where the girl's map is, or you are going to die slowly, *Rubio*. And very bloody."

It suddenly occurred to Colter that Bethel, having heard Machado's men stalking around, might have grabbed the Bible with the map in it and hid. He had to buy her as much time as possible to either hightail it away from here or find a secure hiding spot.

"Go to hell," he said, flaring his nostrils defiantly at the big man. "Besides, you're here, ain't ya? What do you need the map for?"

The Balladeer glanced at the Mexican wearing the green felt sombrero. The man walked over to one of the horses and dipped his hand into a saddlebag pouch. When he pulled his hand out, it was clutching a chunk of rolled burlap. He handed the roll to Machado, who held one end and let the rest of it roll out in the air before him. The burlap was a strip about three feet long. Secured to the burlap with strips of rawhide were two daggers that shone so brightly in the sunlight, stabbing Colter's eyes, that Colter had to look away and blink.

When his eyes had adjusted to the glare, he saw that the perfectly tapering, double-edged blades and the hilts of both knives were solid gold. The cylinder-shaped handles were carved turquoise, each inset with one red, precious-looking stone. From end to end each delicate but savage-looking weapon was probably a foot and a half long.

They were beautiful weapons, both looking as though they'd been handmade only a few hours ago though they both gave off an air of antiquity. Were the daggers what Jed Strange had been looking for?

"We have two of these precious beauties," Machado told Colter. "Stolen out of the old bandit's camp. He hid the third one, we think. The map will tell us where he hid it. And where we might find him . . . unless he is looking for us, maybe." He grinned in delight.

Colter looked away from the precious weapons in disgust. As far as he was concerned, treasure hunting was as foolhardy as gambling. If those knives were what Jed Strange had left his daughter to find, and given his life for, he'd been a damn fool. Colter had no idea know how much the daggers were worth, but it wasn't enough.

"He ain't holed up with that third dagger," Colter said. "And he ain't lookin' for you. He's dead. And there wasn't any map. We just knew to head for the Dragon Range, hopin' we'd run into him somewhere hereabouts."

"No, no, *Rubio,*" Machado clucked reprovingly. "You lie. There are many routes into the Los Montanes del Dragones, some with more water tanks. But you chose the same one we chose. The same one Strange chose — the one that leads to the treasure!"

The Balladeer glanced at the man in the

green felt sombrero, who wound the burlap around the daggers and returned the bundle to the saddlebag pouch. "I am sorry to have to do this to you, *Rojo.*" He opened his coat and pulled out a stout, steel knife with a hide-wrapped wooden handle and a brass hilt. Dropping to one knee beside Colter, he cupped the redhead's chin in one strong hand, holding his head still, while lowering the blade toward Colter's left cheek. "You have obviously endured much misery" — he glanced at the scar in Colter's other cheek — "but I am afraid that, until you tell me where the map is located, you will endure much more . . . an even more repulsive-looking mark to wear to your grave."

As the Balladeer touched the tip of the knife to Colter's left cheek, someone yelled in Spanish from somewhere behind Colter. Machado pulled the knife away and frowned back toward the narrow chasm through which Colter had fled the Apaches and walked into the banditos' trap. Colter heard the sound of horses moving toward him, and spurs trilling.

Finally, he saw another Mexican leading Colter's and Bethel's mounts into the crowd gathered beside the stream. The Mexican — a short man who wore a red bandanna over his head, under a tattered straw sombrero — had Bethel's Bible in his hand.

He dropped the horses' reins and held the Bible aloft, shaking it, with the top of the folded map sticking out of it. He shouted in Spanish, obviously informing his boss of his valuable find. Machado swung away from Colter, grabbed the Bible out of the little man's hand, slipped the map out of the back, tossed the Bible into the stream, and opened the folded paper.

He studied it for a time, shaggy brows furrowed, lips moving, murmuring to himself. Finally, he lifted his eyes and his chin, a smile stretching across his large, savage face. He spoke to his men in Spanish, and they all pricked up their ears, expressions brightening. He handed the map to the man in the green sombrero, and then, while the other men drifted off toward gear strewn along the stream bank, he walked back over to Colter. Lifting a gloved hand, the fingers having been cut out of the glove — he pressed a dirty index finger to his lower lip.

A shrewd light grew in his eyes. He smiled, chuckling with self-satisfaction, making a sharp knife of dread twist in Colter's guts.

"Ricardo! Javier!" He turned to two men who stood downstream a ways, near a freight wagon that Colter just now saw and that sat with its rear to the stream, tongue drooping. "Pull out one of those rifle crates and build *El Rojo* here a casket, huh? We want to give him a proper burial, now, don't we?"

Ricardo and Javier looked at each other. They turned back to the Balladeer and threw their heads back, bending their knees, laughing. Then, quickly, they ran around to the rear of the wagon, and presently they were hauling out a rectangular wooden box.

"What the hell you gonna do?" Colter asked Machado, who sat on a rock nearby, crossing his knees too daintily for a man of his size, casually trimming his fingernails with his big bowie knife while the rest of the men sank down around the several campfires blazing along the stream. He whistled contentedly to himself and ignored Colter's question.

While Ricardo and Javier hauled the box over to Colter, setting it down beside him, Colter's heart began hammering like a wolverine trying to claw its way out of a cage.

"Goddamn it," Colter said tightly, looking at the box whose wooden cover was stamped WINCHESTER REPEATING ARMS CO. NEW HAVEN, CONN. "You got the damn map. Why don't ya just let me go?"

"For two very good reasons, *El Rojo,*" Machado said. "You tried to kill me. That is the best reason I can think of. I will admit you are very fast with your old pistol. Probably faster than anyone I have ever seen. If you had not used your gun on me, I might have even invited you into my gang . . . uh . . . despite the mark of Satan on your cheek there." Indicating his own cheek with the knife, he chuckled. Ricardo and Javier were untying Colter's ankles from the stakes driven into the ground. "But the fact is, you did try to kill me. And what kind of man would I be if I let you go unpunished?"

"A damn reasonable one!" Colter said, watching the two men toss the ropes away from his ankles.

He stared at the box beside him as the two men untied his wrists. He glanced at Northwest cropping grass about twenty yards away, near Bethel's pinto, the reins of both horses dangling. Somehow, as soon as Ricardo and Javier had freed him from the stakes, he had to make a try for his horse. He didn't know what had happened to Bethel — she must have slipped away somehow — but he wasn't going to find her if they buried him alive in that rifle crate.

His left wrist jerked free of the stake. Then the right. Instantly, he tried to make a grab for the pistol on Javier's right hip, but his hand felt like a stone hanging there off the end of his wrist. The rope had cut off his blood supply, and now as the blood hammered back into the appendage, his nerves burned mercilessly. He groaned as he dropped to hands and knees, Javier pulling back and chuckling.

He rolled onto his back, clutching his wrists, feeling the blood trickling back into his feet, as well, his toes tickled by the flames of hell. Easily, Ricardo and Javier crouched over him, lifted him by shoulders and ankles respectively, and, while he feebly struggled, kicking weakly and striving to keep himself out of that damned gaping casket, they dropped him inside.

When they released him, he lunged upward, half turning and trying to climb over the edge of the box. Suddenly, the Balladeer stood over him, laughing, lifting a boot and smashing the heel into Colter's forehead.

Colter flew back against the side of the box. He stared up, heart thundering in his chest.

"No, goddamn it. Godamn you sons o' bitches to *hell*!"

The last thing he saw before Ricardo and Javier lowered the lid quickly onto the box, almost smashing his fingers between the lid and the box's right edge, was Machado's hysterically laughing countenance — laughing so hard that spittle was stringing from his bearded chin, and his beaded braids were dancing wildly beneath the broad brim of his leather sombrero.

"Happy sailing, eh, *El Rojo*!" the big Mex intoned, breaking into another burst of untethered laughter.

The box was small and dark, scrunching his shoulders painfully together. He lay there, miserable beyond imagining, hearing the gunlike thunder of the nails being hammered through the box's lid and into the sides, sealing him up like a sardine in a very small tin.

Horror was a coyote wailing in his head.

Buried alive . . . Wasn't that everyone's worst nightmare?

No . . . not buried alive, he realized now, as the makeshift coffin rocked and pitched from side to side. They were carrying him down a steep incline, and then his head slammed painfully against the coffin lid as they dropped him.

There was a splashing sound. The box spun wickedly. It wobbled, floating. Colter felt the chill of water beneath him, the wetness bleeding between the boards of the box to dampen his clothes.

No, not buried alive. At least not in the earth.

They'd dumped him into the stream.

The coffin rocked and swayed. The current caught it and Colter, panting in the tight confines, in the hot, humid darkness, his hands pressed up flat against the coffin lid, felt himself being hurled downstream.

Buried alive in a watery grave.

The coffin pitched and plunged, Colter's belly lurching into his throat as the coffin tipped up, suspended for a moment straight up and down before plunging down a short falls. The end housing Colter's head smashed against a rock with another sound like a gunshot. The box end with his feet flew up over his head.

"Ahh, shiiiittttt!"

Then he was horizontal again, rocking on down the stream — belly-down in the cold, wet box.

"Have a good trip, *El Rojo!*" the Balladeer called behind him. "If you're lucky, you'll make it to the Gulf of *Mejico!*"

He and the other men laughed raucously.

CHAPTER 26

As the rifle crate was hurled down the narrow but fast-flowing stream, Colter, lying facedown in the overturned coffin, pressed his hands against what was now the crate's bottom and humped his back against the top, trying in some way to break the thing apart. Or at least to pry off the lid.

As the crate spun suddenly, causing Colter's guts to spin, as well, he gave up and merely tried to brace himself, gritting his teeth through which he could hear his own panting breaths raking. He could hear the water rushing and gurgling around him. He could smell the piney odor of the green wood but knew he wouldn't be smelling anything soon if he continued to use up his air.

What would be worse, he vaguely wondered — suffocating or drowning?

Water was oozing from the cracks in the lid and from several other cracks between the crate's pine boards. Colter was soaked. Soaked and confined in horrifying blackness, brains and guts churning as the angry stream hurled down its rocky canyon, bouncing off rocks, the violent collisions causing the ringing in Colter's ears to grow louder.

Ah, shit, he thought. A watery grave in the Mexican desert? He hadn't seen this one coming, and he was glad he hadn't.

Suddenly, the coffin slammed against what he assumed was the stream's stone bank. It must have gotten hung up between rocks, because more water oozed into it, and he could feel a fluttering in the end housing his feet. Just as suddenly as he'd gotten hung up, the coffin jerked free. It spun wildly. Colter groaned and gritted his teeth and squeezed his eyes closed against the water oozing up around him, threatening to cut off his air.

The foot of the crate dropped downward. Colter's head and torso rose, twisted around, and then plunged.

The water in the crate gurgled as it washed this way and that.

Bang!

The true bottom of the crate smashed the stream's rocky bottom, and Colter could hear the crack, feel wood slivers gouging his left thigh. Now he was faceup once more, but the water was coming in fast and filling his nostrils and his mouth. He made the mistake of trying to breathe. The water hit his lungs and burned like coals in a blacksmith's forge.

Only a few seconds left now.

His entire body was submerged.

He was vaguely aware of the crate spinning around him once more. Then *bang*!

Both the side and the floor of the coffin gave way. Colter's feet dropped. His knee smashed against a knobby black rock that he glimpsed amongst a feathery spray of tea-colored water. He rolled sideways, the frenzied current sweeping him along.

Air brushed his face. Instinctively, he drew a breath and got part of it down before the water in his lungs exploded outward. He heard himself choking and gagging. His lungs felt as though they'd burst at the seams. While the current swirled him and pushed him downstream, he tried to gain another breath of the refreshing air washing over him between waves of the rushing rapids.

He managed only a teaspoonful as he continued to cough and choke and vomit the water he'd inhaled when he'd been inside the gun crate.

Ahead, a bird winged out over the frothing stream. No, not a bird. He'd caught only a glimpse of it, but he looked again now, turning his head one way while the river turned him another, and saw a rope. Yes, a rope. It extended out from the right bank and was looped over the end of a black log poking up out of the stream.

A pounding sounded from somewhere atop the bank.

A man's voice shouted, "Grab the rope, kid. Grab the *rope*!"

The rope grew in Colter's eyes until he could see the individual hemp strands twisting and straining as the man took the slack out of it. Colter threw up his left arm. He hooked it over the rope that cut into his ribs just beneath his armpit.

He groaned. But he clung to the rope for all he was worth. Staring at the rope and only at the rope, praying the log didn't break free, Colter used his hands to follow the rope toward the right bank. The whitewater beat against his legs and hips. He had little remaining strength. He used every ounce of it to walk his hands along the rope to the bank.

When he'd gained the bank's grassy lip, a big brown hand reached over it. Colter took it. The man's fingers closed around Colter's hand, and he pulled Colter up and over the bank.

The redhead collapsed, water gurgling in his throat as he tried to breathe. A brusque hand turned him over. Then the man grabbed Colter's ankles and shoved his knees up toward his chest. The water came up in several choking spasms, dribbling over his chin and down his chest.

The man dropped Colter's ankles, turned him over on his belly, and rammed his knee into the small of Colter's back. Colter vomited more water. Finally, he drew a breath. It went in more than halfway. Then he drew another and another . . .

He rolled over. A dark man in a calico shirt and a green flannel headband stared down at him, severe features indecipherable. He had dark brown hair and brown eyes, and those eyes boring into Colter's made the life shrink back down into the redhead's waterlogged boots.

Ah, hell. An Apache.

Then the man's face brightened, brown eyes flashing. He extended his big right hand. "You Colter Farrow?"

Raking air in and out of his lungs, Colter gave the man's hand a halfhearted squeeze, nodding. "Who're you?" he choked.

"Me? Hell, I'm Jed Strange."

Colter just stared at him. He'd misheard. Too much water in his ears.

Movement caught his eye, and he looked behind the crouching man to see Bethel running toward him, weaving around rocks and spindly shrubs from the direction of a high, basalt ridge — probably the backside of the canyon wall. At the same time, hoof thuds drew Colter's head to his right. Running toward him as well was Northwest, galloping along the streambed, head in the air, eyes frantic.

He must have broken away from Machado when he'd seen the banditos toss Colter's makeshift coffin into the stream, and took off after it. He ran up to Colter now, eyes white-ringed, and rose off his hind feet, giving a relieved whinny.

"I take it you know this hoss," the man who had called himself Jed Strange said, straightening to regard the pitching coyote dun. He might have looked like an Apache, but he spoke English with a Texas accent. He appeared in his late forties or early fifties — lean and rugged, his shoulders slightly bowed.

Colter stood and ran a soothing hand along the horse's snout, his head still spinning from the ride down the river and his brush with death. He looked befuddledly from the man dressed as an Apache to the girl running toward him.

"Colter!" Bethel said, running up to him, wrapping her arms around his waist and burying her head in his chest. "I thought you was a goner for sure!"

"Bethel," Colter said, shaking his head slowly, trying to coax his marbles back into place. "Where'd you go? I was —"

"No time for explanations," Jed Strange said, turning to his own horse, a big-boned Appaloosa standing several yards away eyeing Northwest crossly. "We gotta get mounted and hightail it. I been waitin' to lock horns with Machado, but I reckon it can wait!" He walked toward the big Appy, beckoning to Bethel. "Come on, girl — you're ridin' with your old pa!"

Bethel looked at Colter, grinning, eyes fairly flashing like gold coins in the sunshine. "That's my pa!"

Colter frowned, thoroughly confused. "So I heard."

"Come on." Bethel turned and ran off toward her father, who was just now mounting the Appy. "We'll explain later!"

The fire cracked and popped. The two rabbits spitted over it dripped grease into the bed of glowing coals, and sizzle and steamed. The coffeepot sitting on a flat rock to one side of the flames gurgled, spewing smoke from its spout.

It was an old, rusty pot with a dent in its side.

"I just don't understand this," Colter said, hungrily chewing the succulent meat off the first of the three jackrabbit haunches. "We found your gun on that bandito in the roadhouse yonder. At least, Bethel said it was yours, Mr. Strange . . . and it had your initials on it."

Bethel had given the gun back to her father, and he now wore it in the holster thonged low on his right thigh clad in fringed deerskin leggings — pistoleer-style. Sitting crosslegged on the other side of the fire from Colter, Bethel on his right, sticking close to her old man, Jed Strange plucked the silver-chased piece from the sheath and twirled it on his finger twice quickly, expertly.

He stared down at it, pensively, his broad, sun-seasoned face bronzed by the firelight. "Poor Percy."

"Who's Percy, Pa?"

"My partner, Percy Tarwater. Fella whose grave you found, I reckon. I never did know what happened to ole Perc. I gave him my gun because he didn't have one, and he was making a supply run up north to a little village at the north end of the range." Jed Strange scowled across the fire at Colter. "Who killed him?"

"Some Mexican rawhider we run into at Juan Domingo Gutierrez's place up north along the trail."

Strange nodded slightly, pursing his thin lips together, and kept his eyes on Colter. "How'd you get my gun back?"

"I reckon Bethel done that."

Strange turned to his daughter sitting Indian-style, as was the surly-looking old bandit, Jed Strange, himself. She was staring admiringly up at the man. She flushed a little, blinked, and glanced at Colter and then turned back to her father, not sure how to proceed. "I . . . I reckon I shot him, Pa. He said how he cut your throat . . . so I thought you was dead fer sure . . . an' . . . an' . . . I just pulled the trigger. The damn pistol roared like a dragon and lunged like a rattlesnake!"

The deep, dark lines in Strange's leathery face multiplied. "You shot a man?"

"I reckon I did at that, Pa. There were three more of 'em, an' Colter cleaned their clocks before they cleaned mine. It was a helluva dustup." Bethel shook her head as she stared up at her old man, whom Colter judged to be a little older than he'd at first thought — still strong of body, with only a slight paunch, but his face was a road map of hard years and many trails under an unforgiving western sun. "Tough country down here, Pa."

Strange set a big, gnarled hand on his daughter's head. "You shouldn't have come, Bethel. I sure never figured on that."

"You were gone a whole *year,* Pa! You don't know what it was like, livin' with Aunt Kate. Why, she had me goin' to church every Sunday!"

Strange snickered. "Don't doubt it a bit." He shook his head as he stared pensively into the glowing coals, half smiling. "Ole Kate . . ."

After a time, he raised his eyes to Colter's on the other side of the fire. "Sorry about leavin' you to the wolves back there, boy. There's several hidden passageways in that chasm you and Bethel were in. You wouldn't notice 'em less'n you been in and out of that canyon as many times as I was — me an' Percy. I broke off trackin' Machado a few hours ago, when I seen you two. I glassed you an' recognized my daughter. Them Injuns turned back when I started flinging arrows at 'em." He glanced at the ash bow and deerskin quiver of arrows lean-

343

ing against a near piñon. "I reckon you didn't see through the storm."

"I didn't see nothin'," Colter said, shaking his head as he continued to eat hungrily.

"I snuck in behind you and snatched Bethel away because I figured Machado and his men were in that canyon. I wasn't sure who you were — friend or foe. By the time Bethel had told me you were friendly, and I had her in a secure place, I went back for you, but Machado was already pounding nails in your coffin. I hightailed it out to my horse and tried to run you down."

"Well, you did, and I do appreciate it," Colter said, giving another shiver against the bone-deep chill that was still chipping away at him despite the fire's warmth.

"I've been followin' Machado for days. The problem is I'm all out of shells for my Winchester." Strange flicked the Colt Peacemaker's loading gate open and spun the cylinder, looking relieved to see the brass snugged down in all six cylinders. "Forty-four shells were one of the things Percy was headin' out to buy . . . with the last of our gold dust. We popped the last of our caps at the Apaches that haunt these canyons and been makin' our lives pure-dee hell for the six months we been here in the Dragones."

Bethel plucked some meat off the half-eaten rabbit haunch on her tin plate. "Is that what's kept you out here so long, Pa? *Gold?*"

Holding his smoking cup in his hands before him, Strange rested his elbows on his knees. "Not just a few pinches of dust, daughter. But enough gold to see me into my old age and you . . . well, enough to send you back East to a good school. Make a teacher out of you, just like you always wanted." He smiled. "Though with as much gold as we'll have when we finally ride out of here, you likely won't need to work another day in your life. How'd you like that?"

"I'd like that just fine, but I'd like to have you back home even better."

"All in good time, girl. All in good time." Strange ruffled the girl's hair, then glanced at the bedroll spread out beside her, in front of her saddle. "Now, you best finish up and crawl into bed. Big day tomorrow."

"Doin' what?"

"You'll see." Strange looked at Colter. "You best hit the hay, too, son." He slapped the six-shooter on his thigh. "I'll keep watch tonight."

"All night?"

"I sleep like an Apache sleeps," Strange said, winking. "With both eyes open."

CHAPTER 27

Jed Strange poured himself a fresh cup of coffee, then bid his daughter and Colter good night once more and walked out away from the fire's shimmering light, toward the dark wall of a stony ridge.

Colter finished his rabbit and stared over the fire at Bethel. She was staring back at him, a dubious look in her eyes. She tossed a quick glance behind her, then returned her anxious eyes to Colter, leaning forward slightly and keeping her voice down. "You think he's gone off his nut?"

Colter sipped his coffee. "The desert does strange things to people. Add treasure to the mix . . ."

Colter remembered the gold daggers Machado had shown him. Did Strange have the third one? Machado himself was after the third one. If Strange was after the other two, Colter and Bethel had just landed atop a powder keg with a sparking and sputtering fuse.

"Well," Bethel said, wiping her hands on her skirt and leaning back against her saddle. "At least, he's still kickin'. I thought for sure I'd lost him, and, aside from Aunt Kate, he's all I got." She paused a moment, staring at her hands laced on her chest before lifting her eyes once more to his. "And you, I reckon."

Colter tossed another log on the fire. "You don't have to reckon about that, young lady."

Bethel rolled her eyes in frustration. "Dang it, I done told ya — I ain't all that young!"

Colter chuckled as he climbed to his feet and stepped into one of his boots drying by the fire. "Good night, Bethel."

"Where you goin'?"

"Private business."

"Oh." She curled up on her side. "Good night, Colter."

He tossed another mesquite branch on the fire, hitched his empty pistol belt higher on his hips — Machado's men had taken his Remy, but he didn't feel so naked wearing the shell belt and holster — and walked off into the darkness beyond the fire. When his built-in prudence told him he was far enough from Bethel, he unbuttoned his fly and loosed a steady stream. He'd drunk nearly a gallon of hot coffee while drying himself and his clothes out by the fire earlier, and he swore he still had a few gallons of river water swirling around inside him.

Out beyond him in the darkness, someone coughed. It was a rattling expiration. Jed Strange spat, cursed. The coughing came again, lasting longer this time but more muffled, as though the man were coughing into a handkerchief. Colter stared off toward where the man was apparently keeping watch, frowning as the coughing continued.

Colter buttoned up and walked off through the rocks and cedars, in the direction from which the coughs had come. A quarter moon was kiting over the southeastern ridges, limning the shrubs and rocks around him in silver. Ahead stood a low escarpment. Strange was silhouetted against the violet sky, one knee up, one arm draped over the knee. A cigarette made a pink dot at the end of his hand.

"Mr. Strange?" Colter called softly.

Another rattling cough. A sniff. "What it is, Mr. Farrow?"

"You all right up there?"

Another pause. A muffled half cough. Then Strange's pinched voice. "You hear me back at camp?"

"I was off taking a piss."

"Come on up here, boy." Strange beckoned with his hand holding the quirley. "Let's palaver."

Colter continued to the base of the scarp and climbed up the side, stepping into the cracks and ledges. He sat down on a rock beside Strange and planted a boot on the one in front of him. "Nasty cough," he said. "Sounds like pleurisy."

"I wish it was pleurisy."

Strange stared off into the night, beneath the gradually rising moon. They were about five miles from where Colter had so unceremoniously taken leave of Machado's gang, in a shallow canyon surrounded by nearly impenetrable walls of granite and limestone. Strange had a camp here. He seemed to know every inch of this end of the Dragones.

Strange took a drag off the cigarette. That started him coughing again into a balled-up bandanna. When he'd stopped coughing, he ground out the quirley beneath his moccasin. "Reckon I'm gonna have to stop smoking those." He kept grinding the cigarette in frustration, shaking his head. "No, hell, it ain't pleurisy. A few months back I took a Yaqui arrow. Percy got the shaft out, and he dug around for the head but couldn't find it. I know where it is, all right." He thumped his upper right chest with his fist. "Right here — in my wind sack."

Colter didn't say anything.

"I don't want Bethel to know this, Colter, but . . . I don't think I have long left. Every time I cough I give up more blood than last time I coughed, if you get my drift."

"You need to see a doctor."

"I got no time for pill rollers. I have to get what I came down here for."

"The daggers?"

Strange jerked a surprised look at him.

"He showed me the two he had," Colter said. "He's looking for the third one. He took Bethel's map out of her Bible, and he figures the map shows him where that third one is."

Strange chuckled and stared off for a time, stifling another cough. "Good," he said. "Good. Good. Damn good!"

"What's so damn good about it?"

"I got the third dagger. Apparently, he don't know that. Which means I know where he'll be lookin' for it."

Colter studied the man for a time. "Mr. Strange, you got me baffled."

"Call me Jed."

"Jed, you got me baffled."

Strange laughed, coughed into the bandanna, and wiped his mouth. He lowered the bandanna, spat to one side, and said, "I want all three of those daggers for my daughter, Colter. And when I get them, I want you to take her on back to Tucson. Will you do that?"

"What about you?"

"Never mind about me. I'll pay you a thousand dollars to see my daughter and those three daggers back to Tucson." Strange paused, narrowed a grave eye at the redhead. "You see, I know you're an honest man. I know I can trust you even when there's gold involved. Not many men you trust with gold."

"How do you know you can trust me?"

"Because my daughter fancies you. Oh, hell, I can see that." Strange laughed again, and thumped his chest with his fist. "And Bethel is a very good, albeit merciless, judge of character. Just like her mother."

Colter flushed.

"I hear you're good at killin'."

Colter's face turned hotter, and he looked at the man, tongue-tied.

"She told me while we were gatherin' wood and you were dryin' out. Said you shot Machado. Next time, aim lower."

"Good advice," Colter said. "Yeah, I've killed a few. But only because I've had to."

Strange's moonlit, dark eyes flicked to Colter's scar. Then he said, "You want to help me kill a few more? And kill Machado again, only this time make it stick?"

The conversation was moving too fast. Trying to slow it down, Colter said, "Where'd those daggers come from, Jed? How is it that both you and Machado know about 'em, and how much you think they're worth?"

Strange gave a ragged sigh and stared off across the moonlit Mexican desert cut by the shimmering snake of the fast-dropping river, lumpy with black, sawtooth ridges. "A long time ago, I rode with a gang down here along that river — the Rio Yaqui. We called ourselves the Rio Yaqui Raiders." He paused to give a rueful snort. "Anyway, we robbed a bank south of here, in a pueblo called Rio Agave. The bank held mostly loot acquired by several wealthy hacendados who got rich rustling cattle on the other side of the border, so we sorta saw it, the way young tough nuts do, as an act of patriotism.

"Anyway, we robbed the bank in Rio Agave, and in the safe we found those three gold daggers. I've seen such pieces before though not in such good shape — treasure looted from the graves of conquistadores, mostly. Or found on the men buried in the desert. You can find such stuff all through Mexico and as far north as Nebraska."

Strange paused to clamp the bandanna to his mouth, stifling another cough. When he pulled the cloth away, he looked at it, shook his head, and continued.

"A passel of *rurales* got onto our trail about forty miles east of here, shot our group up bad. In fact, four of the gang was shot out of their saddles, leaving only three — me and Percy and one other rider. The *rurales* had extra horses, so we knew they were gonna run us down. After we'd gotten across the Rio Yaqui, our horses were done for, blown out, but the *rurales* were still comin'. Knowing we'd have to split up and try to make it on foot, we each hid a dagger after we crossed the Rio Yaqui and were climbing into the southern reaches of the Dragones. We drew a map on the back of a wanted circular, tore it in thirds, and split up."

Strange wiped a hand down his face and turned to Colter. "I never saw either of those other two men again until about a year ago, when I ran into Machado outside Tucson."

"Machado?"

"He was the third rider. Just a lanky wisp of a young, stringy-haired peon then, a poor bean farmer tryin' to make a name for himself as a bandito, and chasin' all the tail he could find. Had a voice on him, he did. The senoritas loved to hear him sing, and he could hold a right purty tune. But he couldn't shoot for shit."

Strange chuckled, fondly remembering.

"I barely got out of these mountains alive, figured Machado and Percy were long dead. I hung around awhile, waited to see sign of 'em. When I didn't, rather than venture back into the mountains alone, I gave up and headed home. Hell, that was close to twenty years ago, now. A long twenty years that included a stint in Yuma Pen. Last year, I heard Machado was runnin' guns across the border, and I was so damn down and out and tired of bein' a night deputy to a drunken old reprobate of a sheriff that I threw in with him for some easy money. Once we were down in Mexico, guess who else I run into?"

"Percy Tarwater."

"Give the boy a cigar! And he still had his third of the map. So did Machado, by the way. Been carryin' it around with him all these years. But we'd torn the map into thirds in such a way that anyone going back for the daggers would need all three pieces to find them all. So after we sold the rifles to the so-called *revolucionarios* we'd hauled 'em to, Percy an' me stole Machado's third of the map and lit out after the treasure."

"You double-crossed him."

"Sure we did. Before he double-crossed us. Shot us and stole our sections of the map. Bound to happen. You saw him. The Balladeer ain't the scrawny little, silver-tongued peon boy no longer. Hell, no — he's a cold-blooded killer. Shoot you as soon as listen to your spurs sing!"

Colter just stared at the old outlaw, not at all sure what to make of the man's story. His sweet daughter, Bethel, had a bona fide old outlaw for a father. And now that she and Colter had found him, Colter just didn't know what to think about him.

Or his quest to retrieve property that did not belong to him.

Strange studied Colter and quirked his mouth corners up, as though he'd been reading Colter's thoughts. "Probably worth around twelve, fifteen thousand each."

"What's that?" Colter said.

Strange had removed a dagger from inside his coat, and was caressing the gold blade with his hand holding the quirley. "I'd say, judging by the ruby in each hand-carved handle, and the grade of gold, each one of them daggers is worth about fifteen thousand American dollars. Fifteen thousand, give or take. Leastways, that's what Bethel could probably sell one for back East." Strange narrowed an eye at Colter. The gold and the red ruby in the dagger's handle shimmered in the moonlight. "Make sure she has them gold buyers figure in the foreign market. These might be worth more somewhere over in Europe. Spain, say. Make sure she don't get gypped."

"You really think you're not gonna make it, Jed?"

"I do believe, son, that getting those two daggers back from Machado'll do me in. I won't have enough gravel left in my craw to get me back to Tucson. Even if I did, I'd be a goner soon after."

Colter blew a ragged sigh and doffed his cavalry kepi. He ran a hand through his hair, the thin strands of which were still crusted with grime from the river water, then set his hat on his knee and followed Strange's gaze out across the desert. "How'd Machado get those two daggers?"

Strange cursed and tucked the third dagger back inside his coat. "It was a simple matter of him sneakin' into me an' Percy's camp just before we was gonna ride on out of these mountains and head home. Him and his boys snuck into our camp when we was fishin' and stole 'em out of our gear!"

Strange laughed without mirth. That started him coughing again in earnest, holding the bandanna taut against his mouth with both hands, not wanting Bethel to hear how sick he was.

"Percy had the third one on him," he said after a time, in a pinched voice, stifling more coughs. "Kept it to marvel at while he was fishin'. Wish I'd done the same with the other two. Then we'd have all three."

"What happened to the third one?"

"We hid it, Percy an' me. Hid it good, because Machado was on our trail. When we managed to slip away from him with the help of some marauding Apaches, I drew us each a map, rode up to Senor Gutierrez's saloon, and put mine in the mail. Sent my copy to Bethel back in Tucson, in case anything should happen to me. I figured she could maybe hire someone to come down an' fetch it — one of her uncles on her ma's side, say. They're good Christians and not too money-hungry, and were good Indian fighters once. Figure I could trust one o' them. Percy an' me didn't want to keep the dagger on our persons no more for obvious reasons. Believe me, we intended to run into

Machado again. And we was gonna get those two daggers back or die tryin'. We been play-in' cat 'n' mouse with the old Balladeer for nigh on four months now. These is big mountains, and the Apaches have us pinned down half the time."

Strange jerked his head around when a coyote began yammering from a nearby ridge — an eerie, ghostly sound. Turning back to Colter, he said, "Havin' a snake like Machado on your trail makes ya jumpy. A few weeks back, I could hear the bastard singin' all hours of the day and night." He snickered. "'Specially after we double-crossed him. Like teasin' a coiled diamond-back. You must a run into him when him and his boys split up after a run-in with *rurales.* They probably needed fresh horses and supplies."

After a time, Strange drew a rattling breath. "I picked up his trail again two days ago, been shadowin' him ever since . . . till I spied you and Bethel. I'm glad he's back. Damn glad. We'll run into him again, and I'm gonna need some help gettin' those two daggers back."

"How come you got the third one on you now?"

"I fetched it back from where we buried it after Percy never came back from his supply run. I thought maybe Percy got a notion to dig it up himself and ride off alone. No honor amongst thieves, you know." He laughed. "We'll follow Machado up to where Bethel's map leads him. Since he found the map, he must think I buried the third dagger, likely 'cause I didn't trust Percy any more than I trusted him . . . and we'll ambush the sneaky bastard there. He won't be expecting me to try to dig it up until I have the other two. Good place for an ambush, atop that ridge. Hope you got enough ammo. Like I said, I'm out of forty-four rounds."

Colter threw up his hands. "Hold on, Mr. Strange . . . Jed . . . I never agreed to this crazy scheme. And I'm sorry, sir, but that's what this is." He stuffed his hat back on his head. "Machado is one angry killer, and he's got seven other angry killers ridin' with him."

"Seven against two. I've faced longer odds!"

Colter started climbing down off the rocks. "Sorry, Jed. Your game will only get you an' Bethel whipsawed, and me, too, if I bought chips in it. Which I ain't. I'll be headin' back north with Bethel. I'll see to it she gets safely back to Tucson."

After what he'd been through down in

Mexico, he figured he was probably as safe north of the border as he was south of it. Maybe he'd elude the bounty hunters and anyone else after him by heading north to Dakota, or to Canada, say.

Colter climbed down off the rocks and started tramping back to where the campfire glowed dully amongst the rocks and bushes. "Good decision, boy," he heard Jed Strange say behind him, the man's low, gravelly voice clear in the quiet night. "The only right decision, really. Damn glad my daughter ran into ya!"

CHAPTER 28

The sound of someone kicking a rock jerked Colter out of a deep sleep. Instantly, his Henry was in his hand, and he loudly pumped a shell into the chamber.

The figure just now entering the camp stopped suddenly in the false dawn, Jed Strange's slightly stooped figure outlined against the lightening eastern sky. "Damn, boy — you are fast. I'd like to see you shuck a hog leg."

"Machado has it."

Bethel had lifted her head from her saddle when she'd heard the rasp of Colter's rifle. Now she looked around curiously, blinking. "What the hell's all the commotion about?"

"Go back to sleep, darlin'."

"That don't answer my question, Pa."

Strange walked into the camp. He wore a buckskin mackinaw against the high-altitude chill, his breath fogging around his head and green flannel bandanna. Colter assumed the man wore the Indian duds to blend in better with the Apaches, possibly confuse them from a distance. Besides, it was right smart desert attire.

The old outlaw leaned his rifle against a mesquite, then got down on his hands and knees, lowered his head to the fire ring, and blew on last night's coals, stirring a dull pink glow.

"I thought you were out of shells for that," Colter said, glancing at the old '67-model Winchester.

"I was, but I thank you." Strange shunted his glance to Colter's saddlebags, where he kept his last box of .44 rounds, and gave the redhead a wink.

Colter glowered.

Strange continued to blow on the coals. "Boy, you got your hands full with my daughter. Twelve years old an' she's already as sassy as her ma was after fifteen years of marriage." As a couple of small flames began to lick up around the ashes, he gave Colter a shrewd wink. "But you probably already know that, don't you?"

Colter had tossed his covers off him and was pulling his boots on. "I reckon you win the cigar this time, Jed."

"What do you mean Colter's got his hands full, Pa? I don't like the sound of that.

Sounds like you got ideas poppin' around in your head again, and that scares me somethin' fierce."

Colter wanted no part of the conversation. He grabbed his coffeepot out of his saddlebags, draped his bedroll over his shoulders, and headed down to the river for water. When he returned, the fire was popping and snapping amongst the several mesquite branches lying over the old ashes, and Strange was saddling his horse. Two horses had been picketed with Northwest about twenty yards from the camp, at the base of another scarp. Strange's second horse, an oddly yellow-eyed grulla, had belonged to his partner, Percy Tarwater.

"Pa, I just found you," Bethel was arguing, standing near her father, moving around with him as he saddled his horse. "Damn near left you for dead. If I'm goin' back to Tucson, then you are, too. If you ain't, then I ain't, neither!"

"Colter's takin' you back to Tucson, child." Strange set his blanket roll on his paint's back, lashing it behind his saddle. "I'll be along shortly."

Bethel stopped before her father, spreading her feet and planting her fists on her hips. "You can't make me ride back to Tucson with Colter. There ain't no way you can keep me from foggin' your trail to wherever in *hell* you think you're goin'!"

Strange glanced over his shoulder at the redhead, who stood at the edge of the camp, holding the filled coffeepot. Strange had a slit-eyed, knowing expression on his face.

Colter should have known Bethel would never have gone along with his plan for hightailing it back to the border. Her father had certainly known it. And if she stayed down here with the ailing man, Colter would have to, too. He couldn't leave her.

Colter kicked a rock. "Ah, hell!" He shook the coffeepot, sloshing water down its sides and over his hand. To Strange, he said, "You think this gold is worth riskin' your daughter's life for, do ya?"

"No, I don't," Strange said. "But she's here now whether I like it or not." He grabbed his saddlebags, tossed them onto his horse's back. "I intend to tuck Bethel away in a safe spot before you and I go after them daggers. If all goes according to plan, and we get the jump on Machado, we should have those two gold daggers by sundown. A matched set of three!"

He turned to Colter, leaned back against his horse, snaked an ankle behind the other, and grinned.

Bethel turned her head to Colter. She

looked grieved. "Yep," she said, turning her mouth corners down. "He's touched, sure enough. But I can't leave him to die down here alone, Colter."

The redhead was kicking dirt on the fire. "Hell, I know that!"

"Hold on," Bethel said a couple of hours later, sawing back on the grulla's reins. "What was that?"

Riding behind the girl on a switchbacking game trail that wound gradually up the steep mountain wall, Colter stopped Northwest and looked up into the chill gray fog that cloaked the grass, ponderosa pines, and cedars in an eerie gauze that had issued a sporadic drizzle all morning. He heard the loudening thuds, and then a rock bounded out of the gray and tumbled over the slick green-brown grass to pile up against a half-buried boulder about ten feet upslope and ahead of him and Bethel.

"What's it look like? It's a damn rock," Colter said, grumpy. He didn't want to be here. He didn't want her to be here, either.

"I know it's a rock," Bethel said, hipping around in her saddle to give Colter a sneer from beneath the floppy brim of her rain-dark hat. "I'm wondering what set it off."

"It's all right." Strange had stopped his

Appy about twenty yards ahead of his daughter and was staring up through the scattered pines. "Just the rain loosed it, most likely. I been watchin' an' listenin', and I've detected no 'Paches. Believe me, when you've been in Apache country as long as I have, you know where they are and where they're not. I can smell the sons o' bitches."

"Oh, yeah?" Colter said, sneering, already tired of the old outlaw. "What do they smell like?"

"Goat!" came the amused retort.

"Could Machado be up there?" Bethel asked in a dreadful tone, squinting into the gauze.

"Doubt it. We're a jump or two ahead of him, havin' taken that dogleg through that little canyon. Trimmed off about three miles. He won't be to the crest of this here ridge for another hour."

"He won't come this way?"

"Hell, no, daughter," Strange said, turning away suddenly. In the dingy light, Colter thought he saw the man wince, as though stifling a cough. "This is the backside of the mountain. Machado ain't expecting us to meet him at the top, so he'll ride the trail on the mountain's face — a good cart and wagon trail still used by woodcutters from the mission that lies about two ridges to the north." He looked at Bethel. "You all right? How's your horse doin'?"

"He's doin' all right, Pa. Purty sure-footed."

"That's why Percy chose him." Strange stretched his gaze back to Colter. "Colter, how you doin' back there? You look like someone tossed a dead rat in your morning belly wash."

"That's how I feel about this whole damn thing, Jed. I've got enough trouble without huntin' more."

"Damn, boy." Strange grinned and shook his head before turning around and touching spurs to his Appy's flanks. "I thought I was supposed to be the one with all the good sense."

"That's sorta what I thought," Colter groused, booting Northwest on ahead behind Bethel, setting the barrel of his Henry atop his saddlebow.

As he rode, he looked up the slope on his right. Most of the time he could see only a few yards up the steep, rocky incline stippled with occasional cedars and pines. When the great cloud capping the mountain thinned, he could see the vast slab of broken granite that sat over the top of the mountain like a lead bullet over a cartridge casing. From a distance, before he and Bethel and her father had started climbing the mountain — Dragon Ridge — the formation at the top had looked like three giant horse teeth — three granite teeth separated by narrow cracks between them.

Colter heard near footfalls above him, and he tightened his right hand around the neck of his Henry. Then he saw Jed Strange coming toward him on the switchback trail thirty yards up the slope. As Strange rode, swaying easily in his saddle, moccasin-clad feet set loose in his stirrups, Strange pressed his fist to his mouth and coughed softly. His face turned red as he leaned farther forward, and then the man disappeared into a thick snag of pines as he angled farther up the slope.

The trio stopped just beyond the pine snag, on a relatively flat shelf in the mountainside. "Rest here," Strange said, climbing heavily down from his saddle, his face not so much red now as pale. They were deep in the cloud again. Colter could see nothing beyond a dozen yards. The pines stood still and dripping, trunks dark and wet in the iron light.

"What's that cough from, Pa?" Bethel asked him, stepping up close against her horse to loosen her latigo cinch.

"What's that, darlin'?"

"Don't darlin' me. I heard it last night and I heard it several times this mornin'," Bethel said. "What is it — consumption?"

"Oh, hell." Strange hauled his canteen down from his saddle and sat on a rock beside the trail. "Just a little touch of the pleurisy."

He removed the cap from the canteen and took a drink, spilling a little when he coughed around the flask's lip.

"Pleurisy, huh?"

Bethel strode over to her father. He wore his buck-skin coat unbuttoned, as the coat was a little too heavy for the temperature, which was probably around fifty degrees. Bethel reached down and swept the left flap of the man's coat back from his calico shirt. Colter winced when he saw the bloodstain on the left center of the man's chest, beside the hide tobacco pouch that Strange wore on a thong around his neck.

"What in tarnation?" Bethel said with hushed exasperation.

Strange snatched his coat flap back, pressed it taut against him. "You're a damn snoop!"

"What is that? Bullet wound?"

As Colter took his own canteen down from his saddle and Northwest started cropping the green grass along the trail, the redhead saw Strange look off, squinting, his cheeks in the dull light appearing hollow and jaundiced.

Shit, he didn't have long left, Colter thought.

Strange shook his head fatefully. "Arrow."

Bethel glanced at Colter. "Did you know about this?"

"Only since last night." Colter unscrewed the cap on his canteen and took a drink.

"You shoulda told me," she said.

"It wasn't my place." Colter lifted his canteen toward Strange, who was still looking off. "It was his."

Bethel turned back to her father and said in an incriminating tone, "You're dyin', ain't ya, Pa?"

Strange looked at her, then stood and brushed past her as he walked over to his saddlebags. "Hell, I ain't dyin'. I'm too mean to die. I'll be here when the devil comes, an' him and me'll dance in the last flames."

He fished a clear bottle out of the saddlebag pouch, popped the cork, and took a deep pull. He looked up at the trees and then all around before taking another pull and returning the cork to the bottle. He shoved the bottle back down in his saddlebag pouch.

"Come on, girl," he said, grabbing his pinto's reins. "I thought I'd like to rest here awhile, but gold's awaitin'. I'll rest when I'm dead." He chuckled and stepped into the leather.

"Pa?" Bethel was standing in the trail, staring up at the man, tears streaking her cheeks. "I'd like to go home. I'd like to go home right now, Pa. I'm real tired of Mexico. I'd like to sleep in my own bed again."

Strange winked at her. "We'll go home, darlin', when we're about forty thousand dollars richer." He glanced back at Colter, who'd been feeding Northwest a handful of parched corn. "Be a gentleman and help my daughter on her horse, will you, Red?"

Colter walked over and placed a hand on Bethel's shoulder. "There's no stoppin' him, Bethel. We'll get what he's after, and then I'll see to it we all head north."

"Ah, hell," she said, staring off after Strange, who was walking his horse up the trail, slowly disappearing in the slithering tendrils of mist, "he's always been part loco and all bronco. Ma knew it, and I know it. And I reckon it couldn't hurt either one of us to be rich for once in our lives. He's always wanted it so bad." She chuckled, tears still streaking her cheeks, mixing with the light rain. "Just hope he don't drink it all up now, with Ma not here to see that he don't."

"Come on." Colter boosted her up into the saddle and lightly slapped the grulla's rump. She scrubbed her coat sleeve across her face, then bounced on up the trail.

Colter watched her disappear in the mist. He jerked his hat brim down over his eyes, having a sour, colicky feeling about what would happen once they reached the ridge crest.

He swung up onto Northwest's back. The coyote dun glanced back at him, flicking his ears and chewing his bit.

"Yeah, I know, boy," Colter said, touching his spurs to the horse's flanks. "But I reckon we bought chips in the game whether we want 'em or not. Now we gotta play the hand."

CHAPTER 29

From below, the horse-tooth-shaped formations cresting the cloud-covered ridge had appeared solid and impregnable. From close up now, as Colter followed Strange and Bethel out of the trees, he saw that the monoliths were set farther away from one another than he'd thought. The gap between the two southernmost teeth would give passage to a horse and rider.

Northwest crested the ridge and followed Bethel and her father into the gap littered with black-flecked gray boulders, a few hardy cedars growing from cracks in the rocks. There were puddles in the gravelly trail. Water dripped from the stone ledges above and landed with a hollow sound in the puddles.

The clomps of the horses' shod hooves echoed loudly, water splashing.

At the end of the gap, away from the steep slope they'd just climbed, Strange lifted his right hand as he stopped his Appaloosa. Bethel rode up beside him and stopped the grulla. Colter rode up on her right and checked Northwest down, as well. He stared straight out from the gap, where a dilapidated stone wall, about five feet high, stood about forty yards away. Over the top of the wall, he could see grave markers of stone and wood beyond. Beyond the graves lay the back of a stout adobe church.

The church's rear, wooden door hung from one hinge, and just now a bird was flying out the dark gap. That and the general disarray of the graveyard, littered with tumbleweeds and fallen branches and grown up with cactus and rabbitbrush, indicated that the church and grounds were likely long abandoned.

Strange looked around, then turned to Bethel. "Darlin', you lead my Appy and Colter's horse on over that little rise." He canted his head toward the rise shrouded in ponderosas and piñons, various stone escarpments beyond it. "Keep the horses quiet and out of sight. You'll likely hear shootin', but you sit tight till we come for you."

Bethel merely inhaled, her chest rising steeply behind her wool coat.

Strange glanced at Colter. Colter handed

his reins to Bethel and, holding his Henry, stepped down from his saddle. Strange did likewise, palming his silver-chased Peacemaker and rolling the cylinder across his forearm. All the loops in his cartridge belt shone with fresh brass. He shucked his old Winchester and racked a round in the chamber.

Colter seated a shell in the chamber of his own rifle and off-cocked the hammer.

Holding the reins of both men's horses, Bethel stared down at her father from atop the grulla. He turned to her. "Go now, girl. Machado'll be along soon, an' you and the horses have to be holed up tight."

She glanced at Colter, a dark, dreadful cast to her gaze. Then she puffed her cheeks out as she sighed, reined her horse around, and clomped on over the rise, leading the other two horses behind her.

Strange walked ahead to the wall. He was limping slightly, favoring his right side, and breathing hard. Colter followed the man, stood beside him, looking over the wall in the boneyard. He was trying to remember the map. All that he'd seen to mark the treasure was the Dragon, which had obviously indicated the ridge they were now on. In addition, there had been a small cross. Beneath the cross were the initials X and F.

"All right," Colter said, running a gloved finger down his cheek. "The cross was the church yonder. What did the 'X' and the 'F' mean?"

"The grave where Percy and I buried the third dagger. You see, our original camp was right over there." He pointed toward a dilapidated stone stable and tumbledown corral to the right of the cemetery, hunched in a slight clearing in the dripping pines, barely visible in the foggy mist. "The church is where Percy and me and the young Balladeer holed up nigh on twenty years ago now, when the *rurales* were scouring this ridge for us. We were given sanctuary by an old priest. Xavier Franco."

"Ah."

"I'm going to stay here, as the grave is right over yonder. I wanna be close to the son of a bitch."

"Which direction will Machado be riding in from?"

Strange nodded his head toward the church.

Colter looked around carefully, glancing at the grave with the large stone in which FATHER XAVIER BALTHAZAR FRANCO had been chiseled beneath a small, weathered carving of Christ amongst a flock of little lambs. The grave was mounded with fist-sized red rocks.

"All right," Colter said, looking around, his glance catching on a crumbling spot in the wall on the stable side of the graveyard. "I'll head over there." He looked at Strange. "You just gonna bushwhack 'em?"

"Oh, I'll give him a chance to throw down the two daggers." Strange showed his teeth and slitted his brown eyes devilishly. "He won't take it."

Colter moved off along the wall, swerving around tree branches that had grown over it and stepping over those that had fallen dead at its base. When he'd rounded the far corner near the stable, he crouched down beside the V-shaped gap in the ancient wall and set his rifle across his knee.

The mist came down, ticking lightly off his hat brim.

A long, slow, wet hour passed. Then another half hour. Colter was beginning to think Machado had misread the map, or was suspecting a trap, when a horse whinnied back in the direction of where he and Strange had left Bethel. Colter's heart thudded, and he squeezed his rifle tighter.

Sure enough — they must have flanked him and Strange and found Bethel!

He lifted his head above the wall and froze. Strange was looking over the top of the rear wall, motioning for Colter to drop his head back down. Just then, he heard the dull clomp of distant hooves. Riders were coming from the front of the church. Voices rose, indecipherable beneath the soft pelting of the rain.

Colter lowered his head, pressed a shoulder against the wall to the left of the V notch. He removed his hat and slid his right eye far enough into the crack that he could see the graveyard, which horseback riders were entering via the far side of the church from Colter. There was no mistaking the huge lead rider — the Balladeer himself, Santiago Machado, clad all in glistening black leather and a calico shirt behind his vest and crisscrossed bandoliers. Beaded braids buffeted down both sides of his head as he rode slowly, ploddingly amongst the graves, scrutinizing the stones that fronted each one. Water dripped off the brim of his leather sombrero.

Colter drew his eye back behind the wall. Pressing his back against the wall, holding the Henry firmly against his thigh, he waited. The horses thudded. The Mexicans were talking amongst themselves, their wet tack squawking. They were looking for the initials that Strange had marked on his map.

No one called out suddenly, as Colter had

expected when they found the grave. There was merely a cessation of thudding hooves and a dwindling of conversation. Glancing through the V notch once more, he saw all seven of Machado's riders clumped around the grave about thirty yards out from the rear wall and Jed Strange, and angled a little in Colter's direction.

There was the squawk of tack again and the jangling of bridle chains as the men dismounted. Now they were muttering amongst themselves. Three men moved out around the grave, holding Winchester or Spencer rifles up high across their chests, taking sentry positions. Machado was smoking a long black cheroot as he looked down at the stones mounding Padre Franco's last resting place. He leaned a hand atop the padre's tall, rounded marker and kicked at the stones.

Four men stood around him. They'd dropped the reins of the horses, and the horses now milled to the far side of the grave from Colter, one standing and looking suspiciously toward where Strange hunkered behind the wall. Colter winced, hoping no one noticed, but then it didn't matter because Strange's voice called, "Hold it there, Machado. I've got you dead to rights. One sudden move, and you'll be feelin' right at home here!"

That was Colter's cue. He rose quickly, loudly racked a round into his Henry's chamber, and aimed straight out over the wall. The Mexicans turned their heads toward Colter as though they were all joined by the same string. Machado grinned beneath the brim of his wet sombrero, casually lifted his cigar to his mouth, and let the smoke stream out on the damp air through his nostrils.

Remembering his horrific ordeal on the river, Colter felt like wiping the smile off the killer's face with a single slug from his Henry, but he kept his finger steady on the trigger.

"Santiago!" Strange shouted. "I'm gonna ask you once and only once to throw down them daggers and ride on out of here!"

Beyond the Balladeer, one of the sentries jerked his rifle up. Strange's rifle cracked. The sentry screamed and stumbled back, triggering his own rifle into the ground. The man hit the ground, cursing in Spanish and clutching his right knee.

Machado threw his hands in the air and shouted, *"Parada! Nadie tira!"* Stop — nobody shoot! Or some such, Colter figured.

The others froze, crouching, quickly lowering the rifles they'd swung up suddenly as they shuttled wary looks between Strange and Colter. The man on the ground clutched his knee with both hands, groaning through gritted teeth. The horses scattered, trotting amongst the gravestones toward the back of the church.

The Mexicans stood clumped around the padre's grave, dark and wet, the rain dripping from their sombreros.

Machado stepped toward where Strange stood, aiming his Winchester out over the wall, pressing his cheek to the stock. The Balladeer said, "Jed, *mi amigo*! Perhaps we could powwow about this. What do you say, brother?"

"There's nothin' to talk about. I want those two daggers you stole, and I want 'em now, or I'm gonna perforate your big, ugly hide!"

Machado's face hardened and his back tensed. "Stole from you? Oh, you crazy, double-crossing gringo son of a bitch! You stole my third of the map — you and Percy. No?" He kicked a gravestone over. *"Did you not do that?"*

His voice was shrill with untethered fury.

"Only because you woulda done the same to us if you knew we'd kept our own sections of the map. No honor amongst thieves, you stupid bean eater."

No, there was no honor here, Colter thought as he aimed down his rifle at Machado. So what was he doing here?

"You call me names now, huh?"

"Throw down them daggers," Strange ordered.

The two men held each other's glowering stares. The mist continued to fall, the sky hovering low. The other men stood tensely, keeping their rifle barrels aimed at the ground and shunting tense looks between Strange and Colter, knowing they were in a cross fire. But also likely knowing that, because they were seven against two, the odds were still in their favor despite the walls shielding their adversaries.

As Strange and Machado continued to glare at each other in hushed silence, Colter hoped that Jed remembered the Balladeer's steel breastplate.

"You think you can get all seven of us, huh?" Machado asked sneeringly. "Even with *El Rojo* over there, I will say you can't."

Machado did not wait for Strange's reply. Shouting suddenly and incoherently, he crossed his arms and shucked his pistols.

Smoke puffed from the maw of Strange's rifle. Twin puffs spread from both of the Balladeer's pistols, Machado's slugs tearing rock shards from the wall around Strange's head. Colter triggered his Henry at Machado, but at the same time the big man crouched, one of Strange's bullets tearing into his leg above his knee, then threw himself hard to the right. Colter's bullet ricocheted off a headstone beyond the Balladeer.

Machado rolled into the billowing cloud of powder smoke kicked up by the six other Mexicans now firing at both Strange and Colter, pivoting at the hips and pumping cartridges as fast as they could shoot.

Colter pumped the Henry, aiming and firing quickly, dropping two banditos in about three seconds after he'd missed and lost Machado in the wafting powder smoke. Strange dropped another pair, one falling to his knees howling and trying to fire his rifle one-handed before Strange triggered a silencing shot through the man's forehead. The others slung lead at both him and Strange, and, screaming and cursing, dove behind stones and grave mounds.

The hammering pops and screeching ricochets sounded like the barrage of a small battle for two minutes, before Colter's Henry pinged on an empty round. Strange must have emptied his Winchester, as well, because a sudden silence fell back over the cemetery, settling down as heavy as the low clouds and the steady mist.

Colter punched shells through his rifle's loading gate.

"Red!" Strange called. "You got company!"

"Shit!" Colter said, hearing someone running toward him.

CHAPTER 30

Colter looked through the V-shaped break in the wall.

Only one man was moving — running hard down a line of gravestones toward the wall about twenty yards to Colter's right. The man in the green sombrero, Machado's lieutenant, started shooting as he ran, crouching and shouting curses. He had a pistol in each hand, both guns stabbing smoke and flames between gravestones in the dingy grayness.

Colter jerked his head back behind the wall as two slugs slammed into it. He squeezed his eyes shut against the spraying rock shards.

His heart thudded as his wet, cold fingers slipped fresh cartridges from his shell belt and thumbed them through the loading gate. At the same time, the man kept shooting, his boots splashing in puddles, the sounds growing louder as he neared the wall beyond Colter.

In the corner of his left eye, he saw the man leap over the wall, firing both pistols. One slug tore across the nub of Colter's left cheek. The other slammed into the wall only an inch above his head, pelting him with gobs of wet adobe.

The man in the green sombrero had fallen to his knees, wailing furiously, but now as he stumbled to his feet, bringing both pistols to bear once more, Colter leaped up, raised the Henry, and fired three rounds quickly, pumping and shooting.

The bandito screamed and shot himself in the right thigh as he flew backward. He hit the ground hard, his wails thinning, grinding his spurs into the ground as he opened and closed his mouth and blinked his eyes at the sky.

Colter ejected the last spent cartridge, seated fresh, and silenced the man with a round through the underside of his chin, the slug chewing through his skull to exit the top of his head, spitting a great gob of blood and brains onto the wet earth beyond him.

Colter racked a fresh round in the Henry's chamber and turned toward the cemetery. The place was as silent as before they'd come — most of the banditos sprawled amongst the stones. Strange was just now moving through the open gate in the wall to his left, striding into the boneyard with his Peacemaker raised. He waved the gun around, looking for a target.

No one moved. The fog probed at the bloody corpses like the spidery fingers of ghosts.

Colter stepped through the break in the wall and strode slowly toward where Strange stood before the grave of Padre Franco. At his feet, three banditos lay sprawled in bloody heaps. As Colter walked, swinging around, aiming his rifle from his hip, Strange traced a broad half circle around the Padre's grave.

Colter stopped near the grave. Strange stopped then, as well, about thirty yards between the grave and the rear of the church. They looked at each other.

"The only one missing's my friend Machado," Strange said.

His weathered face was grim beneath his green bandanna, his silver-streaked dark brown hair hanging wet to his shoulders. He'd left his buckskin coat behind the wall, and in his deerskin moccasins and leggings he looked every bit the Apache.

The fog was icy witch's fingers snaking over Colter. Pivoting on his hips, expecting a shot from any quarter, he resisted the urge to shudder. He kept swinging his gaze back and forth across the cemetery. Nothing moved. There was no sound except the quietly ticking mist.

He felt deep lines of incredulity slice into his forehead.

How could a man as large as Machado simply disappear?

He had to be here somewhere. Colter had seen at least one bullet plow into him. He was wounded. Likely hunkering behind one of the gravestones — either dead or right now drawing a bead on Colter or Strange. . . .

Colter backed away from Franco's grave, turning his head this way and that, shuttling his glance across the back wall and then the north wall, and from there to the rear of the church. He strode slowly around the graves and stopped near Strange.

"The daggers were on one of the horses," Colter said. "The horse of the man I killed out yonder."

"I'll stay here," Strange said quietly, tensely looking around at the gray stones, both men expecting the Balladeer to bound out blasting from behind any of them at any second. "You go fetch the daggers. Then let's us . . ."

He let his face trail off when Bethel's voice said, "Pa? Colter?"

Colter saw her coming through the pines beyond the cemetery's rear wall. The redhead tensed, gritting his teeth. Strange stepped forward, his voice tight with anxiety as he waved his arm, "Bethel — get down, girl!"

She kept coming — a small brown figure in the grayness, blond hair hanging from her brown hat. She was heading for the break in the rear wall. "You fellas all right?"

Heart hammering, Colter jerked his head around, tightening his hand on his Henry's trigger.

"Goddamn it, Bethel!" Strange started walking toward the gate. Colter followed him, covering the man's back with his Henry.

"What?" Bethel said, stopping just inside the opening in the cemetery's rear wall.

Just then she heard something and turned. But not before the Balladeer, who must have been hunkered down in the trees just outside the wall, leaped up behind her. Blood oozed from his right thigh. Bethel's startled scream was clipped when Machado wrapped his left hand across her mouth and lifted a cocked, pearl-gripped Colt to her temple.

Colter froze. So did Strange.

"Drop those irons, amigos!" Machado shouted.

Bethel said something that was muffled by the big man's hand, her face turning red. At the same time, she lifted one of her short brown boots and stomped it down hard on the big bandito's left boot. She jerked her head back against his gut. It caught the man off guard.

He cursed and, as Bethel threw herself sharply to her left, leaving Machado open, Colter lifted his Henry and began firing and pumping, the gun leaping and roaring in his hands. Strange triggered his Peacemaker, and the barrage of bullets tore through Machado's arms and legs, a couple hammering the steel breastplate behind his vest and shirt. Colter wasn't sure if it was his bullet or Strange's bullet that did it, but one bullet carved a long red line across the right side of his face.

He hit the ground on his back, howling.

Bethel was crouched on one knee, slowly lowering the arm she'd raised to shield her head.

Colter was striding forward with his smoking Henry. Bethel looked from the wailing Balladeer to somewhere behind Colter. That's when the redhead realized that

Strange was no longer at his side, but was down on his hands and knees, hanging his head low, his smoking Peacemaker clamped between his right hand and the ground.

Bethel ran to her father. Colter walked over to Machado, who lay as he had lain before except that he was still now, blood oozing from several wounds in both legs and both shoulders. Two fingers of his right hand were gone, leaving bloody stumps. His left cheek looked like a half pound of freshly ground beef.

His eyes were bright and glassy. A grimace stretched his lips. He groaned and moaned. Between groans and moans, he sang. The lyrics of the Spanish ballad sounded like a dirge. He did not look at Colter but stared past him at the sky as Colter leaned down and disarmed the man, tossing the pistols and knives off into the brush. He found the burlap pouch hanging from a leather thong beneath the man's black vest, felt both daggers in it, cut it loose with the bowie knife in his boot, and straightened.

Machado was fast dying, harmless, though he was gradually doing more singing than moaning and groaning.

"Did you kill Alegria?" he asked the dying bandito.

The Balladeer stopped singing and looked

at Colter, wrinkling the furry skin above the bridge of his nose. "How could I kill her? I love her." He smiled, then returned his gaze to the sky and continued singing the ballad.

Colter turned away from him and walked over to where Strange was now sitting back on the heels of his moccasins, breathing hard, his face pale. Bethel knelt beside him, one hand on his shoulder, tears streaming down her cheeks. Strange looked at Colter, his eyes pain-racked but touched with humor, as well. They looked delighted when he saw the burlap pouch in the redhead's hand.

"That them?"

Colter tossed the pouch down. "I hope this was worth it."

Strange opened the pouch to the two gold daggers and stretched his lips in a grin.

"Don't die, Pa," Bethel said quietly. "Please don't die. I don't care about no treasure. I just want you home again."

"Ah, hell." Strange shook his head and loosed a ragged sigh, clamping his bandanna to his mouth as he coughed up a small gob of blood. "I reckon I done took my last ride, girl."

Bethel frowned, worried. Strange rested the daggers in his lap, set his hand against her cheek, and caressed her smooth skin with his thumb. "My last wild ride, I mean. We got one more ahead. Back to Tucson. I'll make it."

The man looked down at the daggers and then up at Colter. Strange's eyes shone with a devilish, romantic gleam beneath the green bandanna wrapped around his leathery forehead. The old border bandit wasn't dead yet. Maybe soon, but not yet.

Strange said, "You comin', *El Rojo*?"

Colter shrugged. "I got men after me. Bounty hunters. Maybe army."

"Hey, so do I!" Strange laughed, then turned his head to cough into his bandanna.

"I'll fetch the horses."

Colter saw Bethel looking at him. Her blue eyes shone with optimism. She smiled. He winked at her, shouldered his rifle, and started walking away. He stopped, tramped back over to the grave where the three dead banditos lay.

He crouched over one, pulled his trusty though nondescript Remington from behind the dead man's cartridge belt. He chuckled. Lost and retrieved once again. He'd often considered trading in the old hog leg on a newer model, maybe a fancy piece like Strange's silver Colt.

But no.

He and the old Remy must be doomed to

die together.

He wiped it off with his hand, then stuck it down in his holster and fastened the keeper thong over the hammer.

Brushing a hand across his bullet-creased cheek, he strode out of the cemetery, stepping over the Balladeer, who lay bleeding and dying and singing his last, fast-fading song to the sky.

ABOUT THE AUTHOR

Frank Leslie is the pseudonym of an acclaimed Western novelist who has written more than fifty novels and a comic book series. He divides his time between Colorado and Arizona.

CPSIA information can be obtained at www.ICGtesting.com
Printed in the USA
LVOW041634210113

PP7345000004B/3/P